TAINTED

TAINTED

DEMON WITHIN ONE

by

GINNA MORAN

ISBN 978-1-942073-38-3 (soft cover)
ISBN 978-1-942073-40-6 (epub ebooks)

This is a work of fiction. All of the characters, organizations, and events portrayed in this novel are either products of the author's imagination or are used fictitiously.

Cover design by Silver Starlight Designs
Cover images copyright Depositphotos

For Inquiries Contact:
Sunny Palms Press
9663 Santa Monica Blvd Suite 1158
Beverly Hills, CA 90210, USA
www.sunnypalmspress.com
www.GinnaMoran.com

To Jazmin Garcia, I couldn't have asked for a better best friend than you! You truly are an amazing and strong person, and I'm so happy to have you in my life. Even with the distance between us, you never feel far away. Much love to you, BFF!

PROLOGUE

THREE YEARS AGO

"HEY, LOOK AT me. I need you to stay awake for a little while longer." The feminine voice wraps around me, pulling at my consciousness. "Can you tell me what my name is again?"

"Alana." She's made me say her name a dozen times, asking me random questions I don't want to answer.

"And what's your name?"

"Cami."

"Good."

I blink my eyes, my vision hazy through tears and the stinging residue from the smoke of my burning house. Every time I think about it, I start crying all over again. I nearly didn't make it out. If it wasn't for the man—the demon—who tried to kidnap me, I might have perished with my parents.

God, help me.

"We have to go back," I whisper for the hundredth time before she can ask me another question.

"I'm sorry. We can't. That demon will linger nearby to enjoy the destruction he caused. I'm just so dang grateful I found you in time."

"He said he was taking me home." I try to sort through everything that happened. One second I was reading, and the next, my bedroom filled with smoke, my house exploding with a fire so intense it destroyed everything...everyone. Except me.

My head lolls to the side at the thought, and I rest it against the cool glass window, watching my breath fog it. I can't think about this anymore. Demons don't exist. They shouldn't exist. But after seeing the beautiful man with diamond-shaped pupils, emanating what I can only describe as pure evil, I think Alana might be right. If only she didn't also tell me he was after my soul, and that I'm lucky to be with her.

"I know it's a lot to take in, Cami," she says instead of answering my pleas. "But you're gonna get through this."

"You can't know that." Anger rushes over me a second before grief steals my breath away, and I sob into my hands. "My parents are—my parents are dead." I struggle to say the words, making the situation worse than it is. Because saying it out loud makes it utterly and devastatingly real.

She reaches over and squeezes my tender knee, still bleeding from defensive wounds of fighting and from sprawling across the asphalt while trying to get away from the demon. "I know. And I'm sorry I didn't get to you sooner."

"It's whatever, okay," I quip, heaving a shuddering breath. "I just—what do I do now? I don't have any other family. I have nothing. I don't even have clothes. I'm in these stupid pajamas." Pajamas I'm embarrassed to be seen in. They were my last pair because I was too lazy to do laundry, and they're too small from two years ago.

"I'll get you some clothes."

"I want *my* clothes."

"They'll be your clothes when I give them to you."

"It's not the same!" My voice rises through the cab, and Alana swerves at the sudden shriek of my voice.

Tugging on the door handle, I swing it open, surprising Alana. She cusses and locks her fingers to my leg, realizing I'm not wearing my seatbelt. She slams the brakes, jolting me forward. I hit my hands on the dashboard to brace myself, making the pain in my bloody fingers worse.

"Cami, what are you thinking—"

I throw myself from the truck and run, slapping my bare feet on the sidewalk. I don't know what comes over me, but I need to get far away from the woman who speaks of demons. She very well could be out of her mind. I feel out of my own. She says my parents are dead, but I can't be certain. I didn't see them. *Mom was screaming. She never came out. The roof collapsed. No one could have survived the flames.*

But I did. I don't even have a single burn on me.

"Cami! Stop! It's not safe out here. We have to get to the church."

The church? I don't stop to question her. I keep running.

Soft thuds sound out from behind me, and I peek over my shoulder and spot Alana charging after me incredibly fast, faster than I can run. She'll tackle me before I can even make it to the end of the block.

"I'm going home!" I yell, pushing through the burning pain in my chest, making me wheeze at the exertion.

"The hell you are," Alana responds. "Your home is gone. That demon will be waiting for you. I will not let you risk your life."

The world jerks out from under me, and I tumble forward onto the sidewalk, rolling into the damp lawn of a dark house. I don't get back up. I can't. My body revolts, shooting intense pain through me so that I can barely breathe. "I have no life. I have nothing."

I break down and cry again, curling my knees to my chest. Squeezing my eyes shut, I focus on the pain, wanting to lose myself to it so I can forget everything else. I don't want to be here. I want to be home. I want my parents to be alive. I want this all to be a horrifying nightmare.

But the beautiful demon's face flashes through my mind, reminding me that this isn't a dream. This is my life, and it could very well be over.

"Cami?" Alana whispers. "I need you to get to your feet, okay? I don't want to have to drag you."

I don't respond.

Her footsteps tap quietly across the sidewalk, but she doesn't come any closer. I don't have to open my eyes to see that she's walking away from me. And then I hear her whispering—maybe into a phone. But still, I don't move. I couldn't even if I wanted to. My body and mind compete with each other in a game of how to make me more miserable.

The world turns utterly silent as I lose consciousness for who knows how long. The whisper of a voice tickles my ears, deep and smooth, gentle even. It steadies my racing heart to the point that it no longer pounds in my ears.

And then it vanishes, leaving me colder than before. Or maybe it's the chill of the night as the world kicks back to life.

A hot hand touches my cheek, combing my filthy hair from my face. "Cami? Cami can you hear me?" The voice doesn't belong to Alana. It's not the voice from my subconscious either. This voice is new, slightly raspy, and filled with concern. The voice begs me to open my eyes, and I finally manage to flutter them open.

I inhale a small gasp of breath, staring into the prettiest blue eyes I've ever seen in my life. The boy smiles at me, though his gaze glasses over to reflect my own sorrow back at me. He stares at me for a moment, just touching his fingers to my cheek. I realize he's wiping away the streams of never-ending tears still clouding my vision.

"You look like you've had a bad night," he says, clearing his throat.

I can only nod my response.

"Think you can sit up?"

I nod again, digging my elbow into the grass to put my weight on it. My head spins with dizziness, my stomach clenching, and I fall back and flip away from him, afraid I might puke all over his black boots.

Thankfully, my bad night gives me a pass. "I—" I snap my mouth shut and curl back in on myself, sobs threatening me all over again.

The boy gently rubs my back, the smooth circles warming my icy skin. He does so until I choke back my cries and smother the animalistic sound ripping from me with my hand. Any other day, I'd care about breaking down in front of a cute boy. I'd care that he sees me in my stupid pajamas with my hair a mess. I'd care that I can't speak a coherent sentence. But now? I just want to fall asleep and forget everything.

"Cami, please stay with me," he whispers.

I swallow, trying to stop my voice from squeaking. "There's no point. A demon murdered my parents."

The look he gives me, all pouty mouthed and sad eyes makes him look like I hurt his feelings. "And we'll get him. I promise."

"Who's we?"

"The Hunter's Alliance. Me and my partner. We're tracking him now."

I don't respond. I don't even know what to say to that.

"But before I do anything else tonight, I gotta get you inside where it's safe. Will you try getting up again?"

I shake my head.

He sighs. "Can I help you then? I'll be careful. You look pretty roughed up. I bet you hurt."

Shifting, I meet his startling gaze again and shrug. "I think I'm dying."

Puffing air through his lips, he leans over me, trailing his gaze over my injuries. He shrugs from his leather jacket and wraps it around my trembling body. I had no idea how cold I was until I'm engulfed in the warmth clinging to the tough material.

"Not if I can help it," he says.

"Why bother?" I ask, glancing away. If I stare into his eyes a moment longer, I might believe he cares.

"I'm going to help you to your feet, okay?" he says, ignoring my comment.

I force myself to nod. The boy hooks his arm under me

and carefully lifts me with him as he stands. From this position, he seems to have grown, standing over six feet and taller than I expected. He can't be much older than me, but he doesn't look like any of the guys at my high school. Though I can't see his muscles under his shirt, I can feel them bunching against my fingers as I grip him tight enough to make him tilt his head to look at me.

Pain burns from everywhere. Without the adrenaline from trying to run from Alana, I feel every bruise and cut on my body, including the wounds on the bottom of my foot from stepping in the glass from my broken window shattered by the demon.

I wobble and drop back to the ground, but the boy catches me, sliding an arm around my back and one under my knees to pull me against him. I stiffen in his hold for a split second, but he whispers my name, and my muscles relax. Burying my face into his chest, I inhale a long, shuddering breath. His warm scent tickles my nose through the ash still clinging to my nostrils to remind me that my life burned to dust by the hands of a demon. A demon.

I groan.

"I'm sorry if this hurts. The church is only a few blocks away. Think you can hang on?" he shifts me again like he's trying to put space between us, now afraid to touch me.

"You're not hurting me," I whisper, sinking against him. I sniffle, trying not to cry again.

He must sense my oncoming breakdown because he

slowly rubs his hand along my arm, the gesture bringing me more comfort than I expected. Something about this boy seems to ease the deep ache consuming me.

"Good," he responds a little late.

A horn honks from beside us, and the boy shifts me as he turns to glance at the street. Alana drives the truck beside us, motioning for the boy to get in. One look at her sends panic rushing through me again. The boy takes a step toward the truck, and I wiggle in his arms not wanting anything to do with the woman who says I should be thankful I still have my soul.

She puffs her bottom lip out when our eyes meet. "I'll meet you at the church, all right?" she says to the boy. "That okay, Cami?" she adds to me.

I bob my head, surprised she didn't command him to throw me in the bed of the truck to race off again.

"And watch what you say, Evan. Discovering the existence of demons is enough revelations for Cami tonight." Without waiting for the boy to respond, she accelerates and disappears around the corner at the end of the block.

"What did she mean by that?" I ask, turning my gaze away from the empty road to glance at Evan.

His jaw twitches, and he meets my eyes. "Nothing much. It's just a lot to take in. Trust me."

Strangely enough, I do.

"The good news is that you'll get used to it," he adds.

"Doubt it. I mean, demons? Really?"

He responds with a small chuckle that tickles my ear, easing some of the pain radiating through me. "You're right. Your life is going to change."

I stifle a whimper. "It already has."

Rubbing his hand up and down my arm again, he tries to comfort me. "I'm sorry. I really am. I know what it's like to have a demon destroy everything."

I hide my face, my tears soaking into the front of his shirt. "I just don't know what I'm going to do."

"You're going to take a deep breath, see how strong you are, and fight."

"I'm not strong."

"You survived a demon attack."

"Doesn't feel like it."

He hugs me tighter, squeezing away the trembles running through me. "I know, but that'll change. Promise. It's all over now."

Except I don't think it is. A demon killed my parents. The same demon came after me, and I don't even know why. Nothing about this situation makes it feel like it's over. As I stare at the dark sky, taking in the night I now know is filled with demons, I can't help but wonder how I'm going to survive all this.

"Then why doesn't it feel that way?" I ask, trying to suppress my tears.

Evan releases a breath. "I'm sorry. You're right. I was just trying to make you feel better."

I groan. "This sucks."

"That's the Veiled Realm for you," he says.

"The Veiled Realm?" I ask.

"The demon world. Your new life."

DEALING WITH DEMONS

FRIGID DARKNESS COATS my skin in ice, but it doesn't cool the fire running through my veins. I'm trapped in a world of nightmares, hanging on to my sanity for dear life. I'm disoriented, unsure of which way is up. No matter how hard I kick my legs, I don't get anywhere. I'm terrified.

My heartbeat resonates in my eardrums. The comforting thump-thump, thump-thump keeps me from giving up. My soul isn't lost...yet.

"You don't belong here, Cami." A soft voice echoes in my mind.

"Who said that?" I must be going crazy. There is no one here.

"I did." The voice comes from nowhere and everywhere, corking the hopelessness leaking from my soul.

Hazy light shimmers in the distance. Like a shipwreck survivor glimpsing a lighthouse on a faraway shore, it's miles beyond my reach. The light is my last salvation from this barren, black void.

"Please, get me out of here." My voice quivers with desperation. I'd do anything to escape this nightmare.

"I can only help you if you let me in." The voice echoes louder, closer. It's the voice of a boy, not deep enough to be a man. It's a beautiful sound, like a symphony of reassuring emotions creating a heartwarming melody.

"How can I let you in if I can't get out?" I ask.

"It's simple. Open your soul."

I jolt upright, startled from sleep.

A soft glow emanates from my bedside lamp, lighting my room. I can't believe I fell asleep an hour before sunrise. I haven't done that in over a year. Alana decided I was old enough to have my own room if I could handle staying awake all night, prepared for any and all demon invasions. She'd freak if she found out I'd been taking a catnap.

I shake the lingering nightmare from my mind, the same one with the same voice that has haunted me since the death of my parents. I don't remember much of that night, everything that happened now a complete blur. I only remember that Alana came into my life like an explosion and tore apart my world. But I can't think about it now. The pain never goes away, and I can't have her catch me crying, and I have enough to worry about, let alone worrying about stupid, cryptic dreams.

The stench of manure and burning rubber stings my nose, drawing my attention away from my tear-soaked pillow. My heart jumps at the disgusting smell, and I reach for the glass of holy water I have sitting on my bedside table. I can only think of one thing that smells that disgusting—a lower level demon in its true body.

Leaning over the side of my bed, I peer under it for signs of my childhood monsters, but there's only a baseball bat. My closet door hangs wide open, displaying the few shirts and jeans I have. My leather jacket drapes over the back of a folding chair stationed in front of a television tray I use as a desk. Shifting my gaze, I peer at my open curtains, giving me a full view of the walkway outside of my window.

And then I see it.

Beady eyes gawk at me through the glass. The demon looks like a metallic porcupine with sharp, silver spikes protruding from crusty skin. Its body glitters in the soft light emanating from my room. Triangular ears fold against its head and a thin flap of skin sags from its neck, twitching and moving like an antenna. It sits on its haunches like a mangy dog, pressing its flat black nose to the windowpane.

I suppress the scream burning in my throat. The last thing I need is to rile it up and have it smash through my window. I have just one cup of holy water left, and I need to save it for more threatening demons. This one seems content just taunting me.

I scoot to the edge of my bed and give the demon my best death glare. As long as I don't submit to my fear, I won't look like easy prey. This kind of demon won't pick a fight if it knows it'll lose. It makes choices based on animal instinct rather than intelligence. There's not much I can do until sunrise except hold my ground.

"You got a lot of nerve being here," I say. The demon may look like a mutated animal, but I know it can understand me.

The demon's eyelids close and flash open in response.

I tilt the glass of holy water to my lips and drink a small amount. It's not that I'm thirsty, but what I'm hoping is that it will protect me in case the demon decides watching me isn't enough. Blessed water is like acid to demons. A glass of it will distract them long enough to give me time to get a running start. In this case, it will give Alana enough time to come and kill it since she's only a door away.

"Fine. If you're going to play this game, then I'm going to give you three choices. You can wait here while I scream for Alana, and then she can kill you. You can wait until the sun comes up and traps you for the entire day, and then Alana can kill you. Or, you can leave now and bother someone else, and never come back here, or Alana will kill you." I can't believe I'm negotiating with a demon. People lose their souls dealing with demons, but I'm not leaving room for error. Whatever it decides, I'll survive until sunrise.

The demon lifts its hand and drags its spiked fingers across the glass, creating a horrible squeaking sound. I cringe, opening my mouth to yell for help, stopping short when it stands up on two legs and walks backwards in slow-motion rewind.

It disappears around the corner of the apartment, and I sigh in relief. It chose option three, sensing I wasn't joking. I guess the demon was smarter than I thought. It's hard to tell what a lower level demon's capabilities are, and I'm really glad one of them wasn't speech. I still have nightmares from the last demonic animal that could speak. My creep-o-meter almost blew up.

I watch the sky lighten as dawn approaches. My eyes are heavy from my short nap and the demonic stare down.

"Finally," I say out loud to myself as warm sunlight pours into my room. Even though it's been three years since I was introduced to the Veiled Realm, the world of demons, I'm still adjusting to the side effects it has on my life.

Being an ordinary human, instead of a kickass demon hunter like Alana, has left me trapped in Purgatory. I can never live like a normal human, and I can never live safely in the Veiled Realm. It's too dangerous, too foreign. The Veiled Realm is the ridiculous side of life no average human would ever believe in. The exceptions are people like me—those who have become involved with the dark side by accident.

Loud banging outside my door interrupts my thoughts.

I step into the narrow hallway of our tiny apartment, maneuvering around stacked boxes that will never be unpacked. Not if we have to move every couple of months. This is the third time we've moved this year, and it's not even halfway over. It's the only way to avoid demons. If we're not on the run, they'll come after us until I'm either dead or tainted by evil. Or worse—they could leave me without a soul.

Alana perches on the kitchen counter, sifting through the top shelf of the junk cabinet. Her shoulder length blond hair hangs in a ponytail, the front half clinging against her cheeks. She swivels sideways and glances over her shoulder.

"Fantastic morning, isn't it?" she asks. "Another peaceful, uneventful night." Alana's fuchsia pajamas look as fresh and unwrinkled as they did last night, and I don't know why she bothers wearing them. The woman doesn't sleep at night, only in the morning, and even then she has insomnia most of the time.

"For you, maybe. I spent a good thirty minutes convincing a demon that you'd kill it if it didn't stop staring at me through the window." I wince, expecting Alana to start screaming.

She turns on the balls of her feet and jumps from the counter. She looks me up and down, checking for signs of injury.

"You know better than that, Cami," she says. "If you would've told me, I could've killed it. This is bad. It might go after an innocent person or come back here."

"It was only a lower level demon. Not something the average person couldn't fight off," I say, despite my better judgment.

"That kind of thinking will get you killed. I've spent too long keeping you safe to let that happen. You *have* to tell me these things."

"Fine, whatever," I say. Alana is persuasive when it comes to doing the right thing to protect myself from demons. The promise of injury, death, and the loss of my soul always seems to do the job. It's still effective, even though I'm now seventeen and no longer the naïve fourteen year old girl she rescued.

I watch Alana pull an empty water jug out of the refrigerator and shake it. Small droplets of water pelt the sides, creating a soft drumming sound. She tosses it into the trash before looking up at me.

She sighs. "Where's the rest of the holy water?"

"I drank it," I say.

"What? Oh, never mind. Go get dressed. We have to get more supplies."

＊＊＊

The California afternoon sun beats down, warming my skin. I use my hand to shade my eyes, not caring about the possibility of getting sunburned. Alana once told me demons are repelled by sunburns because they can feel the sun's rays emitting from your skin. I'm just not brave enough to test the theory.

"You're quiet." Alana shifts on her feet as we wait for the bus to arrive. It's a nervous habit of hers. She can never be still for longer than a minute.

"I know. I'm just thinking."

"Thinking's good. What about?"

"You'll just get upset."

"Try me."

"I'm thinking about the Veiled Realm. How much I still don't understand," I say. "If you would tell me the truth, we wouldn't have to keep having this same stupid conversation."

"You know I can't." Alana sighs, staring at me from under her light blond lashes. "It would make you a target to more than demons. I want us to live normal lives—at least as normal as we can."

"Hold on. More than demons?"

"Crap. Forget I said anything. Now."

I narrow my eyes. Alana can't back out of this. It's not often that she slips up and says too much. My curiosity is overwhelming. I have to know what other creatures are out there. How will I ever protect myself if I don't know what to look for? There could be brain-eating zombies for all I know. I don't know how to kill something that is already dead.

"No. Tell me. The boogeyman doesn't scare me."

"He should," Alana mutters.

My mouth falls open.

"I was being sarcastic. There's no such thing as the boogeyman...I think."

I blink, smoothing the frown off my face. I shouldn't be surprised. If there are demons, why wouldn't there be other beings like witches and warlocks, even fairies? It's comforting to think the Veiled Realm isn't inhabited only by evil.

The scent of fuel and dirt drifts through the air, trapped in a breeze. The bus rumbles as it pulls to the curb; the brakes squeak when it comes to a stop. Alana drops coins into the dispenser, and I stomp on behind her. She strategically sits by the middle door, and I claim the seat across the aisle from her. I'm not getting trapped by the window if something happens.

I gaze at a boy close to my age, boredom masking his face. His complexion is smooth with no signs of acne. His deep set, chocolate brown eyes stare at the ceiling.

I imagine he's one of the creatures Alana refuses to admit is real. I picture wings sprouting from his back, swooping out like an eagle's, wrapping me in feathery softness. I can almost feel the light breeze from his imaginary wings ruffling my hair.

The boy arches an eyebrow. My cheeks flush, and I roll my eyes, brushing off my embarrassment. He presses his lips together and turns away.

"Not worth it. Some people can sense when something

isn't right. And you, Cami, dance with the dark side," Alana says.

"Not by choice," I say.

"Doesn't matter."

"It should. It's not my fault demons actively seek us out."

"Or is it..."

"Shut up!"

I shift in my seat and stare at the blurry world flying by. If Alana would buy a car, we wouldn't be stuck on this stinky bus for over an hour. Where she would find the money, I have no idea.

Alana taps my shoulder; our stop is next. I stand up and grip the back of the seat, jerking when the bus comes to a halt. I shuffle off after her and notice the boy exits the front of the bus.

Alana strides forward, forcing me to keep a fast pace. Her boots are soundless compared to the constant thud-thud-thud of mine. She moves as gracefully as a ballet danc-er, her back straight and her bare shoulders showing off her athletic muscles.

A breeze gusts from behind, and I stumble. I jerk my neck to look behind me. The boy from the bus lurks ten feet away. At close range, I notice every aspect of him. He's tall and built like a swimmer. His muscles are firm, well-defined, but not overbearing. They're subtle against his slim figure. His chocolate brown eyes shine with mischief and his lips narrow in a cocky grin. His thick black hair lies in loose waves, framing his face, curling around his smooth jawline. A golden halo surrounds him in beautiful, shimmering light. I rub my eyes, clearing away the haze of the sun.

"Cami, get behind me."

I step back. My eyes never waver from the boy. Alana's low voice creates a storm of fluttering moths in my stomach. I haven't seen her act like this during the day since our first day together. I peer over her shoulder, flattening my body against hers.

The boy crosses his arms over his chest and frowns, his soft features creasing in irritation. Turning his attention to me, he curls his lips in an awkward smile, showing a small dimple on his cheek. Everything about his relaxed posture screams he's not a threat, and I wonder why Alana acts like he's going to hurt us.

He shakes his black curls away from his dark eyes. "You're always so on edge, Alana. Lighten up a bit. I'm not here for a fight," the boy says, his soft voice perking up with amusement. Something about his voice sinks into me. It sounds really familiar, almost like the voice from my nightmare.

"Then why are you here, Dylan? Are you trying to put my charge at risk?" Alana says.

"You know him?" I ask.

Dylan shifts, crossing and uncrossing his arms before placing them on his hips. Confusion lines his eyes. I inch away from Alana and step next to her, straightening my shoulders to look him dead in the eyes.

"Poor, poor girl," Dylan says, shaking his head. "You haven't told her anything have you, Alana?"

I give Alana a sidelong glance. "No, she hasn't."

"For your protection!" Alana exclaims, her soft voice going shrill. "Cami, please believe me. This is for the best."

"You can't keep her in the dark forever. She will discover the truth about our world." Dylan swings his eyes to me. "And when you do, I can help you...if you're not obliterated first."

My hands tremble. I clench them into fists, trying to quiet the rolling fear in my mind. Alana always intones that a little fear keeps you alive, too much will be your demise. At the moment, it's going to be the death of me. The grim reaper will be knocking on my door if I don't get myself under control.

"I'll keep you in mind," I say. "If you have nothing else to say to me, then leave. Nightfall is only a couple hours away and we need to get supplies."

Dylan purses his lips in thought, shrugging his shoulders. He probably didn't expect me to speak for Alana. I may be under her care, but she treats me like her equal most of the time.

"Well, if you don't want to talk, at least let me escort you." Dylan says. "It would be a shame for something to happen because I've kept you from your errands."

Alana narrows her eyes. "Fine, but if you even breathe a word about the Veiled Realm, you're going to wish you never got off the bus."

ANGEL BOY

THE SUN HOVERS westward, threatening to disappear sooner than I'd like it to. A cool breeze tickles the back of my neck, rippling loose hair from my messy bun. Alana and Dylan flank my sides, and I'm like a little girl again, striding along with my parents. Actually, Dylan is hot and not even close to being dad-like. As for Alana, well, sometimes she does act like my mom.

"There it is." Alana points to the haven a block away.

A quaint, red bricked church is nestled between two residential homes. Four pristine white pillars decorate the small entryway, and a single spire rises from a white steeple. A copper cross tops the spire, gleaming like it's been recently polished.

I climb the small set of stairs following Alana. Dylan is close behind me. We come to a door where a square plaque is nailed to the doorframe. I stare at the embossed insignia. Two daggers make the shape of a cross. A circle lies to the right of the horizontal dagger. Another circle, with straight lines sticking from it, is directly above the handle of the vertical dagger, representing the moon and sun. At dusk, the plaque will be twisted to the left, turning it into an X. It marks the church as a safe house for people in need of a place to hide when demons are wreaking havoc.

"Stay with Dylan. I'll only be a minute." Alana stretches her arm out to block my entrance.

I roll my eyes. Not allowing me in the church means one of two things. It could mean that Alana is preventing me from meeting someone who might say too much. Or two, it really will only take a minute. *Who am I kidding? She definitely doesn't want me to meet someone.*

"Come on. I'm not going to stand here at the door like a demon that can't cross the barrier," Dylan says. His breath tickles my ear, and I can't help breathing in his fresh scent. He smells good, like a sunny apple orchard laden with ripe fruit.

Dylan turns and leaps to the ground without using the steps. I attempt to do the same, only my foot catches on the last step, and I topple forward, somersaulting onto my back.

I cover my face to suppress my embarrassment. For once, why can't I be graceful like Alana? I've always felt awkward next to her, like a toddler twirling in the middle of a stage full of professional dancers.

Dylan smirks and shakes his head. "I'm surprised by your lack of finesse."

I huff and push to my feet. "Why's that? There are millions of clumsy people in the world who can't jump five feet and land smoothly, let alone walk on a flat surface without tripping."

"Exactly. You are *you*, even though I expected you to be different. Maybe Alana is right about everything. You *are* destined to be normal."

I feel as small as an ant. When did being normal turn into such a bad thing? I've spent the last three years pining for my old life, for the chance to fit in with the kids at school. And now, I feel like being normal is overrated. I should be different, extraordinary. Yes, I *am* different, just not in a good way.

"I don't get it," I say, clenching my fists. "What is it with you people talking in code? If I were destined to be normal, I wouldn't have demons on my back. I'd stay in the same school instead of moving every couple of months. I wouldn't need a demon hunter to protect me. If I were normal, my parents would still be alive. They're not because a powerful demon wants me. And I don't even know why."

I stomp down the sidewalk away from the church and Dylan. I plop down on the curb, not wanting to risk going too far, just far enough so it feels like I'm waiting alone.

Dylan saunters over, making my retreat pointless. Will this guy never give up? He settles down next to me, stretching his long legs into the street. He leans back on the palms of his hands, his head raised to the crystalline sky. A gust of wind plows me to the side, and I fall into him.

"Even the wind is out to get me," I mutter, cradling my face in my hands.

I silently scream into my palms, releasing the tension from my chest. The stiff wind transforms into a light breeze, caressing my shoulders, as if apologizing for making me miserable.

"Sorry. I didn't mean to push you," Dylan says. His eyes focus on the ground like a puppy that has just piddled on the carpet.

"You didn't." I snap my head up and stare at him. "I fell into you, remember?" Confusion lowers my brows.

After a moment, Dylan lifts his gaze to meet mine. He smiles, shaking his head. "Alana's going to kill me for this."

He pushes to his feet, standing in front of me. The sun shines behind him, casting its luminous glow around him. He stretches out his arms, imitating a bird in flight. Wind swirls through my hair. I gawk at the silhouette of wings flapping against the blinding sun. They're huge and iridescent, and sunlight shimmers through them.

My breath catches. Dylan is the most mesmerizing boy I've ever laid eyes on. I stumble to my feet. I stretch out my hand to touch his wings, but they're gone as quickly as they appeared, yet the image is forever imprinted in my mind.

"You're an a-a-angel," I stammer. It's hard to describe what I've just seen. It was amazing.

Dylan's face lights up. "Not quite. I'm only half. Humans call me a nephilim."

I close my eyes and roll the word over my tongue. Dylan locks his fingers around my wrists, forcing me to stare into his eyes.

"I imagined you having wings on the bus," I say.

"Wasn't your imagination."

My heart races as fear builds in the pit of my stomach. I have nothing to be afraid of, yet his heavy stare is too much. It's like he's peering into my soul, looking at all the scars, the pain, the broken pieces. I yank my hands back and turn away. I need to go back to Alana.

"Cami, please," Dylan pleads as I walk away. "Don't tell Alana you know."

I begin to nod my head when Alana's voice booms out nearby. "I already know."

Tears burst from my eyes at the sight of Alana, who is standing with a small box in her hands two houses away. My shoulders shake with my silent sobs. I hiccup and sputter, trying to apologize. Alana rushes to me, wrapping her strong arms around me.

My knees buckle, and I sink to the ground. The hurt and grief from past memories seep into my soul. It suffocates me with thick clouds of regret. *What is wrong with me?*

Alana slaps her hands to her temples. "What did you do to her? I leave her with you for five minutes and you start flashing your wings! Unbelievable."

"I thought she could handle it," Dylan says.

I feel like I'm invisible. The two of them talking like I'm no longer here.

"Most girls swoon over me."

"Those girls already know about your kind, nephilim."

"You're just mad because I'm not—"

Alana lunges at Dylan. They topple to the ground, and Dylan lands flat on his back. Alana grabs his wrists and forces them over his head.

"*Human*," Dylan spits out.

"Then you're right. Cami needs to be with her own kind."

I clear my throat, uncomfortable about them discussing my life without actually including me in the conversation. I grab the back of Alana's shirt and hoist her to her feet. Dylan rises to his, dusting the gritty dirt off his backside.

Dylan opens his mouth to say something. I interrupt him with a wave of my hand. "Don't. I don't want to hear it."

"Cami..." Alana says, her voice trailing off.

I glance at the sky. "I know. The sun is beginning to set. If we catch a bus now, we'll have fifteen minutes to spare."

As we head to the bus stop, Alana walks next to me while Dylan trails behind us. We have to wait five excruciating minutes before the bus roars in the distance. The bus arrives and the stench of exhaust tickles my nostrils, making me sneeze. It jerks to a stop, and I bolt on, dropping change for three into the fare box.

I sit in my usual seat, dead center near the exit and across from Alana. Dylan doesn't sit with us. He seems to be absorbed in his own thoughts. Maybe he's upset because Alana wants me to stick to dating normal boys—humans. That's impossible, though. I'm always on the run for my life. No boy would ever believe the breakup line of, "Sorry, this isn't going to work out. I have to leave town because the demons want my soul." *Right.* It would be nominated for the worst breakup line of all time.

Dylan's interesting and his looks are more devilish than angelic, but I've known him for only a few hours and know nothing about him besides his species. Also, his being so close to me scares the hell out of me—the attraction is almost tangible between us.

"Will you ever forgive me?" Alana leans across the narrow aisle. "I mean, for letting you think he was human." She lifts her chin toward the back of Dylan's shaggy black hair.

"I don't know," I say, knowing I already have. "You let me believe that only demons existed. Now that I know that there are angels, well, I don't know what else to expect. Will an angelic army try to take my soul, too? Would you let them because they're not demons?" I've trusted Alana with my life for so long that it physically hurts to question her. She's never lied to me, but keeping secrets is much worse.

"I'm not going to let anyone take you or your soul. You've lost too much already," Alana says.

I raise my eyebrows. "You'd seriously fight an angel? Are you insane?"

"Sometimes," she says.

I smile. "You mean all the time."

I catch Dylan staring at me, and I get up to sit next to him. I rest my hand on his knee, and he places his hand on top of mine. The heat between our fingers is electrifying, and I imagine his lips on mine.

"Are you busy tonight, angel boy?" I ask.

He shakes his head.

"You're welcome to have dinner with us. I'd love to know more about you."

"Alana wouldn't mind?" he asks.

I'm sure she will, but I don't say it. She owes me this. "No, she'll be happy to have you over."

"I doubt it," he says, looking over his shoulder at Alana glaring at us.

"I'll be happy. It's not every day I get to hang out with an angel."

His lack of enthusiasm makes me regret asking him. What if he says no? It's not like I'm anything special. He did say I was destined to be normal...

He smiles, surprising me. "Okay."

Yes! I resist doing a happy dance because I'd hate for him to change his mind. Alana's going to kill me for this, but she'll get over it.

"Cool." I don't want to sound too excited.

I ignore Alana's death glare. I hope she doesn't do anything stupid to ruin this for me. I don't want to have to protect Dylan from my protector.

I push the thoughts about what could go wrong to the back of my mind. Dylan stares at me, and I wonder what is going on behind his eyes. I could look at him forever, but forever is interrupted when Alana taps my shoulder and the bus comes to a stop.

I guess forever will just have to wait.

THE TRUTH CAN KILL

ON NIGHTS LIKE this, I wish the apartment had air conditioning. After being closed up most of the day, the air is stuffy, and the five minutes of opening all the windows didn't help any.

The smell of melted cheese and toasted bread has settled into my clothing. The remnants of the luxurious dinner Alana had prepared, grilled cheese sandwiches, sits on the plates in front of us. I hope Dylan wasn't expecting a gourmet meal.

He hasn't said more than two words since he entered the apartment. His eyes dart to the door every now and again, planning an escape route. This was a bad idea. I shouldn't have asked him to come over. I didn't think he would shut down the moment the door clicked closed.

"You didn't have to accept my offer," I say, annoyed by Dylan's anxious I-need-to-get-out expression. He reminds me of the kids at my school who panic when a teacher holds the class an extra minute after the bell. I would know that face. I've made it many times.

"I wanted to come. It's just—being away from my sanctuary after the sun sets is nerve-wracking. Aren't you ever afraid a demon will knock down your door? You don't even have a dead bolt."

"Like that would stop a demon," I say. "We're pretty safe here. Demons don't come knocking that often, except for the occasional peeping Tom demon, and they're easy for Alana to kill."

Dylan looks a tiny bit relieved. "I guess that's a good thing. I'm not really prepared to fight demons. I'm more of an onlooker—an errand boy."

I raise my brows wondering if he has had any experience at all in combat. I don't even think he's carrying a weapon. Maybe he doesn't need one. He could be hiding his super-human powers from me like he hides his wings.

"Now that I think of it, Cami, there was that one de-mon who crashed through our wall, which was kind of like popping in." Alana smiles as she turns to face Dylan. "It was a beast, like a hellhound on steroids. I bet the Hunter's Academy didn't teach you about them."

I laugh, smacking Alana's arm. She can be cruel when

she wants to be. She smiles and winks at Dylan. Poor boy doesn't have a chance against her.

"Can you stop?" I want Dylan to stay here long enough for me to learn about nephilim. It's one of the reasons I've invited him over for dinner.

Dylan gives me a tight-lipped smile, flashing his adorable dimples. "It's fine. I'm used to it."

I glare at Alana. I wonder how long they've known each other. Their casual banter feels like it hasn't been three years since they've seen each other. A lot must happen when I'm at school.

Alana pushes away from the table and pats my head like I'm a good little girl. She puts a slender hand on Dylan's shoulder, making him wince. "I can sense my presence is no longer welcome. Stick to nephilim if you want to live to see tomorrow," Alana says. "Good night."

Thank God! I thought she'd never leave.

Alana pads down the hallway and doesn't close her door. Unlike a normal guardian, she is more concerned about what Dylan will say than what he'll do.

"For once I wish I weren't on her bad side," Dylan mumbles, brushing his hair out of his eyes. He looks more comfortable with Alana out of the room. It would be nice if he'd just open up to me already. It shouldn't be this hard since I've already seen his wings.

"That's her good side."

I force myself to laugh to fill the silence bound to take

hold of Dylan. He stares at nothing in particular, avoiding my eyes like I've turned into Medusa. He fidgets with his shirt sleeves before leaning on his elbows.

"So..." I adjust my loose bun, tightening it. Awkward silence settles between us for a moment as I figure out what to say next. "I don't want to be blunt, but how are you even possible? I've always thought angels were ethereal, androgynous beings. Not exactly the type to hook up with mortals."

"I guess Alana has never explained the mechanics in making a baby," Dylan says, smirking.

My mouth drops open. I'm absolutely mortified. "Wh-what?" I stammer, covering my heated cheeks with my hands. "I know that already. She saved me three years ago, not ten. I mean—"

"I was joking." Dylan's lips curl into a mischievous grin. "You're cute when you're embarrassed, you know."

I swallow hard to calm my nerves. "Yeah, well, you're not so hot when you're making fun of me." *Could I be any more of a dork?*

Dylan smiles, his adorable dimples flashing again. I begin to wonder if he has any flaws; maybe a scar or a freckle to show his human half. It would make me feel better about my Plain Jane features. I guess it's better than sticking out in a crowd. I get enough attention from demons as it is. There isn't a big need for me to get attention from humans too.

"Good to know," he chuckles. "And to answer your question, some angels decide that freewill and mundane emotions are the way to go. The Veiled Realm is full of possibilities."

"I thought angels were—were *pure*," I say.

"Forget everything you've heard. It's usually a distorted version of the truth. And remember to be careful. The truth really can kill you." Dylan crosses his arms over his chest. His eyes darken like he's haunted by the secrets he keeps locked inside him.

I nod my head. "Stop skipping around the subject. I'm not new to the Veiled Realm."

"New enough. I usually don't have to explain the possibility of my existence," Dylan retorts.

"Sorry," I mumble. It's not like this is easy for me either. I feel ridiculous asking questions that he assumes everyone knows the answers to.

"If I can be honest, I don't know how much of a help I'm going to be about nephilim. Yeah, I'm half angel, but it's not like my dad raised me."

"Your father is an angel?" I ask.

"Was. And from what I hear, not a very nice one. I'd love to tell you some romantic story about my mom falling in love with her guardian angel, but it was nothing like that. As far as I know, my dad was assigned to be a Demon Watcher and had a little too much fun indulging in human pleasures. He knocked my mom up."

"That's terrible. I bet that's what happened to the angel who was supposed to watch my demon."

Dylan shakes his head. "Angels don't necessarily watch demons. They try to intervene and save souls before demons can take them. If you willingly give up your soul, you've lost. It's like when angels become unfocused and distracted. Instead of losing their souls, they lose their wings. It happened to my father. Demons probably dragged him to Hell after that."

The truth isn't as good as I thought. It's sad. I wish he would've made up a romantic story. I hate the idea of the fallen. It means more demons to worry about.

"Is your mom okay?" I wish I could change the subject to save Dylan from feeling obligated to tell me his personal story, but I can't. I want to know everything about him.

"I don't know. She gave me to the hunters when I was a baby for my safety. I only know this because it's in the file the Hunter's Alliance created for me."

I wipe a tear from my cheek before he sees it. It must be awful learning about your life from a file. I squelch the urge to hug Dylan even though it breaks my heart, knowing he didn't have what I had with my parents.

Dylan reaches out and runs his finger along my cheek. "Don't feel sad on my account," he whispers. "I don't even know if what I told you is true. The alliance could've gotten it wrong."

I cover his hand with mine, interlocking our fingers. I

imagine what my file would say if the alliance knew of my existence; something along the lines of wrong place, wrong time, unsure of what to do with her.

"Yeah..." My voice trails off. Now at a loss for words, I rub my free hand over my face. I feel naked and vulnerable. It was too easy to let my guard down with Dylan. I straighten my shoulders. It's not like me to show my fragility to a stranger. This little chink in my armor could be the end of me.

"I think this is enough talk about me. I'm sure you've had enough sadness in your life to fill an ocean," Dylan says.

"I don't know what's wrong with me. Something about you opens me up to everything that has hurt me in the past." I know I shouldn't be ashamed to show my softer side in front of Dylan. He's a freaking angel. I can see my pain reflected in his eyes like his power is empathy, absorbing the weakening emotions I feel.

"I think it has to do with the angel thing. You know the harmonious voice, the halo, the wings. Humans are more likely to let down their guards with the nephilim than with anyone else."

I nod my head and smile. "You're full of it. You don't have a halo, Angel Boy."

Dylan laughs, caught by surprise. "I was just trying to make you feel better."

"And it worked," I say.

ON THE RUN

THE CLANKING OF the water pipes breaks the silence of the apartment. I tread across the small living room, turning off light switches. I push aside the curtains and morning light spills in, bathing the room in a soft glow.

Dylan lies half asleep on the couch. His legs sprawl over the coffee table, giving me room to curl up on the cushion next to him. His messy hair curls in every direction. I plop down beside him, running my fingers through his adorable bed head.

Dylan gazes at me through his dark eyelashes. Fighting off exhaustion, he blinks through half closed lids. I can tell he isn't used to staying up all night. After I gave up on keeping him awake, he's been dozing for the last hour.

Talking to him was nice while it lasted. I didn't realize I'd been starving for another person to talk to. I'm accustomed to talking only to Alana.

"You look tired." A small smile creeps onto my lips. I hope he doesn't have anything important to do today. "Are you going to be okay getting home?"

Dylan covers his mouth, hiding a yawn. "I'm fine. Next time I'm sent out on an errand like this, I'll remember to sleep my day away first."

My heart sinks into my stomach. "What kind of errand?" It's hard to believe our meeting wasn't fate, and that it was planned out by people I'll never get to meet. "Were you sent to take me away from Alana like she accused you of?"

"No." Dylan shakes his head. "I wasn't even supposed to reveal myself to you. I just—I just got distracted on the bus. I didn't think you'd even notice me. I was sent to give Alana this." Dylan reaches into his pocket and pulls out a small white envelope. "And then, well, you know the rest."

"Oh." My heart hammers as I stare into Dylan's pleading eyes. Paranoia strikes me like a hot lightning bolt. If Dylan was able to find me, anyone could. "How did you track us down?"

"It's kind of my specialty, but that's beside the point. The moment I saw you and our eyes met, I couldn't resist showing you the real me. I needed to meet you." Dylan rubs the top of my hand. I could sit with him like this forever.

"And then suddenly, I wanted to protect you; your innocence, your will to live. The protective wall you've built around yourself called to me. Alana is right about not wanting you to be involved with the Veiled Realm, but you are meant for it. It's the only place you'll ever fit in, even if it doesn't seem that way now."

My hands begin to tremble. Fear and anger crawl up my spine. I would love to be comforted by his words, but they bother me. I should be the one who knows my deepest, darkest secrets. I should never have to wonder if someone knows more things about me than I'm even aware of. It's as if Dylan breaks through the barriers I built around my heart after my parents died. It's like he's reaching into the giant cracks and touching the barely healed scar tissue on my soul. He's intruding and discovering places I never wanted to remember again. Yet, I want to open up and let him see the damage the demons caused so he can heal me and make me whole again.

My breath catches as Dylan's fingers rub my cheek. I flinch away. His worry for my suffering is too hard to grasp. Could he really know where I fit or who I should be? My pounding heart echoes in my ears. I swallow the sour taste of my pride and bury my anger and vulnerability deep inside. It takes every ounce of my strength to stay still. I'm not sure if I should slap him and make him stop or simply run away with him.

"Cami," he says. "Look at me."

I lift my gaze, staring into his eyes. And then a thought hits me like a burning comet falling from the sky. Dylan isn't trying to rouse the pain in my soul or carry me into a new life. He is showing me options I have that I was never aware of. I don't have to run forever. I can find my place in the world. My cheeks warm, and my nerves settle.

Yet, his efforts are futile. I would never leave Alana, and that's why my emotions have gotten out of control. I refuse to live a life without her, even if it makes me an outcast in both worlds.

"You're beautiful." Dylan tucks strands of my dark hair behind my ear. "I wish I didn't have to go."

"Me too." My shoulders hunch in disappointment. I knew this moment would come. Dylan has a life to go back to. I should be used to meeting people and never seeing them again, but I'm tired of that. *Why can't I be normal?*

"You could come with me." Dylan cups my face in his hands. "Alana isn't the only one who can keep you safe."

"It isn't possible. This is the only way I can try to be normal. It's for the best." I would love to run away from this life, but I can't trust Dylan. I've known him a few hours, and it would be crazy to even consider it. I like him, but I also like chocolate, reading, and not being bothered by demons, too.

"Yeah, for the best," Dylan mumbles. I don't think he really believes my words.

I wrap the cozy throw blanket around my shoulders and

walk Dylan to the door. He hands me the envelope for Alana and kisses my cheek.

He hovers inches away from me. "Remember what I told you yesterday. I'm here for you when the time comes."

I nod my head, not fully believing that the time will ever come. Alana has done a pretty good job at keeping me on the edge of the Veiled Realm for the last three years, until yesterday.

I watch from the doorway as Dylan meanders down the narrow path that leads to the street. The wind blows through my tousled hair, and I glimpse the outline of his invisible wings. He turns the corner and disappears.

Deep in my heart, I know I'll never see Dylan again, not if Alana has anything to do with it. She works hard to keep me safe. She'll never put my life in jeopardy for a half-angel. It's never been this difficult watching a potential friend, maybe even a boyfriend, exit my life, and I know I won't ever forget him.

⁓ ◦◦ ⁓

I wake up mid-afternoon to Alana shuffling around her bedroom. She slams her door several times, wanting me to get up without bothering to knock on my door like a normal person. I roll out of bed and stroll the five feet it takes to get to her room.

A partially full duffle bag sits on the edge of Alana's bed. She separates her tiny wardrobe into two piles, creating a mound of clothing to keep while throwing the rest off the bed in a shower of inappropriate hunting attire—the clothes she wears that leave her vulnerable during fights, like tank tops and shorts and even her favorite summer dress. This routine is all too familiar.

"We're leaving again." I was right about never getting to see Dylan again.

Alana jerks her head up and nods. She doesn't say a word, continuing to pack. I should've known living here for even a month longer was too good to be true. We're always on the run.

I turn on my heels and stomp back to my bedroom. I open my closet door and yank my sparse wardrobe from the hangers. It's useless to argue with Alana. Her mind is set. We're leaving again because of Dylan. I should've let him leave us at the bus stop.

Alana has always told me it's imperative that no one knows where we live. I assumed because she knew Dylan, this time would be different. I was wrong. I want to be angry with her, furious even. The little voice in the back of my mind prevents me. It begs me to be reasonable because the less a person knows, the harder it is for demons to track us. They use humans as pawns in their games to keep an upper hand. The last thing I want is for Dylan to become a pawn that aids in my destruction. Even if he isn't human, there is a possibility that he could be used. I'd hate myself if that ever happened.

I stuff what few belongings I have into my backpack,

leaving out a pair of blue jeans, a long black sweater, and my leather jacket, before heading to the bathroom.

I comb my fingers through my messy chocolate hair, the curls more frizzy than bouncy, and then poke at the puffy skin under my green eyes. My pouty bottom lip quivers as I try to pull myself together. *God! I don't want to move again!*

I hop into the shower to let the hot water wash away my anger and unease. I try to enjoy the sound of pouring water because I don't know when my next shower will be. There have been way too many times I had to clean off in the sink of a fast food restaurant. When you are on the run, daily luxuries are hard to come by.

I turn off the water when I hear Alana make her way into the kitchen. I towel dry my hair and pull it into a soppy bun because I haven't had a hair dryer in months.

My fresh, lavender-scented clothes cling to my damp skin as I head back to my bedroom to get my backpack. I glance one last time at my room and slam the door, glad I haven't had the chance to personalize it since I'll never see it again.

I sling my backpack over my tense shoulders and lean against the white wall adjacent to the front door. My chest tightens. My heart feels as if it may explode this time. At least I still have Alana to pick up the pieces.

"The cab is meeting us at the front office," Alana says.

I stroll behind her without a single glance back at our quaint apartment because it will only make me feel worse.

We reach the bright blue building surrounded by beautiful flowerbeds full of bright white daisies. I wait outside as Alana hands an envelope to the receptionist. I'm sure it has instructions to donate the furniture we can't take.

A shabby cab pulls into a space marked for visitors. The driver's face hides behind a long, scraggly beard. His red and black shirt is unbuttoned at the collar, showing off a chest full of orangey hair that matches his head.

Straightening my shoulders, I stomp down the sidewalk to get in before Alana. I slide across the splitting, dirty brown cloth bench seat. The putrid smell of feet wafts around me, and I cover my nose with my sleeve to keep from breathing in the smell.

Alana jogs over and hops in next to me like she's jumping into the getaway car after a bank heist. Now that we are away from the comfort of our apartment, she'll be on high alert. Everything and everyone is a threat to us. It's hard to know the enemy until it's almost too late.

Alana mumbles to the driver to take us to the nearest bank and then gives him an address I'm not familiar with, a safe house far from here. I hunch forward, leaning my head on my hands. We have about two hours until dark according to the clock. I truly trust only the sun, but it's hidden behind a thick blanket of clouds. The sky matches my mood. It looks like a storm is brewing, readying to rain on my already miserable day.

"Don't worry so much." Alana's breath tickles my ear.

"We'll find a new place to live in no time."

"I liked where we were," I say through clenched teeth.

"I know you did, and I'm sorry. It's just that Dylan knows where we live now."

I glare out the window. "Dylan would never hurt me. I think he actually liked me."

"You know that after a day? You've got to be kidding me!" She wrings her hands together. "You don't know anything."

"Because you won't let me know anything!" I yell. The cab driver stares at us in his rearview mirror. I slump out of his view and force the anger from my voice. "It's like you're trying to protect me from the inevitable. I'm not a little girl anymore, Alana. I survived the fire that killed my parents. I survived every demon that has tried to attack me. I'm pretty damn sure I can survive the truth."

"I can't take that chance," she whispers. "You mean the world to me."

I lean in closer. "I think it's more than that. What are you so afraid of?"

Alana sighs, drawing her eyes to mine. "That you'll want to leave me."

I release the breath I've been holding. "I could never do that."

"I hope not."

DESERTVILLE

DEAD PATCHES OF shrubbery fly by the dirty window. We've been on this bland freeway for more than an hour and the setting sun slinks lower on the horizon every minute.

A green-and-white lettered sign declares we are now entering Desertville. I shiver as we exit onto Highway 395. The name of the town doesn't lie. The measly view consists of clumps of track homes and barren lots. It seems like everything has been tinted brown—the road, the shrubs, the houses—even the clouds look brown.

"I gotta stop for gas," the cab driver mumbles as he pulls into a truck stop.

"Good. My legs are cramping," I say. My back is killing

me from the ride. I shift in my seat to stretch my legs.

Alana glances out the window and back to me. Her eyebrows furrow, absorbed in the same internal debate as always—stay with the cab or follow me. The choice would be easy if it were past dusk, she'd come with me no matter what. But night isn't here yet. I can handle being alone.

I push open the door and step out. Alana slides across the seat, hovering just outside of the cab. Due to the long drive, the cab driver insisted on receiving advance payment to make sure we wouldn't stiff him when we arrived at our destination. It's the only reason Alana doesn't want to leave the driver unattended.

"I'll be fine," I say, rolling my eyes. "I'm only going to the bathroom."

Alana nods her head. "Be quick."

I walk inside the convenience store. My stomach rumbles, overwhelmed by rows of delicious junk food. I enter through the bathroom door marked for women and lock it behind me.

I cringe, taking in the tiny bathroom. It smells as bad as it looks. The grimy tile walls should've been cleaned and disinfected months ago. The cracked, rectangular mirror is covered in graffiti. I stare through the haze of black permanent marker at my reflection. Puffy, bluish circles surround my eyes, making it look like I haven't slept in days. My bun rests limply against the back of my neck. Half of my hair is out of place, falling over my shoulders.

I splash cold water on my face and wipe away the day's travels with a coarse paper towel. I wrap the paper towel around my hand and push the door handle down to leave, but it doesn't open. The lock is jammed. I'm stuck.

"A little help here!" I yell. Sweat beads on my forehead. My fear of being locked in a room without a way to escape is coming true.

I kick the door with enough force that should've knocked the flimsy thing off its hinges. I pound my fists as hard as I can. Someone is bound to hear all the noise I'm making. I jiggle the handle, slapping my open palm against the door.

My heart stops as the lights flash off, leaving me in utter darkness. My heart bangs against my ribcage. I blink to adjust to the darkness without success. It's too dark; even the fluorescent lights in the store refuse to shine through under the door.

"Help!" The sound of my voice echoes around me and fades. Are these walls soundproof? Is this someone's twisted idea of a joke? *So. Not. Funny.*

My breath quickens, the air feeling like it's seeping out of the room. Goosebumps form on my arms, and I close my eyes to suppress my jittery nerves. I can sense another presence nearby. Alana has never mentioned ghosts. It's possible she has never encountered them, but it's not like she has ever been forthcoming with those kinds of details. My stomach churns in anticipation. The unknown is taking its toll on me.

A loud scratching noise comes from the far wall, and I take a step back. The pressure in the room thickens like the walls are closing in on me, suffocating me with my worst fears. The noise is too obnoxiously loud to be mice. I can only hope that it's coming from rats and not something else, something from the Veiled Realm.

I nearly jump out of my skin when the sound of tinkling bells rings out in my pitch black prison. I slap my hand against my forehead, remembering the cell phone in my jacket pocket. I slide my hand in and retrieve it. I flip it open and look around at the empty bathroom in the faint glow of the phone.

"Cami?" Alana questions.

"I'm locked in the bathroom!" I yell. "And the lights are off."

"Crap," Alana breathes. "I'm coming."

I hang up, but keep my phone open to allow the built-in flashlight to fill up the small room. I stay next to the door with my eyes trained on the shadows. I glance at my startled expression in the mirror and freeze when I notice movement behind me. A dark cloud forms by the disgusting toilet.

"Cami," Alana says through the door.

My response dies in my throat as the cloud begins moving toward me. I hold my phone out farther with a scream ripping from my throat. The cloud is an army of black spiders. They move and flow with an insect's grace, like a silent wave drifting closer to me.

I slam my fists against the door. "Get me out of here!" Hot tears roll down my cheeks. "Th-there's spiders."

"Oh, God," Alana says. "Can you climb up on the toilet?"

"They're coming from that direction." Fear pulses through my veins. "And the sink doesn't look like it can hold my weight."

The door shakes as Alana tries to force it open. The spiders scatter, some rushing in my direction. I squish the closest one to me, hearing a small pop as it explodes under my boot.

I lean against the pedestal sink and push myself up. It wobbles under my weight, and I try to stay as still as possible. The spiders begin to swarm around the base of the sink, skittering up the walls like they have been trained to seek and destroy.

"Hurry up. I'm pretty sure these aren't normal spiders. They're huge."

"I think you're right. Don't let them on you. They'll either eat you alive or lay eggs in your blood stream," Alana says.

"What? Get me out of here!"

My stomach flips, nausea coming at the worst moment. *I do not want to die like this.* I scream again, muting the crashing at the door. My throat burns, but I can't stop.

The spiders freeze. I wonder if it's possible that my

screams stunned them. I watch in awe as they begin crawling backwards like someone has hit the rewind button. It's eerie and disturbing but somehow fascinating.

The banging racket at the door continues as Alana tries to break it down. I don't want to stop screaming, even if she thinks I'm being devoured alive. I'd rather let her worry than stop the only thing I can do to save myself.

My scream dies as the last spider disappears through a tiny hole in the wall next to the toilet. If banshees really exist, they'll be begging me to join them.

I slump against the mirror out of breath. The door flies open with a thud. I jump, startled. The quick movement topples me onto the floor. My cell phone flies from my hand, the screen shattering into a million pieces. *Great!* I won't get another phone for who knows how long.

Bright fluorescent light pours in and Alana grabs my hands, dragging me out of the bathroom. She pushes the frazzled employee away, and we rush from the store. "I thought you became spider food." She pulls me to my feet and wraps her arms around me.

"Almost," I say. "My screams scared them off."

"Impossible." She tenses. "Not even the most potent bug spray can do that. You should know it's not that easy."

"Then why..." My words trail off. I stare out the windows at the nearly dark sky. The sun is gone, and so is our cab.

A lone figure stands in the middle of the desert field

across the highway. I bring up my hand and point, unable to form any words. Alana jerks her head up to look where I am pointing.

"The spiders knew a bigger predator was in town," Alana says.

The beautiful demon glides across the empty two-lane road, closer to us—closer to me. My heart races, the realization sinking in. We are stuck in the middle of nowhere, after dark, with the demon from my past who wants my soul.

NEVER FORGET

MY BLOOD BOILS. Rage and anger consume me. My vision tints a crimson so deep and so dark, it's like blood vessels have burst in my eyes, preventing me from seeing anything but *him*. He's not going to get away this time. This demon, posed as a man, murdered my parents. He's the one who took my entire world and set it on fire, leaving a broken heart and painful memories as my only possessions.

The demon narrows his eyes and smiles, showing off his perfectly straight teeth. He doesn't move. He's breathtaking, like a wingless angel statue in a graveyard, and just as eerie. And I hate him. I hate that I want to talk to him, to know about him. It's like part of me is dying to let him win so I can be with him and learn from him. It's not the same feeling I had with Dylan. This is more powerful, darker. It doesn't involve lust or romance. I just want to know his secrets and understand why I've been chosen to be tormented. Why he wants me so much.

I hate him because he is the key to unlocking everything Alana has kept from me. He's the only string that ties me to my past, preventing me from moving forward with my life—the reason I can never forget.

Alana braces herself next to me as she prepares to fight, even though she would rather run. It's the best way to protect me, to keep me from being thrown into battle. I don't possess her combat skills or her ability to look evil straight in the eyes. It's hard to overlook the demon's perfection and see the evil Alana does.

All I see is a handsome man who knows information about me that I don't—a man hell-bent on acquiring my soul. At this moment, I'd rather be trapped in the room with the flesh-eating spiders because at least my soul would remain intact.

The power swelling within the demon's brilliant green eyes is almost tangible. I sense it's a power so great even the best hunters can't defeat him.

I back up, moving behind Alana, using her as my shield. She can protect me from the front while I watch her back. I never know what kind of tactics a demon will use to get to me.

I peer over Alana's shoulder. The demon curls his lips into a lopsided frown. He clenches his fists, jerking his hands to his chest. He thrusts his arms out, and a flashing ball of light zooms over our heads, smashing into the side of the convenience store in a fireworks show of sparkles.

"We need to move," Alana whispers, pressing her back into my chest.

I shuffle backwards until my back presses against the pillar of the metal awning. I duck behind it, crouching low. Alana stands tall behind me, sandwiching me between the pillar and her, shielding me more effectively.

My loosened hair swirls in the desert wind. The hot air heats my skin. The scent of cinnamon caresses my nostrils as the breeze carries the demon's seductive aroma my way.

The wind blows, sweeping a layer of dirt through the air to obscure my vision. I wince as another glowing ball of energy heads in our direction. The pillar next to ours vibrates as the ball collides with it. The demon isn't trying to kill us. He's attempting to get us back into the open where he can get a clear shot to snatch me. If he wanted us dead, we would be. His aim is never off.

"He's going to fry us if he doesn't stop," I mutter.

"Those aren't for us," Alana says.

I look up at her, but her eyes never leave the demon. "Then who are they for?"

"Another hunter."

I'm not sure whether I should be afraid for the hunter

or relieved for the reinforcement. This isn't anyone's battle but my own, with the exception of Alana. I'd be dead without her.

"Get to my car," a feminine voice says.

I glance around and see a girl no older than I am tucked behind the pillar parallel to ours. I can't get a good look at her through the glare of the overhead lights, just her dark hair swirling around her.

"Where is it?" Alana asks, unperturbed by a stranger being on our side. It could be because the hunter is less of a threat than the demon.

The girl points at an old pastel green Jaguar parked in the small three-spaced lot facing a chain-link fence.

I jump to my feet, catching the demon's attention. He glides closer, tantalizing me with his spicy smell. He lifts his hand, beckoning me to join him. His eyes shine in the light, and I notice his expanding diamond-shaped pupils.

"It's been so long," the demon says. My knees buckle at the sound of his deep, sugary voice. "I don't see why you're always running from me, Camilla. I won't hurt you. I promise."

My heart flutters in excitement, conflicting with the fear racing through my mind. It wouldn't be hard to resist if he wasn't this good looking.

"Liar," I growl, composing myself. I can't let him hypnotize me. "You want my soul."

"If I wanted your soul, I'd already have it. I want you in

your entirety. You're very important to me," he says.

I grab Alana's hand. "Why?"

The demon opens his mouth to answer when Alana lunges. I fall backwards, crashing into the rocky cement. I scurry away on all fours, moving closer to the Jaguar. Pebbles embed in the palms of my hands the faster I move. My shoulder hits the front bumper, and I curl up next to the tire, unable to take my eyes off the impending battle.

Alana's leather jacket flows behind her. She dances around the demon, ducking out of his reach. I hold my breath, waiting for the demon to throw an energy ball, but he doesn't.

She grunts as the demon's fist connects with her shoulder, throwing her off balance. Crouching low, her arms extend out like a bird of prey before she launches forward into the demon's knees. He topples to the dirt with Alana on top of him. She forces his hands above his head, restricting his movement with one hand as she reaches for the tiny dagger tucked in her waistband.

The sharp blade glints in the light. My brows scrunch as the demon's lips move. I watch in shock as Alana has a silent conversation with the demon. *What the heck is going on?*

Firm hands grip my shoulder, and I jump. I've forgotten about the other hunter. She pulls me to my feet and shoves me into the front seat of the Jaguar.

"Stay here," the girl says. She slams the door shut and hustles to Alana.

I watch in horror as the demon twists out of Alana's grasp. She flies through the air and skids across the ground like a discarded toy. My heart stops, seeing her crumpled in the dirt, unmoving.

I jump at a flash of light brighter than electrifying lightning. The hunter must've reached the demon. I bolt from the car, disobeying the hunter's orders, not caring if it kills me. Alana is hurt. She needs me.

Loose rocks scrape against the cement as I jog over to her. I release the breath I've been holding. She's blinking, dazed. I grab her hands and pull her to her feet and support her weight as I help her to the waiting car.

"How badly are you injured?" I ask, afraid to hear the answer.

"Only bruises," Alana mumbles. "Out of breath."

Alana crawls into the backseat, and I take my position behind the wheel. Escaping has been a lot easier since I got my license last year.

"What did you say to him?" I ask, referring to what I saw happen between Alana and the demon.

"Not a lot. I demanded he leave us alone. That you were mine, and he could never have you."

"Oh," I say.

A screeching sound, like nails on a chalkboard, pierces my ears, nearly causing my soul to jump out of my skin. Hands slam against the passenger side window, and I scream. The door flies open and the hunter falls into the front seat. I stare in awe, amazed that she's still alive.

"Drive!" she yells. "I didn't kill it."

I fumble with the keys already in the ignition. I don't bother reversing out of the spot. I hit the throttle, jolting the Jaguar forward, crashing through the flimsy fence. Dirt sprays from under the tires as I floor the gas pedal, sending a cloud of dust up in our wake. The car bumps and jerks on the uneven field. I don't slow down for fear of not making it to the road.

I barrel onto the two-lane highway. I clench my fists as I look in the rearview mirror. The demon stands motionless in the middle of the road, the hilt of a dagger protruding from his stomach.

He raises his arm, and I hunch down in my seat, anticipating an energy ball plowing into the car, but nothing happens. He twitches his fingers, waving at us. There won't be any more fighting tonight, but the battle has just begun.

7

STORYTELLER

I DON'T SPEAK as the hunter guides me through an old neighborhood, where I hope a safe house is located. I pull into a gravel driveway. The girl grabs a small remote from the glove compartment to open the wrought iron gate. Weed infested dirt fields surround the looming Victorian house. We've left civilization behind at the last street. The worrisome barren lot is as brown as the rest of the town. I suppose if a hunter lives here, it has to be safe, right? The iron fence encasing the property makes me feel somewhat protected even though it's most likely only there to keep animals and trespassers out, not demons.

The faded yellow house has dirty, white chipped shutters and siding. Old, rickety stairs lead to the wooden porch.

Dim lights shine through lace curtained windows, giving the house a haunted feel. Luxuriant potted plants line the front and add the warmth the house needs to make it appear lived in. Though the house is in serious need of a makeover, a fresh coat of paint and some care could restore it to its glory days.

I park the Jaguar in front of the wooden steps and hand the keys to the girl. I help Alana from the backseat, stumbling over the uneven ground with her added body weight as I follow the girl up the stairs.

The door creaks open and I brace myself for a knife-wielding murderer, but to my relief, an elderly woman hovers in the entryway. Her honey brown eyes dart from me to Alana and then into the distance at nothing in particular, probably scouting the land for demons. She doesn't appear to be a hunter, at least not now, but maybe back when she was blossoming with youth.

"Come in, come in," the woman says, pulling me by the sleeve. The girl shuts the door with a thud, locking the deadbolt.

The woman leads us down a narrow hallway into a tidy kitchen. It smells like a picnic in a garden soaked in sunlight—a mixture of freshly cut peonies and warm bread straight from the oven. I'm surprised by the modern appliances tucked into light gray cabinetry. A simple table decked with a sheer, ruby tablecloth sits in a round kitchen nook next to a large curtained window.

Alana slumps into a floral-patterned chair at the table, leaning her chin on her hands. I plop down next to her, staring at the dirt and pebbles embedded in my palms. *It could be worse.*

The woman pours four cups of tea from a whistling kettle on the gas range and sets them in front of us. Alana grimaces, preferring coffee, but takes a courtesy sip of steaming lemon scented tea.

"Are you hungry?" the woman asks. "I have some leftovers I can heat up."

I nod without saying a word. I didn't realize I was hungry until she mentioned food. The girl sits across from me, looking less like a fearless hunter.

What I thought was dark brown hair is actually deep purple. It curls down her back almost touching her waist. Shorter pieces frame her delicate heart shaped face while side swept bangs cover one of her honey brown eyes, the same color as the woman's. Black eyeliner and heavy mascara line her eyes, and pink lip stain highlights the bow of her pouty mouth.

A black pearl necklace winds around her neck, and black metallic bangles clank on her wrists. Her black lace T-shirt hugs her curves, showing off a burgundy tank top underneath.

"I'm Cadence Dubois," she says, extending her delicate hand out to mine. Her black nail polish glistens in the light, making me self-conscious of my dirty, in-desperate-need-of-a-manicure hands.

"Cami Anders." I tilt my head toward Alana. "This is my guardian, Alana O'Neil." I shake Cadence's hand while Alana smiles over the top of her mug.

"This is my grandmother." Cadence motions to the old woman.

"Thank you for your kind hospitality, Mrs. Dubois," Alana says, setting her mug on the table.

"Please, call me Vivian. And your kind is always welcome."

Our kind? It's hard to get used to people referring to Alana and me as a kind, like we are aliens from another planet. It feels wrong. We are as human as anyone else. Does that mean she and Cadence aren't human?

"I'm glad you like humans," I say in response. Maybe she thinks Cadence rescued us, and that we are something else. "I don't know how I'd feel if you didn't."

Vivian beams a smile and glances at Alana. "I'm a human myself. I only meant that hunters are always welcome. That's all."

Goosebumps prickle on my arms as Vivian stares at me. She can't possibly think I'm a demon hunter like Alana or her granddaughter. Nothing about me indicates I'm a fighter. I don't even carry a weapon—not like that means anything.

My thoughts are interrupted by the scent of dinner. My stomach growls when Vivian sets three plates of meatloaf and mixed vegetables in front of us. I'm tempted to start digging in with my hands but stop myself when Alana shoots me a don't-you-dare look.

I push away from the table and walk to the sink to wash my hands. The cuts and scrapes burn as I squeeze a dime-sized amount of soap onto my palm. I wash my hands, using my short nails to pull out most of the larger pebbles, saving the rest for tweezers and a first-aid kit. I rejoin the others at the table and start taking small bites of the meat, savoring the hearty flavor.

"May I ask why a hunter, fresh from the academy, is living in the middle of nowhere?" Alana asks Cadence. "Most graduates like to hit the big cities on a hunting spree."

"I'm needed here," Cadence says. "My grandmother can't protect herself from the Veiled Realm—not since my father was elected to the Hunter's Alliance."

"I told you I can take care of myself," Vivian says, sounding much younger than her years. She pats down the stray dark gray hairs of her pixie cut, tucking the loose strands behind her ears. Deep lines form on her forehead as she glares at her granddaughter. "You should join these sweet girls when they leave. Let me have some peace. You know the demons don't bother me."

Cadence rolls her eyes, and I feel like I'm intruding on a private family moment.

"I gave up hunting long ago," Alana says, interrupting. "Your granddaughter would be better serving this town than following us around."

"What a shame." Vivian shrugs her petite shoulders. "I suppose everyone must live their own lives. And yes, I'm talking to you too, Cadence. You're not living your life. You're living mine."

Alana chuckles. She sips her tea, refraining from getting involved. Vivian could teach her a thing or two. She's right about people living their own lives. Alana should let me live mine.

I set my fork down and push my empty plate away. "You were really good tonight." I smile at Cadence. "I wish they would teach those moves in public school."

"I wondered why you didn't join in. I thought that may have been your first time seeing a demon." Cadence raises her eyebrows, looking at Alana.

"I wish. That demon has been after me for years. Alana's the only reason why I'm still alive."

Alana glances down at her half eaten plate. "Cami was never meant for this. I gave up hunting to give her a normal life after her parents were murdered. It's very important to me that she remain protected."

"But you can't escape her—"

Vivian slams her hands on the table, cutting off whatever Cadence was about to say. I hunker in my chair, feeling invisible once again because Alana talks about me as if I'm not in the room.

"I think it's time to move into the living room. My back

is aching from these old chairs," Vivian says.

Cadence rolls her eyes and helps her grandmother up. I follow impatiently behind them, not used to the slow pace. Alana wraps her arm around my shoulders, treating me like my world will come crashing down tonight unless I stay by her side.

I take a seat next to her on a plush, red upholstered couch. It's out of place among the antique furniture, reminding me of myself. The couch can't help that it doesn't fit in, even though it's trying so hard. I must be exhausted. I'm comparing my life to a freaking couch!

Vivian settles into a worn rocking chair and places her feet on an ottoman. Cadence sits cross-legged on the thick rug, leaning against a small loveseat.

"If you don't mind me asking, how did you end up here?" Vivian asks. "This town isn't exactly a tourist spot."

Alana relaxes with the change of topic.

"Well, I met my first nephilim yesterday, invited him for dinner, woke up this afternoon to Alana packing, and now here we are. I know to never invite guests over now," I grumble.

"That's not exactly how it went," Alana says. "You know the reason we couldn't stay."

Vivian nods her head, agreeing with Alana. I cross my arms and stare at the floor. I don't care if Alana was protecting me. Dylan would never have hurt us. At least I hope not.

"I think you have issues with non-humans," I say.

"That's not it," Alana says. "I have nothing against half-humans or anyone else of the non-evil variety. It's just that Dylan has been helping someone I've been avoiding for quite some time. I'm not ready to face that person just yet."

I sigh. I can't be angry at Alana for this. Her reasons for running have always been good, and I can't start questioning them now. When she's ready to talk about it, she'll tell me.

"Okay," I mumble. "Sorry for the family dramatics." I glance at Vivian and Cadence.

"No worries," Cadence says. "I know how that goes."

I fidget, wishing for this night to be over.

"Now that you know about us, why don't you tell us a little about yourselves?" Alana asks, taking the focus away from our personal lives. She's always been good at getting out of awkward moments.

"That's a wonderful idea," Vivian says. Her honey brown eyes light with excitement. "I don't get company often, and I'm sure Cadence is tired of all my stories."

"Stories?" I'm not so sure I want to spend the rest of the night listening to Vivian reminiscing about the good ol' days.

"Of course. I'm not just a little old lady with children who fell into demon hunting. I've been part of the Veiled Realm for a very long time," Vivian says.

"You're a demon hunter?"

"Oh, no, nothing like that. I was born with the ability of knowing the Veiled Realm—and it's darkest secrets. The Hunter's Alliance calls me the storyteller because not many people believe me until it's too late."

HUNTER'S ALLIANCE

"YOU TELL STORIES," I say, pausing. I imagine Vivian sitting in front of a campfire, whispering ghost stories to children. She looks serious enough, and it scares the hell out of me. I bet people like her were the ones to start the myths and legends that have turned out to be true. "About the Veiled Realm? Why doesn't the alliance believe you?"

"Fear. My visions don't always make sense. The alliance only believes things they've experienced and documented. Their humanity blinds them. It keeps them closed-minded, prevents them from accepting all possibilities. It's how humans cope with the Veiled Realm," Vivian says. "It's also what keeps them safe and unnoticed."

"That's stupid of the alliance. Their inability to accept

the unknown is going to get them killed." The more I learn about the Hunter's Alliance, the more I disapprove of their ways, even if they're efficient in training hunters to kill demons. Alana should run for a position with them. She understands how debilitating fear is.

"I agree wholeheartedly, which is why they don't take me seriously," Vivian says.

"I know the feeling." I glance at Alana. "I mean about being taken seriously...and maybe the getting killed part. I don't even know how to tell who's human and who isn't."

"I can help you with that. It's like a sixth sense. If you come in contact with a species from the Veiled Realm, your soul knows. You may be repulsed by that person or extremely attracted. You may feel just a little off. It's a struggle between your brain and your soul. Your brain uses your five senses, your soul, the sixth," Vivian says.

That explains my attraction to Dylan.

"You said other species...are you saying there are more than just angels and demons?" I finally have the opportunity to probe the mind of someone who is willing to answer my questions. And Alana can do nothing to stop her. *Ha!*

"Yes." She stares at my guardian for a moment, and Alana gives her the *look,* the one that'll stop Vivian from saying much more. She isn't willing to provide the answers I yearn for, not without Alana's consent. Her overprotectiveness is getting on my nerves.

I roll my eyes and stand up. "Thanks for sharing your

knowledge with me. Save the rest for when Alana actually lets me hear the truth." I glare down my protector.

I walk to the doorway and pause, turning back to the others.

"Third door on the left, dear," Vivian says. "Get some sleep. You don't have to worry about demons tonight. They can't cross our gates. They've been blessed."

I clomp down the hallway, counting the doors on the left side. The others continue to converse, and I swear I hear Vivian say, "You can't protect her forever. Her time is coming."

Her words unnerve me after everything she has said. I only hope Alana believes her before it's too late.

I lie in a gigantic, four-poster bed with a soft quilted comforter pulled all the way to my chin. I'm small compared to the open space built for a family. The scent of roses wafts through the air, soothing my tense, aching muscles and hurt ego. Paintings of luscious garden scenes framed in gold adorn the burgundy walls, and a cherry wood dresser sits against the wall near the closet. I'm too young to be sleeping in this time-warped room, screaming of Vivian's antique taste.

I turn on my side and stare out the window. The curtains are drawn open, allowing me to watch the black, moonless night. I'm not going to let myself be surprised by an enemy. Not in a stranger's home where I'm only aware of one escape route.

A quiet tap on the door jolts me upright. So much for being left alone to wallow in my self-pity. I bet Alana is coming to check on me.

"Come in," I say after the knocking becomes insistent, refusing to be ignored.

The door cracks open. I'm surprised to see Cadence in the doorway. She struts in barefooted and closes the door behind her.

She stands awkwardly in the middle of the room. Her purple hair looks black in the low lighting. She shuffles forward, and I notice her tan complexion now that it isn't layered in pale makeup.

"I don't trust the fence either," she says, pointing at the window.

I nod my head before saying, "What's up?" I'm positive Cadence didn't decide to pop in without reason.

"I thought I'd keep you company. It's nice not having to hang out with Grams for once."

Living here must be boring, surrounded by the dry, dead desert. "I know what you mean. Alana doesn't believe in the need to keep me entertained, only safe. Don't get me wrong, I love her to death, but after living most of my life with my family and having friends...well, it's lonely. It also doesn't help that she's stricter than a prison guard."

"I'm sure she'll lighten up eventually," Cadence says, shrugging her shoulders.

"Maybe when I'm fifty." I roll my eyes. "Her stubbornness drives me insane. The one time I think I might actually like a boy, and we run." I don't care if I sound childish. Alana's irrational decision caused us to end up here.

"The nephilim?" Cadence asks, sitting on the edge of the bed. I'm surprised she remembers.

"Yeah, the nephilim," I say.

Referring to Dylan as a nephilim leaves a bitter taste on my tongue. I couldn't imagine him being anything other than human. It's rude in a way. He's just as human as I am, even with his glorious wings. "Do all hunters emphasize on species? Dylan could pass for human."

"It's not our choice. Other non-humans get offended when they're called human. Anyway, I wouldn't waste too much time thinking about him. Most nephilim are nothing but a pretty face and a quick way to get around." Cadence's pouty lips curl into a smirk like she's met a half-angel or two.

"I don't think that was true with Dylan. He went out of his way to talk to me, to teach me about his kind. But, I'll never be able to find out for sure."

"Yes, you can. Why don't you call him?" Cadence asks. "Alana can keep hiding you from the world, but she can't stop you from talking to him, not if you're determined enough."

Butterflies beat in my stomach. It never even occurred to me to call him. It would be as simple as catching a bus, or better yet, flying to meet me somewhere. Alana has to sleep at some point. She can't watch over me twenty-four seven.

I open my mouth to ask Cadence for a phone when I realize there's a colossal, heart-stopping issue. Dylan never gave me his number, and I have no idea how to get it. I'm pretty sure nephilim don't have a specific section in the phone book.

"Small problem. He didn't give me his number," I say, hiding the disappointment in my voice.

"I bet I could get it," Cadence says, unfazed. It makes sense. Cadence hasn't gone rogue like Alana. With her father a part of the Hunter's Alliance, she probably has great connections.

I flash my brightest smile. Not because Cadence can find Dylan's number but because she is willing to help me. It's not often that I meet a person I can trust to help me. My luck must be changing.

"Has anyone ever told you that you're a rock star?" I say.

"Actually, yes. I tell myself that every time I kill a demon." Cadence laughs. I admire her self-confidence.

I laugh a real shoulder-shaking laugh. It has been so long since I've laughed like this. I wish Cadence would come with us to guarantee our friendship isn't only temporary. I'll have to convince Alana that if she teams up with Cadence, they'd be able to get rid of my stalker demon once and for all.

Cadence reaches for my hands and pulls me off the bed. She gives me a once over, noticing that I'm still in my jeans and long-sleeved shirt.

"Let's go to my room. You can find something else to wear while I use my resources to find this nephilim's number."

I follow her back to the living room and up the stairs. Her quick pace stops me from taking in much of the decor. When we reach her room and she thrusts the door open, I can't help but gape.

"You really are a rock star," I say, closing the door behind us.

MORE THAN HUNTED

CADENCE'S MASSIVE, ECLECTIC wardrobe is like a mini-mall. I spin around and around in her walk-in closet, astonished at its size. My last bedroom is tiny in comparison. As it turns out, Cadence's room is a new addition to the house, giving her the luxury of more space than the original master bedroom, along with her own spa-worthy bathroom.

"You can borrow anything you want," Cadence says from the doorway.

"Thanks." I run my fingers over the soft cotton fabric she seems to favor.

I yank a black halter top from its hanger and rub my fingers over the sparkling rhinestones dazzling the bodice in an intricate swirling pattern. Her wardrobe contrasts usual hunting attire, but I wouldn't doubt her wearing it to slaughter demons. I can tell from her outfit tonight that Cadence can kick ass while looking sexy. I wouldn't mind her teaching me a thing or two.

I lay the shirt across my arm and pluck a couple more less seductive ones off their hangers. I add black skinny jeans and a miniskirt to my small pile, throwing my practicality to the floor with other discarded clothing. I've never worn anything so impractical in my life, but Cadence has inspired me to be daring, to be in control of who I am. It's a relief knowing that I'm still capable of making my own decisions. I don't have to rely on Alana to make them for me.

I skip barefooted across the plush black carpet to the sitting area. Cadence reclines in her chair stationed in front of a gleaming oak desk. She scours the content displayed on her monitor. She motions to a pair of flimsy pajamas folded on a small, circular table. I strip out of my jeans and slip into the vibrant, magenta pajama bottoms.

"Great choices," Cadence says, looking over her shoulder.

I plop down in the chair next to hers to see what she's looking at. There's a message board on the screen flashing black and crimson. It looks like a place where people pretend to be vampires to find their soul mates—or maybe not pretend. I scan the page reading mini-profiles of strangers. This is the last place I'd expect to find Dylan's number. Cadence clicks on a name and the familiar safe house crest flashes and disappears.

"Demon hunters have their own website?" I say to break the silence.

"It's the easiest way to keep track of people...among other things. It's not a public domain though. It won't pop up in any search engines. You also need a password, which is assigned by the alliance, to gain access."

"Can you look anyone up?"

"As long as they want to be found. I searched for Alana, and she currently isn't listed if you're wondering. The only document associated with her name is her resignation letter. Everything else is most likely hidden in the archives, which only alliance leaders can access. I checked earlier."

My spirit deflates like a raft sinking in shark-infested waters. Alana's past is locked up tight. I trust Alana, I really do, but I'm afraid her past will come back to haunt us like mine has.

I search the screen for glimpses of Alana's name anyway. It doesn't hurt to double check. Cadence types the name Dylan into the search engine to filter the majority of the hunters.

"Lucky you! There are only seven people listed with the name Dylan," Cadence says.

I bite my lip, imagining having to call and ask each one if he remembers me. It's been less than twenty-four hours since I've laid eyes on him, so I know he would, but asking is the only way I'd know it's him for sure. *How embarrassing!*

"Four are over the age of twenty five and two are human. That leaves us with Dylan Davidoff, age eighteen, nephilim."

"That's him!" I bounce in my seat.

Cadence writes a phone number on a notepad and hands it to me. The area code is very familiar. Alana and I once lived in it. I'd never forget San Diego. It was the first place I lived without my parents. My palms begin to sweat in nervousness. Now that I have his number, a string of negative thoughts zing through my mind.

"I can't call him," I say. "It would be weird. He'll think I'm stalking him."

"No, he won't," she says.

"How do you know? He didn't even give me his number. He had plenty of opportunities, but he didn't. He was probably just being nice."

"Maybe he was, but what if he wasn't. You can face evil demons but are too chicken to call a boy?"

"A nephilim," I correct. "You were right about that. Dylan is only half human. Why would he even bother with me? I'm not even a demon hunter. I'm just demon *hunted*."

"Stop putting yourself down and call. You may not realize it yet, but you're more than just hunted. You are something special. If you weren't, that upper level demon wouldn't even bother with trying to take you alive."

I'm not sure whether I should be relieved that I'm not ordinary or completely out of my mind terrified. Besides my parents, Alana is the only one who has ever called me special, and that was their job. Cadence is a stranger, a really cool stranger, but still, someone who wouldn't go out of her way to make me feel better. Maybe she is right.

"Fine. Give me your phone."

Cadence hands me her hot pink-cased smart phone. I shift away from her. I can't let her see how hard my hands are shaking. I press each digit on the screen and hit the call button.

I clear my throat. My heart races faster than the quick rings. I'm about to hang up after the fifth ring when a smooth, deep voice answers.

"Hello."

I hesitate. The voice isn't Dylan's. His is a tone higher, softer.

"D-Dylan," I stammer. I swallow hard, unsure of what to say. The surprise of a stranger answering has thrown me off, leaving me numb.

"No. This is Evan. Dylan went back to the academy."

"Oh. Sorry for bothering you. I know it's late and all," I say.

I'm about to hang up when Evan says, "Wait. I can let Dylan know you called."

"That would be great. Tell him Cami Anders called. I'm Alana's friend."

"Alana O'Neil?" Evan asks.

This is not what I expected to happen. The only way he could know Alana is if he had previously worked with her. As far as I know, she doesn't have a family.

"Yes." I rake my teeth over my bottom lip. "She's my guardian."

"My partner has been searching everywhere for her. Any time we get a lead, she disappears again. You're the reason why." Evan's voice is soft, not accusatory. He seems more excited than anything. "You have to tell me where you are."

I knew this was too good to be true. The last thing I'd ever do is give away our location. I don't know if this is a trap. Alana may have enemies she's never told me about.

"No." My voice echoes louder than it should. "I won't break Alana's trust like that. And don't bother asking Dylan. We've moved since this morning."

"I understand." By the sound of his voice, I think he really means it. "Could you at least tell me how everything is? I know I might be pushing it, but I have to ask."

"Taking into account that I'm homeless now, I've had better days." It's weird. I never thought I'd be comfortable talking with a stranger over the phone. It's like Evan is an old friend.

"I'm sure Alana will figure things out. Did Dylan at least give you the money?"

A frown glides on my face. I glance at Cadence next to me. She is leaning closely, eavesdropping on my conversation. She puts her hand on my arm, aware of my misguided thoughts. I was under the impression that the Hunter's Alliance had given us the money and not a boy from Alana's past. Without this mysterious benefactor, we'd be in a horrible position. The alliance probably couldn't care less about Alana. Heck, they probably don't even know I exist.

"That was from you?" I ask.

"No, from my partner. Even after all these years, he still loves and cares about Alana. It's tough without the backing and funds from the Hunter's Alliance. Since Alana abandoned her position, well, all I can say is that the alliance disapproves of her reasons."

It's hard to imagine Alana ever having had a romantic life. It's not because she's unlovable, but she has a tendency to keep people at a distance. I'm lucky that she's determined and strong-willed—and maybe lucky that she found me when I was still clinging to my childhood. If not, I'd be totally lost.

My stomach clenches with tightly wound knots. I'm uneasy about this entire conversation. I'm afraid that I've already said too much. Evan's partner could be some stalker ex-boyfriend, and she could be too desperate to deny the financial support.

I let a moment of silence pass. "I can't do this. I can't talk about Alana. I have to go. Please, tell Dylan I called."

"Don't hang up. I promise not to ask anymore about Alana. It's just been a really long time since I've heard any news firsthand." He sighs, creating static in the phone. "I've waited even longer to talk to you. You left quite an impression the time we met."

I grab Cadence's arm for comfort as the creep-factor skyrockets. "I don't know you."

"Not really, but we did meet once. After that, Alana took off, only sending me the occasional letter and picture of the two of you." *Why don't I remember him?* Alana has a lot of explaining to do.

"Wow. This is a little much. I really have to go now."

I end the phone call and throw the phone back to her like it might explode in my hands. I wrap my arms around myself and bury my face in my crossed arms to try to stop the sudden urge to throw up. I shouldn't have let my guard down. I feel nauseated. Evan has left me more confused than ever, like the screw holding my sanity in place has been loosened.

"That was unexpected," Cadence says, yanking my arms away from me. "Sorry it wasn't Dylan."

The cell phone chimes, startling my frail nerves. I grab onto the desk to keep from falling over. I shake my head before Cadence can hand the phone over. It has to be Evan calling back, and I really don't want to talk to him. Stupid technology and Caller ID.

"It's just a text message." Cadence sets the phone on my knee, and I pick it up before it falls. "If you don't read it, I will."

I glare at the new number on the screen, the one listed for Dylan probably a landline. "It's from Evan," I say more to myself. My mind is still muddled from the shock of Evan's unwavering persistence to talking to me. I find my voice and read the text message out loud. "I didn't mean to freak you out. Here is a picture of me to help you put a face to my name."

I scroll down. My heart races as I stare at a boy around my age. His bright blue eyes sparkle in the dim lighting. His light brown hair curls around his ears. I bet it would be soft if I ran my fingers through it. He seems familiar, but I still can't place him in my memories. Who could forget those deliciously pouty lips? My unease melts away as I stare at the mysterious boy who is my only connection to Alana's past. Just because I don't want to talk about Alana doesn't mean he can't.

"God, he's hot," Cadence says, leaning close to me. "He's nephilim. No full human can look that good."

"Yeah," I say.

"Text him back," Cadence encourages.

I laugh. "And say what? I changed my mind about talking to you because my friend thinks you're sexy?"

Cadence nods her head. "Sounds good to me." She laughs, wagging her perfect eyebrows up and down.

I lightly punch her in the arm. She's insane if she thinks I'm that audacious. I hit the respond button and punch the buttons before closing the phone.

"What did you say?" Cadence asks.

"It's okay, and I would call him later to explain." I set the phone down, shifting in the chair. I hope I'm not making a mistake.

HELL'S PALACE

THE OLD CREAKY house settles into silence as the sun begins to rise. The unexplainable magic fades from the walls as if the house knows it no longer has to protect us from lurking demons. I've never felt this safe outside of a church before, even with Alana always a door away.

Cadence dabs my lips with shiny lip gloss, the finishing touch to my fully made up face. I slip on the black halter top with the rhinestones, maneuvering into it without messing my loosely curled hair. I lace up my black boots, finishing my classy meets tough-chick look. Cadence wears her black, jewel-studded miniskirt with a fiery red tank top. A thin, long-sleeved fishnet shirt covers her sinewy muscled arms.

We've been up all night planning, and I'm sure I'll eventually be exhausted, but I don't really care. I'm a solid ball of excitement. I've never had the opportunity to hang out with someone my own age who knows about the Veiled Realm.

I know I should be concerned about what the night will have in store for me, even terrified for my soul—yet, none of this bothers me. The only thing I'm worried about at this point is Alana discovering our plans before we can leave the premises.

"We can leave through my window." Cadence pulls her red velvet curtains open. I blink, adjusting my eyes to the blinding sunlight.

"Perfect. I'd rather not ask Alana if it's okay. She'd probably want to come, being my body guard and all."

She opens the window, and I step onto a balcony with a drop down ladder. Sneaking away is a lot easier than I thought it would be. It's almost ridiculous that I'm doing this during the day.

"I've never liked being on the second floor so I made sure to have an alternative escape route. Ironic that I'm using it to sneak out, though," Cadence says, closing the window behind her. "Maybe we should've worn lighter colors like day time ninjas."

I shake my head, grinning. I'm going to miss Cadence when Alana decides we have to go. I'll have to convince her to come with us. It would be better if Alana decides we should stay. Vivian seems like someone who would allow it. In a perfect world, my wishes would come true, but I won't hold my breath because I might suffocate waiting. I suppose it's a good thing, though, that we don't stay, not with my demon here to cause trouble in town. It wouldn't be fair to the innocent townspeople—or Cadence. She'd have to work double time for me to keep the populace safe.

We sneak down the gravel drive to the Jaguar. Cadence presses her key fob, unlocking her car with a blink of the headlights. It's reassuring having a vehicle instead of having to walk. I don't think I'd survive without one in the desert. Demons may not be able to lurk around in the sun, but other animals can.

I hop into the passenger's seat while Cadence starts the engine. She maneuvers through the gravel, opening the gate with the small remote.

I roll down the window, allowing the hot wind to kiss my face. Cadence smiles and turns on the air conditioning. We barrel down Highway 395 past newly built housing communities until dry, desert landscape surrounds us.

Cadence turns onto an unmarked dirt road. The Jag bumps and kicks up dust as she tries to avoid dips and large rocks. I'm excited and scared all at the same time. I have no clue where we are headed. But anything is better than being on lockdown in a house in the middle of nowhere—unless we're headed to Nowheresville...then I may have to reconsider.

"Almost there," Cadence says.

I peer through the windshield, scoping the area for a mall or even a tiny shopping center. A rundown shed is the only building in sight. Cadence puts the car into park and gets out. I stare at the peeling, muddy brown paint of the door and watch as she pulls it open. I swear I see someone moving inside.

A short, scraggly man steps out of the shed. His long, blond hair sparkles a shade lighter than mine in the sun. His uniform consists of a blue suit with a crest embroidered over his chest pocket. He races to the car, opens the door, and gets behind the wheel.

I yelp in surprise and scramble out of the car before he can take off. I almost lose my balance when my boot kicks a baseball-sized rock. I steady my wobbly legs, resting my hand on the hood of the Jag. The car lurches forward, barely missing my foot, and dust swirls into the air, leaving me standing startled and awkward, covering my face.

The little man manages to maneuver the car through the shed door without a scratch, driving it into a magical void. It disappears, compacting to fit in such a small space. I'm not over being surprised like I thought I was. I can't grasp how this little magical shed is even possible.

I dust off my jeans and adjust my top. Cadence smiles at me with raised eyebrows and then motions me to join her. I jog the twenty feet it takes to get to the entrance of the shed, anxious to take a look inside. I'm turning around and leaving if it leads to another dimension.

"What the heck?" I'm irritated over the lack of warning.

"Don't worry about Vinny. He's just doing his job. You know how it goes with..." Her voice trails off. "Never mind." *Nice way to change the subject.*

I grasp Cadence's arm and let her guide me into the dark shed. As soon as my eyes adjust, I gasp at the enormity of the space. It isn't magical or a secret dimension, and we don't shrink in size to fit. The shed is an entrance to an underground facility.

A paved road slopes down into the earth to a parking garage. A narrow doorway to the left shares the same small sign of a safe house, the alliance's insignia embossed on it.

Cadence presses a small button that illuminates a glowing green. The elevator doors swoosh open, and she strides in. She winks at an indiscreet camera in the corner, and I press a hand to my forehead to cover my face, not keen to the idea of a stranger watching us.

"What is this place?" A tiny window on the door, like a ship porthole, displays a solid wall of shimmering rock as the elevator descends deeper into the earth.

"Think of it as happy hour for people who work the night shift. It's a club for people like us to hang out after work. That's why we're coming in the morning."

"I thought you were the only hunter in this area," I say.

"Oh, I am. You won't find many humans down here," she says.

The elevator jerks to a stop without the comforting thud of hitting the ground. It wobbles on its suspension cables like we're in between floors on a high-rise with only air above and below us. The doors slide open, revealing a spacious room accented in dark colors. A bar is tucked in the back with patrons drinking from embellished goblets fit for the medieval times. Music blasts like rolling thunder, echoing off the vaulted ceiling. Rainbow colored lights flash on and off at random like a strobe light being controlled by a toddler. The club is clouded with fake fog, which creates a weird, ominous atmosphere. The air is different here—cool and stale and oddly humid. The earthy smell is diluted with other scents. It's potent and refreshing, yet slightly feral with a mixture of expensive perfumes and nature.

People are everywhere. Some dancing, some quietly talking against the walls, some look to have taken permanent residency at the bar, drinking unknown beverages from the spectacular goblets. Large, erratically placed, red vinyl booths scatter the perimeter of the club like the designer tossed everything in the air and where it landed it stayed.

Cadence holds my hand, guiding me around groups of people who stare in my direction. She spots a vacant booth, and I slide in across from her. She yanks out a tattered menu from between the condiments on the table and hands it to me.

"I'd advise you to pick something from the front unless you're feeling daring," Cadence says over the music.

I read the menu with the name Hell's Palace in script font arching across the top. Below the name is a list of menu items without pictures or prices. Each item is creatively named. There's a cheese burger named Mortal Desire. *Mmm, sounds tempting.*

Everything on the menu can be found at any bar and grill, but the names make them more appetizing. That's until I flip the menu over. The item titles are just as fun as the front; it's the descriptions that make my stomach churn in disgust. I've never seen such strange ingredients consisting of exotic animals I've always thought were made up.

"Freshly churned unicorn ice cream?" I laugh. "Sounds delicious." I flip the menu back to the normal food selection.

"Crazy, huh?" Cadence says with a shrug. "I once ordered the Witches Brew and was sick for over a week. I don't have a stomach made of steel like most customers, but you could try your luck."

"No, thanks. Most of my luck is bad."

"I doubt it. You've escaped from I don't even know how many demon attacks. You have more than one guy interested in you, you're at a really cool club with an awesome friend, and there's another hot guy headed our way. I'd say you have really good luck."

"Phone guy doesn't count, Alana does the majority of the ass kicking, and I think that guy is coming to talk to you." I drop my gaze to the table. "Though, you're right about the other things."

Cadence winks before glancing back at her menu. I run my fingers through my hair, making sure there isn't any dust in it from almost being run over by Vinny.

I can't stop my eyes from looking at the boy heading our way again. He appears taller the closer he gets, towering over the crowd as he glides through clusters of people dancing. I'm tiny in comparison, sitting in the booth. His eye color is lost in the strobe lights—dark one moment, a reflective blue, green, and purple the next. His dark hair is styled in short, perfect spikes fit for a rocker. His tan skin makes me think he works outdoors, and the shadows from the flickering lights enhance the curves of each bulging muscle on his bare arms.

I kick Cadence under the table to get her to stop playing coy. Unlike her, I can't pretend not to notice the enormous presence now blocking my view of the rest of the club.

The boy leans against the table with his huge hands pressed palms down. A sapphire glints from the black metal ring on his middle finger. His tight, plain white T-shirt and fitted jeans don't leave much to the imagination. He leans closer with an easy-going, crooked smile, refusing to respect the three feet of space normal people give each other to prevent awkwardness.

"I've lived here all my life, and I've never seen you two here before," he remarks, staring back and forth. "I'm Drake."

Cadence reaches out her hand and clasps her slender fingers in Drake's. "Cadence," she says, "and this is Cami."

I force a narrow, closed-lip smile onto my mouth and bob my head instead of shaking Drake's hand. Cadence slides around the circular booth next to me, inviting Drake to join us. He slinks in, leaning his elbows on the table. The bend in his arms flexes the bulge of his muscles, and I can't help appreciating the curvature of his strong, blocky build.

"Do you come here often?" Drake asks, using the most unoriginal pickup line in existence. He looks back and forth between me and Cadence again, determining who is more responsive to his charms.

"Only after a good night," Cadence says without elaborating. The mystery surrounding her is her strongest weapon.

Drake's eyes stop on mine expectantly. "Never. It's my first time. I'm new to the area."

"That's cool. When'd you arrive?" Drake is a little persistent for my liking, especially since I hate talking about myself. I'm content to watch him and Cadence without getting involved.

Instead of responding, I glance at Cadence for help.

"Last night," Cadence says for me. "I helped her out with a pesky demon." *Meaning, she helped Alana out.*

Drake rubs his hands together. "I didn't think there were any demons left out here. Not with the new hunter in town."

I push the menu away. "I was unaware of him following me."

"Not to burst your bubble, but it isn't always sunny in Desertville, so this place will never be demon-free. And don't worry your pretty face over it. I'm that gorgeous hunter you spoke of." Cadence beams a stunning smile.

Drake raises his eyebrows. "You? By yourself?"

Cadence huffs in agitation.

"Oh, wait. You said Cami was new in town. I knew the alliance wouldn't send you here alone." Is this guy for real? One, Cadence is badass and could probably throw him across the room. Secondly, I don't exactly exude the aura of a fierce fighter. My hands shake even thinking about demons.

Shockingly, Cadence glares across the table, and her hands clench into fists in her lap. She sits up straighter and leans forward, showing off her cleavage. "Right. She's my partner. And isn't it funny that the two of us can protect your ass from demons?" Why she lies about me, I have no idea. Maybe to make things easier. Alana stays away from everyone involved in the Veiled Realm. Might as well not dish that she's gone rogue to protect me from all things Veiled Realm related, including every person who lives within it.

I open my mouth to tell Drake the truth, that Cadence doesn't need my help at all, when a waitress in tight black leather saunters over, creating a grateful distraction. I order chili-cheese fries and a Coke. Cadence agrees to share some-thing called a Howler's Feast with Drake, and thankfully the discussion is forgotten.

The conversation stays mundane and we begin to relax. My hope of finding out more about the Veiled Realm is shattered because everything and everyone looks so dang human apart from the menu. My sixth sense must be broken. My pride and need to fit in keeps me from asking questions. I don't want to sound like an outsider, and I refuse to draw any more attention to myself.

I sit and listen to the flirtatious banter between Drake and Cadence. I hear a chiming melody coming from Cadence's pocket, barely audible over the blasting music. I nudge her shoulder with mine and tap her pocket. She digs out her phone, glances at it, and then hands it to me.

Our disappearance has finally been noticed. There are three missed calls from Alana and two text messages. My heart skips a beat when I see one of them from Evan.

I click on his text message and read: *I hope you have a good morning.* I text him back that I'll call him tonight. I read through Alana's angry text message and push the green button to call her. I cover my ear with my hand to muffle the noise.

Alana picks up on the first ring. "Where the hell are you?"

I press my mouth against the phone to talk over the music. "I'm with Cadence."

"What?" Alana says. "I can't hear you."

"Hold on," I say.

I scoot out of the booth and saunter to the restrooms on the opposite side. I wave to Cadence to stay, slipping into the quieter room.

"I said, I'm with Cadence. We decided to go out to eat," I say.

"Why didn't you tell me? I would've come with you."

"You don't have to be my shadow," I mutter. "Cadence is a hunter. She can protect me, too. And don't worry. We'll be back before dark."

Alana sighs. "Cami."

"I'm fine," I say before she can demand that I come back. "I'll see you later."

I hang up the phone, shoving it into the pocket of my black skinny jeans. I stomp from the restroom and smile as Cadence stares wide-eyed at me. She waves her hands, and I copy her to show my excitement. I'm halfway across the dance floor when someone pushes me hard in the back.

I drop to my knees, holding my chest in an attempt to catch my sudden loss of breath. I twist my shoulder to look behind me when small hands grab my hair and begin to drag me toward the elevator. My boots can't get a grip on the smooth dance floor. I claw at the slick metal door of the elevator as it closes to keep it from shutting. Cadence and Drake both run through the oblivious crowd to me. But it's too late. The door slides shut, leaving me with my attacker.

DEAD BEFORE DARK

THE SPACE IN the elevator seems smaller. The air is permeated with my fear, and I cower in the corner like a frightened, trapped animal. I'm dizzy with claustrophobia and can barely focus on the figure towering over me.

A beautiful woman with sharp, narrow features blocks my only exit by standing in front of the sliding doors to prevent me from bolting the moment we surface. She places her hand on the gun holster at her hip. She is prepared to kill anyone who stands in her way.

She doesn't look at or talk to me. I open my mouth to demand she tell me what's going on when the elevator doors slide open. No one waits on the other side to save me and my heart sinks. Cadence is either stuck waiting for the elevator to go back down, or she is rushing up the stairs I never had a chance to see. The fire marshal would have shut this place down if there wasn't a stairway unless...he was one of *them.*

The woman wraps her slender hands around my wrists and yanks me to my feet. She's a lot stronger than she looks. Her strength is unnatural for her petite build. It stems from something otherworldly, something demonic. The potency of her perfume couldn't hide the odor of demon, yet I know she couldn't be one. They don't carry guns, and it's daylight.

Her bright red nail polish glitters in pale rays of sunlight drifting through the shed's open door. As she pulls my back to her chest, her nails dig into my arms. I breathe in the familiar scent of doom and my nostrils burn. She doesn't smell like just any demon—she stinks of *my* demon. The sweet spiciness lingers in her pores.

I search for the small man, Vinny, but he's vanished. I contemplate whether I should yell or not, afraid the woman will kill me on the spot if I do. Her chin digs into my shoulder while she struggles to keep my arms behind me.

The headlights on a black sedan blink. The trunk pops open with a small click. *Oh God, no!* I'm terrified of the idea of being locked in the small, lightless space.

I kick my leg behind me, the heel of my boot hitting the woman in her shin. Wrestling from her faltering grip I dash away, dodging her as she tries to pummel me into submission again.

She yells in frustration. I zigzag as I run to the outside door. I'm afraid she'll shoot me given the opportunity. It's a relief she knows nothing about me, or she'd be better prepared for when I escape. Choosing between fleeing and fighting, fleeing always wins without question. It's what I'm good at. Apparently strength is the only power she acquired from dealing with my demon; she's slower than I am.

"Get away from me!" I scream, finding my voice.

The woman laughs. "No." Her sugary voice echoes through the garage, the kind of voice a pediatrician uses right before they stick you with a long needle.

I duck behind a pillar to catch my breath. The parking garage is silent. I don't even hear the click-clack of the woman's heels. I risk sneaking a peek at my surroundings—empty cars and concrete walls. It's an underground prison. I turn on my heels and break into a sprint. The woman jumps out from behind another pillar. I scream as she tackles me, shoving my face into the gritty asphalt.

"If you try that again, I will kill you. I don't care if I was told to bring you in alive," the woman growls.

Her words send pain into my chest like a jagged knife stabbing my heart. My arms fall to my sides in defeat. I don't want to die, and this woman won't even think twice before killing me. *This is so not good!*

The woman yanks me to the car. Her nails bite into my bare skin, and I wince in pain. Staring at the empty trunk of her sedan, I take shallow breaths. Panic seeps into me. It's as if I'm gazing into a dark abyss before freefalling for all eternity. I contemplate my options. I could try escaping again at the risk of meeting my maker, or I can give up. It's either die now or die later. *Later it is!* At least I may still have a chance.

The woman shoves me into the trunk.

"Cami!"

Hearing Cadence's voice, my hopes rise. She bolts down the slope of the road. The woman slams the trunk shut, cutting me off from my rescuer. I hear a door slam, and the car rumbles to life. I'm thrown forward into the backside of the backseat as the car races in reverse.

Something slams into the trunk, and my stomach drops at the sound of Cadence's screams. I pray for her safety. The noise didn't sound loud enough to be a body, but I can't say for sure.

I jump when the chime of Cadence's cell phone echoes in the small space. I shove my hand into my pocket in relief. The woman didn't think to search me. I ignore the text from Evan and dial Alana's number. Again, she picks up on the first ring.

"I've been kidnapped," I whisper, afraid of the woman hearing me. "I'm stuck in the trunk of a car."

"Oh, God. And Cadence?"

"She couldn't get to me. It happened so fast. Alana, I'm scared."

The phone flies from my hand when the car bounces. We won't hit the highway for a little while...I hope. I scramble around, twisting to grab onto the small, glowing phone.

"It's going to be okay." The fear in her voice makes it hard for me to believe her. We've never had to deal with non-demon kidnappers before.

She talks frantically to Vivian about what has happened. She breathes into the phone before continuing. "We can track you. Cadence has a tracking device in her phone because she loses it so often. I'm coming to get you."

I sigh in relief. I've never been so thankful for technology.

A sudden thought hits me. What if Evan tracks Cadence's phone for his partner? No, I don't think he would.

"I'm in the middle of nowhere," I say. "It might be a while before we reach a road if we're heading in the direction I think we are."

"Where?"

"We were at a place called Hell's Palace. We turned off Highway 395 onto a dirt road. It was past all of the housing communities."

"I'm leaving now. I have to hang up so Vivian can guide me. Just hang on tight, Cami. If the car stops I want you to fight for your life. Do *not* go quietly."

"Alana," I say, tears rimming my eyes. "Sorry for getting into this mess."

"Don't worry. I'll be there soon."

The line goes dead. I shine the flashlight of the cell phone around the trunk for anything I could use as a weapon. I shift my legs and dig my fingers into the small space between the carpet and the wall of the trunk. The carpet pulls up, and I stick my hand into the spare tire compartment. I cover my mouth before I scream out in joy as my fingers wrap around a tire iron. This woman's obvious lack of experience in the art of kidnapping is working in my favor. *Stupid, stupid woman.*

I maneuver the tire iron out of the hole and press it against my chest. The carpet falls back into place with a quiet thump. I twist back onto my side, preparing to jump up as soon as the trunk opens. I rub my fingers over the back panel, feeling the knob of the quick release switch. I yank the lever but nothing happens. The woman is more prepared than I thought.

I'm not sure what to do with myself besides wait. I stare at another text message from Evan waiting for me. It says, *I can't wait,* with a smiley face icon.

I press the call button. I can't take the silence and fear of being trapped in a trunk. I have to talk to someone, anyone, and Evan is the only one available since I have Cadence's phone, and Alana is talking to Vivian. The phone rings several times before he answers.

"Hey," he says. "I wasn't expecting you to call so soon."

"I don't know how long I can talk," I whisper. "I'm

kind of in a really bad situation, and I didn't know what else to do."

"How bad?" he asks.

"I'm probably going to be dead before dark."

"What?" He sounds concerned or more likely shocked. The line goes quiet. I'm scared he has hung up, leaving me alone with my thoughts, until he sighs.

"It's a long story," I say before he speaks. "Some stupid woman tackled me while I was in a club with my friend. Now, I'm trapped in a trunk awaiting my death or rescue. Hopefully the latter."

"Try the quick release," Evan suggests.

"It's been disabled."

"What kind of car is it?" he asks.

"A four door sedan. It was too dark to tell anything else."

I never thought I'd be spending my last hours talking on the phone with a stranger. It was never on the top of my list of things to do before I die, but it'll have to do. I think I'd go crazy otherwise.

"Most new sedans have a lever on the back of the seat that you can pull to push the seats forward. You could possibly escape through the front," Evan says.

I feel the back of the seat until my fingers bump into a tiny knob.

"It has it," I whisper. Adrenaline rushes through my veins, giving me the boost I need to not give up. I will fight like Alana demanded. "I think you've just saved my life."

A weird beep chirps in my ear, and I glance at the face of the phone. There's an incoming call from Alana.

"Alana's calling me. If you don't hear from me then you know what happened. Thank you for giving me my last chance." I click the phone over.

"I'm here, Cami," Alana says. "Cadence is nearby, too. She followed the woman from the club, staying out of view."

"Thank God," I whisper. "I thought I was alone."

"I'd never let that happen. Now, I need you to listen to me. Cadence is going to cut the woman off, and I'm going to have to rear-end her. You need to hold onto anything you can and stay away from the rear of the car."

I nod my head even though she can't see me. "Okay."

"On the count of three—one. Two. Thr—"

My whole world shakes as I hit the top of the trunk hard. I scream with pain as my nose slams into the roof. Tears sting my eyes. The sound of metal scraping metal cancels all other noise, leaving me deaf. I wince, unable to cover my ears because I'm holding onto the tiny knob and floor panel. The car jerks to a halt, and the trunk space has shrunken. I can no longer turn around. It has been crushed by Alana's vehicle.

The woman curses. I take this welcomed distraction to pop the backseat down. I crawl through the tiny space un-noticed by my complaining kidnapper.

I watch in horror as the woman pulls her gun out of its holster, aiming it at Cadence through the windshield. The woman pulls the trigger, and the gunshot resonates as it blasts through the windshield. I slam the tire iron I've been clutching against the back of her skull. Glass shatters from the side window, spraying onto me.

Suddenly, sharp teeth nick the skin of my arm and I yelp as I'm dragged out of the car by a huge dog. A rumble erupts in its throat, and I scream. *Hellhounds can't come out during the day!*

I hit the pavement and scamper back on all fours, pressing my back against the wrecked sedan. The dog bares its teeth and slinks closer. Hot breath beats against my face; my muscles freeze.

"Alana!" I manage to find my voice. My stomach knots, while the echo of the gunshot still rings in my ears, muting the hound's low growl.

Cadence dashes into view, and I'm relieved she wasn't shot. She stops short of the dog, biting her bottom lip.

"A little help here." I nudge my chin at the dog, unwilling to move and give it a reason to attack me.

"He won't hurt you." Cadence approaches the dog and rubs behind its ears.

"How do you know?"

The dog's long, wet tongue slurps out of its mouth and licks the side of my face, leaving a trail of slobber.

"Because it's Drake."

UNRAVELING SECRETS

I NURSE THE swollen pink welts on my arm from the dog's, I mean Drake's, teeth. They're not bleeding, but I may need to get a tetanus shot. Maybe not. I don't know what the protocol is when a person gets bitten by a man who shifts into a dog. What if I transform, too? And I thought the idea of half angels was ludicrous. This is just plain absurd.

Drake's thick coat shines silver in the sunlight. I scratch his ears while Alana and Cadence pull the woman from her car. I knocked her out cold. And it felt good—almost too good.

I inhale the dry air and release it to loosen the bunched nerves in my stomach. An overabundance of adrenaline courses through my veins. I'm tempted to see if I can pick up the woman's wrecked car like a distressed mother doing the impossible to save her child.

Instead, I fumble in the backseat for Cadence's phone. It's on the floor, half hidden. I scoop it up along with the woman's gun.

Alana runs to me once the woman is strapped into the backseat of the Jag with Cadence standing guard in case she wakes up. Alana wraps her arms around me with her head resting on my shoulder. She shakes as she cries in relief. I rub my hand over her back until she pulls herself together.

"I could kill you," she cries. "Never, and I mean *never* do that to me again."

"It wasn't my fault!" I exclaim. "I didn't know I'd be kidnapped."

"I'm not talking about that," she says. "I understand you want your freedom but at least do it safely. You *have* to tell me where you're going. I can't lose you."

I train my eyes on the ground. I put Alana through hell today. I could've prevented the pain and fear if I'd just talked to her.

I couldn't be sorrier. I could've died. Her efforts to keep me safe would've been wasted. "It's just that...you treat me like a kid. You've kept me in a bubble for three years, and the one time I needed to protect myself, I couldn't. It's not fair for you to have to be by my side twenty-four seven."

"You're right. It's just hard, okay?"

"It wouldn't be this hard if you would stop keeping so many secrets. I wish you could tell me everything like I can with you."

"I can't," Alana says.

"You can," I argue. "Start small."

Alana kicks at the dirt with the toe of her boot. "Okay, I can do that. Once we take care of this mess." She motions to the three car wreckage.

"Deal."

<hr>

I sit on the plush sofa in Vivian's living room. Drake transformed into his human self and is now chowing down on sandwiches Vivian made. Alana and Cadence are in another room, doing whatever hunters do with a captive. I'm not exactly sure what that entails. I just hope it's humane. If they harm that woman, it wouldn't make them any better than a demon. We're supposed to be the good guys. And the woman is human. Cadence is positive because of the gun. People in the Veiled Realm don't use human-made weapons unless they're hunters, and this woman is not.

I pick at half of a turkey sandwich, disappointed over my chili-cheese fries going to waste. I never even had the chance to see them. I bet they were delicious.

"You're not really Cadence's partner," Drake says through huge bites of sandwich.

"Nope," I say.

"I thought you were, you know, because you reek like a

demon. I assumed you did a lot of the dirty work." His nostrils flare as he takes a big breath of air. He shrugs his shoulders and continues to eat.

I laugh in embarrassment. I sniff my arm to pick up my scent. I would know if I smelled like a demon, I have a heightened recollection of what they smell like, and I only smell like me. Drake can probably pick up the scents that linger in my pores from previous contact—kind of how I was able to smell my demon on the woman.

"It could be because demons are attracted to me, always wanting to take me down. I've also had a lot of contact with them the last two days. Hence the reason I ended up in this town."

"That's good to know. I'll make sure to stay away from you come nightfall, Demon Bait."

I gasp in exasperation. I've never been rejected because of the demons, and it hurts my feelings. It's not my fault. I push myself off the sofa, glaring at Drake.

"Well, I don't want to be seen with a—a dog either!" I yell, irritated.

Drake jumps from his chair and with inhuman speed, he grabs my arm. I yelp in fear, uncomfortable with his invasion of my personal space. He smells like raw nature— lush greenery and oak mixed with wild animal. It's the same feral smell I got a whiff of at the club before I was kidnapped. I attempt to tug away, afraid he'll rip off my face.

Vivian storms into the room and courageously slaps the

beast of a boy on the arm. "Let her go. She doesn't know anything. She's never met a werewolf before."

Drake's eyebrows knit together, and he glowers at Vivian. He releases his grip on me but doesn't back up. My hands tremble and my knees go weak. I slump to the floor. *Werewolf? Drake is a freaking werewolf.*

"I—I really thought you were a dog," I stammer. "I only said that because you made me mad by rejecting me so easily because of the demons."

"You really have no idea. You been living under a rock or somethin'?" Drake says, taking a step back.

"No, I've been hiding behind Alana. She said the more I knew, the more vulnerable I'd be to the Veiled Realm. She's overprotective."

"Then you don't know why I can't be around you at night," Drake says, the anger melting from his voice.

Vivian shuffles out of the room, sensing I'm no longer in danger. Drake helps me off the floor and guides me back to the sofa. He takes a seat next to me.

"No, I don't. And it sucks. I didn't even know the Veiled Realm existed until my parents were killed by a demon. What is so bad about hanging out with me?"

"Demons like to have pets," he says.

I purse my lips, narrowing my eyes. What does that have to do with anything? The thought hits me hard. *Drake turns into a wolf. He could be the pet.*

"I'd rather chew off my own foot than turn into a hellhound," he adds.

So that's where hellhounds come from...demon-broken werewolves. I thought they came from some twisted breeder in Hell. "I don't blame you. I'm no help in that matter either. I can't even help myself in that kind of situation. I'm not a demon hunter."

A loud thump and an angry yell force my attention down the hallway. Drake rises to his feet and stands in front of me. I glance around his broad shoulders and see the woman stumbling down the hallway. Alana and Cadence stroll behind her. She isn't going anywhere.

"He'll kill me!" she screams. Thick lines of smudged mascara mar her tear-stained cheeks. "And then he'll take my soul!"

I've never heard a human howl like that.

"You should've thought about that before making a deal with a demon," Cadence says.

"He said it'd be easy!"

"I bet he forgot to mention that Cami is protected by hunters. But why would he? It's a win-win situation for him. Either you get the mark or he gets your soul. Sounds like a good deal to me." Cadence crosses her arms.

I step out from behind the mountain of a boy and stare into the woman's defeated eyes. She falls to the floor and crawls to me, throwing her arms around my legs like a lost child, terrified of the boogeyman.

"You'll help me won't you? You're young and you have

a good soul. Please, don't let them toss me to the monsters."

"I—I don't know how," I stutter.

"You'll come with me. He doesn't want to hurt you. He wants you alive," she says. *Maybe not physically hurt me. This lady is crazy!*

I shake my head. "No."

I struggle under the woman's grip on my legs. Her wild eyes hint to the evil that taints her soul. A haze of black fogs over the dark blue color, and I can see the death and deterioration of her spirit.

The woman claws at me with her fiery red nails, and I stumble to the ground. Before anyone has time to react, she sits on my chest, crushing my ribs. Her delicate hands squeeze around my neck, cutting off my air supply. My eyes bulge from their sockets, and I can't move to throw her off me.

In a flash, Drake yanks the woman away from me. Her ear-piercing screams echo in the suddenly small room. She flails in his tight hold, swinging her arms and legs, out for someone's blood. My blood.

"I'll get you, you little brat!" she screams.

Drake drops the woman a foot, holding her by her head. Her face is a mess of smeared makeup, tears, and anger. In one quick motion, he breaks her neck, dropping her lifeless body like a sack of potatoes.

Fear consumes me. I stumble to the corner of the room and slide down the wall, making myself as small as possible.

I swallow my rising bile. Now's not the time to get sick.

I shouldn't feel this way. Drake was trying to protect me, but the woman didn't deserve to die. I don't want anyone to die because of me. My parents' deaths are enough. This nameless woman will forever haunt my conscience.

"You killed her." My heart aches in despair.

Drake looms over the woman's body. "I had to."

"No, you didn't. She didn't have to die." My neck throbs with pain from where the woman tried to choke the life out of me.

"It was the only way to save her soul." Alana kneels next to me. "She's better off now. She can still find redemption."

TRUST

I LIE ACROSS Cadence's bed unwilling to be in the older section of the house. Here, it feels like I'm somewhere else. Like today didn't really happen.

My hair hangs in a knotted ponytail at the nape of my neck, and I rub my hands over my makeup-free face. If only I could rinse out my head and forget the dark shadows clouding the poor woman's eyes.

I've locked the door, not caring that this isn't my room. I doubt Cadence would mind. She and Drake left about thirty minutes ago to dispose of the body. Alana and Vivian are holed up somewhere in another part of the house, preparing for the night. Once the demon figures out that his minion got away with her soul intact and without me, he'll attack again with an army from Hell.

I roll my sore shoulders, aching from being trapped in the trunk of the car during the collision. My neck has small bruises shaped like butterfly wings where the woman choked me. I'm miserable and alone, yet I prefer it this way. I'm tired of being told that everything will be okay.

The chime of Cadence's phone startles me, and I remember I never called Evan to tell him I was alive. Even though I don't know him, I owe it to him to tell him that he helped save my life. Cadence would've been injured or worse, if not for him.

I grab the phone from the bedside table. There is a text from Evan, and I call him without reading it.

"Please, say this is Cami. Please, tell me you're alive," Evan says.

"Would I be calling you if I weren't?" I ask, a smirk playing on my lips. It's a good feeling to have Evan praying for my life.

"Well..."

I flinch. "Never mind, don't answer that." Goosebumps break out on my arms. "And yes, I'm alive. You saved me."

"You saved yourself," he says. "And I'm glad you did. It's nice talking to you, even if we'll probably never get to meet on good terms."

"You never know. There was a shift in my guardian-charge relationship with Alana. I think she'll warm up to the idea eventually. I'm going to ask her about you tonight."

"You'll tell me if she says anything bad, right?"

I laugh. It's a wonderful feeling that has been lost to me all afternoon. "It depends. Is there anything you need to tell me?"

"Maybe after you talk to Alana," he says. *What's he hiding? Do I want to know?*

A knock sounds on the door and I groan into the phone. I struggle to ignore it, but my visitor is insistent. I pad to the door and unlock it, expecting to see Cadence back early. Alana struts in, her shoulders hunched, and I twist, hiding the phone against my ear.

"Speaking of Alana—she's here. I'll talk to you later." I hang up the phone.

"Who were you talking to?" Alana asks.

Crap! I've been caught.

"Wait, let me guess. It was Dylan wasn't it?"

"No." The moment the word slips from my tongue, I regret it. It would be easier to lie and say it was Dylan. But the truth is, Dylan led me on. Unless... No, I think Evan would've passed on the message.

"Then who?"

"I've never met him, really," I say.

"You were talking to a stranger? Didn't today teach you anything?" Alana's cheeks redden in anger.

I grab her hands, forcing her to look at me. "He saved my life today. He kept me calm when I was trapped in a freaking trunk. He told me how to escape. And—" I take a deep breath. "You know him. So, technically he isn't a stranger. Does the name Evan ring any bells?"

Alana's face scrunches in confusion. Her hands fall from mine, hitting her legs with a quiet thump. She twists her fingers, shifting her eyes back to mine.

"I don't understand. Out of all of the boys in the world, you happen upon Evan's number. How is he?" I'm surprised by her sincerity. Her eyes glaze over like she has stepped back in time to a joyous memory she thought she'd lost forever.

Her face smoothes as she comes back to the present. I didn't expect her to act like this. I was prepared for rage, anger, and tears, not acceptance.

I lift and drop my shoulders. "Good, I think. He wanted to know how you were doing. Apparently, his partner has been looking for you."

"Figures," Alana says.

"An ex-boyfriend, huh?" I say.

"Something like that." Alana rolls her eyes, and I know her well enough to know that this new information bothers her, yet I can't tell whether it's good or bad. "But anyway, there is something else I've wanted to tell you to help you understand why I've kept so many secrets."

I lean back on the bed, allowing Alana to lie next to me. She wraps her arm around my shoulders the way a mother comforts a child. I fiddle with the loose threads on my T-shirt, giving Alana a moment to gather her thoughts.

After a long pause, she says, "I didn't always know about the Veiled Realm. I still don't know everything about it. And what I do know is bad. I'm not like most demon hunters. I wasn't born to be a warrior. I was on my own taking care of my younger sister when I was your age because our grandmother had passed away. I never knew my parents."

I squeeze Alana's hand. This has to be difficult to talk about. I didn't even know she had family, particularly a younger sister.

"Is that why you are so protective of me?" I ask. "Because of your sister?"

"Yes," she says. "We were two teenage girls living on our own, unafraid of anything. A couple of weeks after Lizzy turned fourteen, things began to change between us. She would stay out all night and come home not remembering where she was. She became really moody, and we fought a lot. She turned into someone I didn't recognize. And then she was gone. I searched everywhere for her, and just when I had given up, she came back...to kill me. Her soul was soiled beyond repair. Her eyes blackened with demonic taint. She was a monster, and there was nothing I could do about it except fight to keep my own soul. I won at the expense of her life. It was the only way to salvage what was left of her soul, and it haunts me. I couldn't save the only person I should have. Instead, her blood is on my hands."

Tears drip from her eyes, and Alana wipes her face with the back of her hand. "After that, I was contacted by this mysterious man, a total Van Helsing. He brought me to the academy, and that's where I learned the truth."

My mouth drops open, all words lost to me. I can't imagine having gone through what Alana has. I'm like the sister she lost. I'm the one she had a chance to save. I feel even worse about today. I don't even think an apology will make up for it. Not this time.

"I wish you would've told me this sooner," I say.

She squeezes my arm. "I wanted you to trust me. I didn't want to scare you into listening."

I purse my lips. "I do trust you, but I want you to trust me. Trust that I can handle what the world throws at me. You taught me how."

"I didn't teach you enough. But I promise I will."

"Good," I say. "I'd really like that."

⚬⚬⚬

I'm sitting on the carpet of my old apartment. Opaque tendrils of asphalt smelling fog swirl around me, coating my skin in cool dew. The white walls lack the details of ever having anything hung on them. My room is as blank and cold as the day I moved into it. The swirling fog encloses me in a world of no escape. I can only see the brown carpet and the bare walls. The window and door no longer exist.

"I'm surprised Alana told you about poor Lizzy. I guess it was her way of dealing with her past before getting to yours."

A bright light appears in the corner and fades into the

boy that opened my eyes to the more enjoyable facets of the Veiled Realm. Dylan raises a single eyebrow before folding his knees to sit next to me.

"What about my past?" My low voice fades into the thickening fog, and it comes out as a whisper.

Dylan places his hand on my knee. "I would love to tell you all about yourself, love, but it isn't my place."

"Then what is your place? You haven't called me or anything. What interest do you have in me?" I squeeze my eyes shut, willing the fog to dissipate so I can leave. I'm in no mood for deciphering Dylan's cryptic words.

"You're fascinating, and I'd like to get to know you." Dylan leans forward and kisses me softly on the lips. "But it'll have to wait. Stay safe tonight, Cami."

I wake with a start to a silhouette tapping on Cadence's keyboard. I sit up, rubbing the sleep from my eyes. My dream about Dylan was so vivid that the fog smell lingers in the air. I push the image of Dylan to the back of my mind.

Cadence's back is stick straight in her computer chair. Her purple hair, hidden under a hooded sweatshirt, blends in with the low lighting of the room.

"You should have woken me up." My throat burns, and my neck and shoulders throb.

"I tried, but you were totally out of it, mumbling about Dylan not calling you. You know, if I meet him, I'm totally going to smack him."

Oh, geez. I need to stop obsessing.

The small printer on the edge of her desk whirs to life, shooting out sheet after sheet of paper. I move off the bed and sit in the chair next to her, curious about what she's doing.

"Research," she says, answering my silent question. "Drake asked me out on a date. I'm just checking him out."

"Do you do this for all your potential boyfriends?"

"Only the ones that aren't purebred human. No pun intended."

I cover my mouth, hiding my smile. She stacks the printed pages, stapling them together. She reads through the first three before setting the packet down on the desk.

"No random mauling of humans, steady job, no crazy ex-girlfriends. I think it just may work out," she says.

"It says all of that?" *Having a werewolf for a boyfriend is a lot of work...mauling humans? Really?* "Who writes these things?"

"The Hunter's Alliance," she says. "They handle all of the archives and history. Not everyone is cut out for field work."

I lean back in my chair. I could get a desk job, working for the demon hunters. I should ask Alana about that. She'll be happy that I don't want to go charging into battle. Books are safer. I'd rather get a paper cut over a demon scratch any day.

"Like me." I expect Cadence to agree, but she doesn't.

She turns her head sharply, the glow of the monitor

highlighting her perfect complexion. "You'd make a great hunter. I'd take you as a partner if Alana would allow it."

She must have a lot of things going on in her mind. I'd be a terrible hunter. And a dreadful hunting partner.

"When Alana trains me to fight, we'll talk," I say. I might suck at combat, but how cool would it be getting to hang out with Cadence all the time, kicking demon ass together? Well, I'd watch her do the butt kicking. But, dang, we'd make a sexy team.

"Cool," Cadence says.

A bang on the door interrupts our conversation. Vivian shuffles in. Her silvery hair sticks up in all directions as if she had just rolled out of bed. She grabs the door frame, fear deepening the wrinkles around her honey brown eyes.

"The Hell's Palace is under attack." Her eyes glisten in the glare of the computer monitor. "It's time to get to work."

Cadence jumps from her chair and flies out of the room. Vivian slumps her shoulders, and I help her sit down. She runs her fingers through her hair before taking my hand.

"I'll be fine, dear. I'm not so sure about the people trapped in the club though," she says.

"Is Cadence okay going alone?" I ask.

She shakes her head. "She's outnumbered."

"Then I need to get dressed," I say, running to Cadence's closet. I throw on jeans and a plain T-shirt and rush to swipe my leather jacket off the chair.

Vivian grabs my arm, yanking me to a halt. She unclasps a small silver cross necklace from her neck, handing it to me. "Be careful," she says. "And make sure Cadence gives you a weapon. You don't have any power yet."

I nod my head, not really understanding what Vivian means by power. Maybe she meant that I don't have any skills.

I dash to the living room and see Alana standing by the door with Cadence. She doesn't protest or tell me to go back to my room. Instead, she hands me a long, sheathed dagger.

She motions me out the door. "I guess I'll start your lessons tonight. Now let's go."

FIRST DEMON KILL

THE JAG'S SINGLE headlight barely illuminates the road as we zoom down Highway 395. When Cadence pulled out to block the woman's car, only the front bumper was clipped. On the other hand, Vivian's car, an old, yellow El Camino, took most of damage. It's a good thing Vivian hasn't driven in years.

I grip the grab handle when Cadence turns onto a dirt road. The back end of the Jag fishtails, spitting up dirt and rocks with a cloud of dust.

"I'm going to park." Cadence taps the brakes, pulls into a small clearing, and kills the engine. "We have to walk from here."

I unlatch my seatbelt. I'm not enthusiastic about what

happens now, so I don't attempt to rush out of the car. I'd rather let the professionals do their jobs. I'm a worst-case scenario backup. I crack my knuckles, waiting for Cadence to make a move. I shift in my seat to look back at Alana. She sits erect with her hands clasped in her lap. She frowns at me, displaying her regret about letting me tag along.

Cadence clicks off the remaining headlight, leaving us in pitch black darkness. It's as if someone turned off the electricity. Even the moon and stars are in hiding, refusing to cast a dim glow to light our way.

"Lesson number one, don't get killed," Alana says like it's the easiest of all the lessons I'll be learning.

So, don't die. Check.

"Lesson number two, if you are outmatched by a demon, run."

If fighting fails, run as usual. Check.

"And lastly, lesson number three, humans are to be saved first."

What? No check.

My heart sinks into my stomach. I know I should be standing up for humankind, but what about the rest of the people in the Veiled Realm? They need protectors, too. Dylan and Drake flash through my mind. Dylan could handle himself in a situation like this, but Drake and other werewolves can be turned into Hellhounds.

"I can't tell who's human and who isn't," I say.

"You'll know. Humans are more likely to panic and hesitate, unable to handle the truth so suddenly. Creatures will fight because they're used to the danger."

I bob my head up and down in understanding. When put in a situation consisting of humans verses non-humans, creatures will fight for their lives, leaving humans as easier targets.

I slip my dagger from its sheath. The hilt rests heavy in my palm. I take a few practice swipes and jabs, mimicking all of the times I've watched Alana kill. I wish I had more time to get used to the feel of the dagger. I grip the handle, uncertain if I can do this. Alana and Cadence have had years of experience. Me? Well, I've had none—not in fighting at least. *This is a bad idea.*

With my free hand, I play with the small cross around my neck. I wish Alana or Cadence would make the first move. We've been sitting here for what seems like forever. After a long moment of silence, Cadence opens her door, leaving the keys to the Jag in the ignition. The car will hopefully still be here when we get back. A person would have to be crazy to take a stroll down a dirt road at four in the morning to find it.

I open my door, quietly clicking it shut behind me. It isn't much of a surprise attack if the demons hear us coming. Alana grabs my hand and guides me in front of her, with Cadence leading the way. I'm safely tucked in a demon hunter sandwich, protected from the front and the rear.

I keep pace with Cadence, watching her feet to keep

from tripping over pesky rocks and shrubs. We run parallel with the road, shielding ourselves the best we can in the barren desert landscape.

The ground is like an obstacle course. Every hole, stick, and furry little animal is determined to be in our way to slow us down. Without the moon, I can't determine how much time we have until dawn, but I hope it comes sooner than later. If nothing else can stop a demon, the sun can. If caught outside at dawn, the demon pops right out of existence to who knows where. And I pray I'll never find out. I've seen it happen to some of the more inferior demons. It's like the light wraps around them until they vanish. I've never stayed long enough to find out if they pop back to the same spot as before when the sun sets, but I'm sure they do. The only way to get rid of a demon is to kill it and send it back to where it came from, and even that isn't always guaranteed.

"Trouble," Cadence whispers.

Beady eyes flash like a cat's, but that's no normal animal. The hairs on my arms prickle. The scent of decaying wood intrudes into my nostrils. I immediately cover my nose with my sleeve. The demon smell reminds me of what Drake said to me earlier. I really hope I don't smell like this, or I'm going to have to buy the most potent perfume to cover it. I bet I smell sweeter though, like the upper level demon that can't get enough of me.

I freeze when Cadence comes to a stop. She will only attack if it comes after us. If only we could be so lucky.

The demon squeals, sounding like a raging pig. It crawls through the shrubbery, taking its time to bask in the fear radiating from my pores.

I take a small step back, bumping into Alana. She places a hand on my shoulder to steady me. My palms begin to sweat, and I switch the dagger to my left hand to wipe my right hand on my jeans. I'm going to wear leather gloves the next time I have to use a dagger so I don't have to worry about it slipping from my grip.

The demon goes silent. I watch its silhouette move, darker than the night around us. It's like a black hole sucking every bit of light into it.

The rustling sound starts again and then stops. The demon teases us. The moon peeks out from behind a cloud, and its soft, bluish light seeps through the darkness.

The landscape lights enough for me to get a good look at what I'm about to face. I hate demons like this. I prefer upper lever demons that can at least appear to be human if they want to. Unfortunately, this one can't, and it's freaky.

The only way my brain can make sense of this evil creature is to compare it to something I know. It looks like a mutated version of a forty pound guinea pig, lacking the soft fur. It has two sharp elephant-like tusks, which are a deep burgundy color as if they've been coated in blood. Its eyes are two small circles that look like flat, dime-sized onyx stones have been shoved into its round face. A hairless tail sticks out from what I assume is its backside, sweeping the dirt. Without its tail, we'd never have heard it coming.

"Who wants dibs?" Cadence whispers as it continues moving closer. The swooshing sound of its tail gets louder by the second.

"I vote for Cami," Alana says.

I open my mouth to argue and then snap it shut. I did sign up for this. Backing out now isn't an option. My teeth chatter, and I clench my jaw to muffle the noise. Cadence shifts to the left of me, opposite my dagger, to give me a clear view of the terrifying beast.

"You can do this. Just watch out for the tusks," Alana whispers.

I swallow hard, but the knot in my throat refuses to go down. As I step forward, I slip on a rock and almost lose my balance. I really need to work on my coordination, or I'm going to be the laughingstock of demon hunters and demons alike.

I shouldn't be as nervous as I am, not with Alana and Cadence only a couple feet behind me to jump in if I need assistance, but this guinea pig demon makes me want to throw up.

It squeals again, and I almost jump out of my skin. The swooshing of the tail sounds faster as the demon charges like a bull going after a red flag. It lowers its head, ready to ram its razor sharp tusks into my shins. I side step and thrust my dagger out. It slices through the flesh on the demon's back.

The rotting smell of wood thickens as black goo sizzles from the gaping wound.

The demon twists, catching its tusk on my jeans, ripping the denim. Before I have a chance to catch my balance, it yanks its head back hard. I hit the ground with a thud. My lungs burn as my breath rushes out. *Oh, crap!*

I somersault backwards, throwing my legs over my head before the demon shoves its tusks into my side. I land on my knees and jump back to my feet, disoriented from the sudden movement.

The demon roars.

I watch in horror as it rises on two legs. Its small forelegs now look like T-Rex arms except its claws don't look like they can bend to grab onto me. They look like chicken feet with talon-sharp nails.

The demon waddles toward me, and I crouch low, spreading my arms wide to maintain my balance. I angle my arm into a hook and thrust my dagger out, ripping the demon's underbelly. Black goo sprays out like a fountain, coating my face and hair with its awful smelling slime. My chest heaves as I fight the urge to gag. I swipe my sleeve over my mouth to wipe away the demon blood as best I can.

The demon falls over, its legs twitching, trying to stabilize itself. I jump to my feet and kick it onto its stomach to let the blood pour out faster. It claws at the ground, realizing that it can't outmatch me. Before it can flee, I ram my dagger straight into the back of its skull. The demon drops to the ground, unmoving. *God, this is disgusting.*

I step back and watch the demon dissolve into a runny mess. Come dawn, the sun will take care of the rest of the cleanup. At least it's one less thing I'll have to worry about.

I can't believe it—my first demon kill!

"Nice work, newbie," Cadence says.

I offer a closed-lip smile, afraid of getting demon guts in my mouth. Alana tugs a rag from her pocket and hands it to me. I wipe off as much sludge as I can manage. I'll have to remember to keep wet naps in my pocket from now on.

"I bet you knew it was going to explode like that." I glower at Alana.

"Yep," she says with a small laugh. "But hey, you passed your first test."

"Gee, thanks," I mumble.

I use the rag to clean my dagger and slap it back into Alana's hand. She shoves it into her pocket, unfazed by the mess, and gives Cadence a quick nod.

Once again, with me in the middle, we begin to jog. Adrenaline pumps through my veins, giving me the boost I need to take on an entire fleet of demons.

We sprint through the night for what seems like miles when Cadence jerks to a stop. The tiny, rundown shed that hides the club is in the distance, lit by a bare bulb. I take a breath in relief. There isn't an army of demons waiting for us—only four. And they don't have a clue that we're closing in on them.

PERSONAL DEMON

"OUR ODDS ARE good," Alana mouths.

Cadence nods once in agreement. She makes a few hand signals that look like a plan, except I have no idea what the signals mean. It must be a code learned at the academy. She must've forgotten that I'm not one of them. I'm strictly volunteering for tonight. And after the demon I took down, a desk job is looking really good at the moment.

Cadence gives me the thumbs up signal, and I stare at her with confusion marring my face. I shrug my shoulders, causing her to sigh under her breath.

"We're going to surround them," she says, her voice no more than a whisper in my ear.

I pick at the demon mush in my hair. I'm afraid of being separated from them. What if I can't kill the next demon? I'll get hurt or murdered or worse, lose my soul. No one can wait and watch to jump in to save me if I need it.

Alana places a firm hand on my shoulder. "I have faith in you," she mouths, not trusting her voice.

Without giving me time to back down, Alana jogs to the left and Cadence to the right. My only option is straight ahead. I don't charge into battle, though. I linger, watching the shadows of Alana and Cadence until they start closing in.

I glide through the dry brush, only stepping in patches of dirt. Any sudden noise will bring the demons to me. I'd rather get noticed last, or it'll turn into a save Cami mission instead of a rescue mission for the townspeople of Desertville.

This situation is strange and terrifying because demons don't work together. They just don't. They're fierce competitors, always seeking the most power. Alana once told me demons will fight each other first to eliminate the opposition before going after what they think is prey. It makes it easier for hunters.

I don't think it'll happen like that tonight. Not when their numbers are slim, and there's an overabundance of people to hunt.

My heart pounds like a sledgehammer. Each beat vibrates through my body, resonating to my soul. The shed door opens and fear churns in my stomach when I see shapes moving inside. Besides illuminating the demons outside, the dim lighting prevents me from determining if the shapes are demons or their captives.

Alana hovers in the darkness just outside the ring of glowing light. She pitches a rock as far as she can, and a muffled thud sounds through the crisp air.

Two demons jerk their heads up, showing off their beautiful, inhuman faces. If I didn't know they were demons, I'd think that club goers were hanging outside, enjoying the fresh air. I hope they remain in human form long enough to get this over with. It's repulsive seeing a demon in all its demonic glory.

"I smell a stray human," a demon with long, flowing black hair says. Her smooth voice, like creamy chocolate chimes out, and she flicks her tongue over her lips.

"Indeed," her companion says. "Female."

The man straightens his suit, stepping away from the light to peer into the darkness. I drop into a crouch, concealing myself behind a bush of prickly weeds. Sweat beads on my forehead as he heads in my direction. I hear him breathe deeply, swallowing a mouthful of air to track the scent.

My knees buckle when he smiles in my direction. He doesn't see me though and spins, walking to the spot where Alana had thrown the rock. I cringe at the sharp snapping that sounds like bubble wrap popping as the man shifts into his true form. The darkness swirls, concealing him, except for one distinguishable, creepy feature—spikes now protrude from his club-like hands, with no more fingers in sight.

I sneak closer as Alana takes the demon out. She decapitates his head with two swipes of her long dagger before he can use any demonic power to attack her. One down, three to go. *She makes it look so easy!*

Before I reach the shed, Cadence jumps into battle, dancing around two demons while Alana faces off with the women who had smelled her. It doesn't look as simple now that the demons are aware of us.

I grip my dagger and swerve away from the view of the demons surrounding Cadence. I charge forward, my boots thumping against the compacted dirt. I raise my arm to stab down into the bald demon's back when he swivels sideways, back-handing me in the face. My dagger flies from my fingers, leaving me without a weapon.

My eyes tear as agonizing pain erupts in my cheek and nose. Bile rises in my throat from the pain. I fall to my knees, cupping my bloody nose in my hand. My eyes widen as I get a closer look at my enemy. His flat red eyes, which are too far apart, are situated on his temples. A sheer film slides up and down over his eyes and they bore into my soul. His pointed nose inhabits most of his face; it looks like the beak of a bird with tight skin pulled over it. His lipless mouth displays dull oval teeth.

I crab-walk on all fours, inches out of his reach. A jagged rock slices into my palm, and I hesitate long enough for the demon to grab my leg. He yanks me closer, slamming my back on the ground. A dust cloud engulfs me, stinging my eyes.

"No!" I scream.

I kick my free leg to loosen his grip. As my boot brushes the demon's shoulder, he chuckles. He snags my foot as I attempt to kick him in the face, yanking me off the ground. I flail my arms as the demon dangles me upside down just out of his reach. He reminds me of a cat playing with its prey before it decides to kill it. *This is just great.*

The world spins as the demon tosses me into the air and then catches me in his arms. He smells of rosemary dipped in honey, a fresh, sugary scent to lure innocent people. Only lower level demons smell of death and decay.

I stifle a whimper when his moist, black tongue glides over my cheek to taste the terror spilling from my pores. I yank my face away, afraid to scream. Hot breath tickles my ear, and I jerk in repulsion, slamming my head against his pointy nose in the process.

The demon drops me, violently thrashing from the pain of his injured nose. My backside hits the ground, and I kick my legs out, hitting the demon in the knees. He loses balance and topples backwards. I vault to my feet and kick him again. The steel toe of my boot cracks the bone in his already injured nose, and he wails like a banshee. I kick him over and over again, pulverizing his nose until he doesn't have one. He convulses in anger and lashes out at me with his nails, ripping the fabric of my already frayed jeans.

"Will you destroy it already?" Alana asks from behind me.

"I'm trying," I say. "I lost my dagger."

"Well, you're just pissing it off." She lunges, stabbing the demon through his flattened nose into his brain. The demon stops moving and begins to melt. As the stench of rotting flesh billows through the night air, I gag and turn away.

"I would've kicked him until the sun came up," I say, noticing that all four demons are now gooey blobs, waiting for the sun to vaporize their remains.

"Another reason why I love you," Alana says. "You have such determination."

"Well, running wasn't an option. Neither was dying."

"That makes me extremely happy."

A murmur of voices breaks the heavy silence. I glance up and see several people, mostly tough looking men, hovering in the doorway to the shed. Cadence jogs over, huffing for breath.

"I've never seen anything like this," she says. "So many demons and not a single casualty."

"We made it just in time." Alana wraps her arm around my shoulders.

The scent of cinnamon and clove swirls in the breeze, and my muscles tense. Alana and Cadence are too worn out from the battle to notice. I shift from foot to foot, watching as a steady flow of cars emerge from the underground parking structure.

"It's a trap!" I exclaim.

I spin in a circle, scouring the ground for my dagger. A flash of headlights illuminates the ground for a split second, and I see the glint of the blade only a couple of feet away. I leap for it and swoop it off the ground, squeezing the handle in my hand.

"We have to get everyone back inside."

I dash to the shed. Alana and Cadence fall into place, flanking my sides. I push away the sticky strands of hair from my face, clearing my vision.

A chorus of low growls sends shivers up my spine. I spin in place with my back to the innocent club goers. In the distance, a pack of flaming dogs lights up the night like bonfires burning out of control. *Hellhounds.*

The murmur of voices grows quiet behind me. My stomach clenches, thinking about how many werewolves are still inside and how many of them will end up part of this fiery pack tonight.

And it's not my fault.

Drake was wrong. I'm not demon bait—he and all of the other werewolves are. My demon isn't interested in the Hell's Palace. He used my concern for others to lure me from the safety of Vivian's house. He knew I would stay there forever after dark, and he refuses to give up and let me go.

"He's come back for me with his trackers," I whisper.

Alana pushes me behind her as if she alone can protect me from the pack of hellhounds and my own personal demon. If anything, she'll die trying, and I can't let that happen. I don't want anyone to die for me. My life is no more precious than that of any of the others in the club, humans and creatures alike. If anything, I will fight and give my life for them.

The leader of the pack begins to howl. The deep, guttural sound seeps into my mind, bound to return later to haunt my nightmares. The pack moves in unison, slinking toward us.

A man behind me growls in his throat. The sound of grainy, shaken sand in a metal coffee can blocks out the beating of my heart as he begins his transformation into a wolf. *Please, don't let him get taken.*

The screech of metal being sawed apart rips through the air, deafening me, as I tackle Alana to the floor. I stare in horror between my fingers as a car zooms at us from the sky like a comet from space about to annihilate the earth. And we are the only thing in its way.

ALLURE OF DEMONS

THE EARTH QUAKES as the crumpled car collides with the shed, smashing it to pieces. A man screams in pain, trapped under the sharp debris. People scatter down the open tunnel into the parking garage, afraid for their lives. Cadence kneels at the man's side, doing her best to lift the car to free his smashed leg.

Alana jumps into action, flying to her feet to try to save the man. I lie paralyzed, gaping at the hellhounds. They look like oversized wolves with fiery fur, blazing so hot the yellow flames appear almost white.

"Snap out of it!" Alana yells. The corners of her eyes scrunch in concentration as she wills her muscles to strengthen.

I push to my feet and stumble to the others. I peer through the bloodstained window of the empty car at the pack of hellhounds, measuring the length of their slow strides and how much time we have. I hope the owner of the car is okay, but I can't think about it.

"Please, help me," the man begs.

I grab his hands and then almost drop them immediately. His stumpy fingers remain half transformed into paws. The car interrupted his change into a wolf. I swallow my repulsion, convincing myself that the change is normal, even though I've never seen anything like it. What should I have expected? The man can't just magically poof into a wolf. A lot of shifting and relocating has to happen.

"What's your name?" I ask.

"Darrius." He releases a long, low growl through his elongated canines.

"Well, Darrius, we have two options," Cadence says, interrupting. "We can only lift the car a couple of inches, so you need to either complete your change and slide out your little wolf leg, or you can wait to see if you survive the hellhounds, so we can get a crane to lift this hunk of junk."

The man stares wild-eyed at Cadence.

"Oh, I just thought of a third option. I could kill you now and save you from an eternity of demon servitude."

The man howls inhumanly. "I'll try to complete my transformation. If I can't do it, kill me."

"Good call." Cadence doesn't beat around the bush.

I dig my fingers under the pile of metal next to Darrius' leg. He shifts sideways to keep his soon to be wolf leg from being at an odd angle. Sweat pours down his dirty face, and I shiver at the weird crackle of shifting bones. I look away as his face contorts. I wouldn't want strangers staring at me in the in-between stages of shifting.

My pulse quickens as the world begins to glow brighter. My attention jerks back to the hellhounds waiting in the distance for a command of some sort.

The metal feels heavier as it loses the support of the werewolf's leg. As the metal cuts into my palms, I clench my teeth to stop myself from yelping.

The wolf whimpers behind me, and I drop the car at the same time as Cadence and Alana. The wolf nuzzles my arm in thanks and limps away with his injured leg tucked against his stomach. I try not to gag at the sight of the bloody bone sticking out from his skin.

"What now? I've never fought hellhounds before," Cadence whispers, eyeing the flaming dogs in the distance.

"You need to go inside and protect those people. They need you," Alana says.

Cadence opens her mouth to argue. I raise my hand cutting her off. "She's right. This isn't your fight. It's mine. And Alana's by default."

Cadence crosses her arms. "But this is my town."

"That's why you need to go inside and be with those people. You're the only hunter they have." Alana nudges her away.

A look of pain crosses Cadence's face. Without saying a word, she wraps her arms around us in a group hug. She turns, her leather jacket swooping behind her. Sprinting down the road leading underground, she leaves us to face the pack of hellhounds and the demon out for my soul.

The scent of cinnamon burns my eyes, clouding around me. It smells like an exploded Cinnabon with its sticky pastries burning on a dirtied floor, at once sickening and delicious.

I raise my eyes to meet my tormentor. His vibrant green eyes reflect the fire of his pets like Hell peeking out from his soulless stare. He opens his arms and chuckles, amused by the destruction, enjoying the fear emanating from me.

"This is wonderful, Camilla," the demon says. "Marvelous. You just can't resist the allure of demons can you? Scream demon attack and the hunters come running. And to think, I sent a human to do my dirty work." The demon clicks his tongue.

"I think you have that backward. Demons are drawn to me." My voice quivers, but I have to keep him talking.

The demon has let me go hundreds of times before, enjoying the chase. If I can keep him distracted long enough, the sun will rise, and he'll either have to leave or get trapped in the daylight dimension.

"The girl has spunk," he says to his hellhounds. "All these years I thought I'd have to toughen her up. What's changed, my dear?" The demon isn't asking me, but thinking out loud because his eyes focus on the fiery dogs.

"The demon blood on my hands," I answer against my better judgment. "That's what's changed."

The demon claps. He shows off a mouthful of straight, blocky teeth like he's proud of my accomplishments. I place my hands on my hips, waiting for his next move.

"You are getting better and better with age—like a fine wine. Absolutely mouthwatering," he drawls.

I grab Alana's hand to stabilize myself. I'd rather the demon not compare me to a drink. On the other hand, it's better to be compared and not actually tasted. He can shoot compliments at me until sunrise, but it doesn't mean I'll be joining him anytime soon.

"Thanks...I think." I bat my eyelashes. *Whatever buys us more time.*

I nudge Alana back. I can tell by her stiff posture that she is unhappy that I'm having a casual conversation with the demon. Yet, I think she understands my motives because she hasn't interrupted.

Alana follows my lead. Inch by inch, we creep away from the entrance to the parking garage. The demon continues chatting, and I occasionally smile, pretending I'm listening. The second we're clear of what is left of the demolished shed, Alana drags me with her, and we run for our lives.

The demon chuckles, and yells, "My hounds just love a

game of chase!"

I glace over my shoulder. The entire pack bolts forward to take us down, leaving Cadence and the innocent people alone. The demon doesn't care about anyone other than me. I should be afraid, but all I can feel is relief. There will be no more deaths on my soul tonight.

The compacted dirt gives way to sand, and it's difficult to keep a quick pace. The muscles in my calves begin to ache as I'm not used to these tough conditions. It's easier running on a paved street than out in the middle of the desert.

"Run faster or they'll set you on fire," Alana yells.

I sneak a peek behind me. Three hellhounds run hot on our trail. Their eyes glow red as burning coals. Frothing saliva steams from their glistening jowls, and I shake off the horrible image of being bitten and burned all at once. I'd take a tusk to my gut any day.

Alana jerks my arm, tugging me next to her as she turns sharply, changing direction away from the other half of the pack that has run around to cut us off.

"If we survive this, I'm getting a desk job with the alliance," I say, despite my burning lungs.

Alana bursts into laughter, startling me, and I lose my footing, tumbling forward. She leaps over me like a dancer, landing on her feet. She yanks me up by my wrists, unfazed by my inability to talk and run at the same time.

I spit out a mouthful of powdery dirt, leaving a perfect

trail for the hellhounds to follow. With my sleeve, I wipe away the sand glued to my cheeks by demon blood. I wonder if I yell timeout, would the demonic dogs give me a moment to clean myself off? *Quit dreaming and run!*

As the burning hellhounds close in, my pants sizzle from the fiery heat. Ironically, the sensation freezes my blood. The hounds growl and snap at the back of my legs in an attempt to disable me. Alana locks hands with me, forcing me to keep up with her.

I breathe through my nose to ease the cramp forming in my side. It's been a few months since I've had to run this fast and it shows. I'm not physically cut out for this. If it weren't for Alana, I might give up.

The hellhound closest to me barks as if giving a command to the others. Their pace slows, and I cry out in relief when one by one they back off. I jerk my head to glance back when one of the smaller hellhounds vaults through the air and attacks me from behind.

I'm knocked from Alana's grip and slammed sideways into the ground. I take a deep breath to scream for her to save herself, but before the words can escape, another hellhound tackles the first, nipping its neck. The two dogs tumble over one another until the smaller one is forced into submission.

A deep, blood curdling growl echoes through the night and the other hellhounds back off. I scurry backwards, and Alana picks me up, her dagger in her hand.

The hellhound releases its pack mate. I shiver as it swivels its head toward us. I'm awestruck by its human-like brown eyes, untainted by the fire that consumes the rest of it. I scrunch my brows as it wags its tail. This hellhound didn't want to have me for itself. It was protecting me from the others. The demon hadn't conquered this one's strong will.

"Thank you," I whisper.

The hellhound zooms away to catch up to his pack mates. A pinprick of light grows on the horizon as the sun begins to rise. *Saved by the sun.*

I pat down my smoldering jacket. The leather is still in good shape, thank God. As I dust off my jeans, Alana surveys the land to determine the direction we need to head in. She turns to hug me.

"You were amazing tonight. Are you sure you want a desk job?"

"No doubt about it," I say.

The sky lightens to a glorious purple while we walk back. I'm amazed we ran more than three miles.

A chorus of howling makes my heart skip a beat. I jerk to a stop and scan the horizon for the hellhounds, but they are officially gone until nightfall.

In the distance, two wolves—I mean werewolves—stand in plain sight to guide us the rest of the way back. I mimic a howl, not caring how much my lungs ache, in an attempt to communicate.

Exhausted, I follow Alana back to what is left of Hell's Palace. Cadence pulls up in the Jag, and I'm thankful not to have to walk all the way back. I'm so over physical activity. For the next twelve hours, I'm going to catch up on doing nothing. It's the best plan I've ever made.

MOVING FORWARD

"I HAVEN'T ABANDONED you, love." Dylan's soft voice caresses my ears, wiping my fear and frustration away.

"Then where are you?" I'm hovering in a void. The black abyss coats my body, my eyes, and my soul with foreboding.

"I'm with you always."

"I don't believe you."

"It doesn't matter because it's true." Dylan slides his arms around my waist, and the darkness melts into his golden light.

My body tingles under his touch. "It does matter. You left me to the demons."

"You don't need my protection. Your soul is strong

enough to fight them away," he says, his breath tickling my ear.

"But I'm scared."

"Don't be, love. I'll keep the darkness away."

<hr>

The dream lingers after I open my eyes. I can't shake the feeling of reality, like Dylan was with me again for the second time, and it wasn't just another dream. But he isn't here. I'm alone, half awake, and exhausted. Dylan disappears from my thoughts as the events of last night replay in my mind. The demons, the blood, the fiery bodies of demon-broken werewolves; I can't fathom the idea of hunting willingly. I don't like being an unofficial demon hunter.

The sun shines through an open window, bathing the room in light. A halo of sunlight engulfs the computer, and I sit by it to bask in the heat like a lizard absorbing warmth to help it endure the cooler nights.

Cadence is on her date with Drake, already over the demonic battle. After her success last night, she's the hottest girl in town because of her lethal skills and quick actions. She's a hero in the pack's eyes and considered an honorary member. What werewolf wouldn't want her? She is the best protection from demons.

Cadence left the hunters website logged into her account to give me something to do until she gets back. I browse through news articles, miffed that Cadence received all the fame for the battle last night. I'm only the unidentified person at fault for the high demonic activity. I wish Cadence would've lied when submitting her paperwork, but she said there would be an investigation if she reported the cause unknown. The lack of answers would look like a shoddy investigation on her part. *Whatever.*

A soft knock on the door draws my attention from the screen. Vivian pokes her head in, her eyes creased in the corners as she smiles at me. She shuffles in wearing a house dress with thick white socks bunched around her ankles. She looks like the epitome of what grandmothers should look like with pink curlers in her gray hair and glasses perched on the end of her thin nose. Deep down, Vivian can take on the world. I bet she could throw a mean punch if she had to.

"Don't let that stuff bother you, dear. The alliance is full of people who don't know what they're talking about. And they don't listen to those who do. I should know," Vivian says, reading the article over my shoulder.

I shrug, minimizing the page. Vivian's right. I shouldn't let a stupid article get to me. I know the truth and that's what counts, right? Part of me says to let it go, that there's no point in being upset that I wasn't mentioned as a hero. Yet, a more dominant part of me wants to scream to the world that I killed a demon. I drew the hellhounds away, risking my own life for people I don't even know. If only it wouldn't cause an uproar, because I did bring the demons here in the first place.

"I can't help it. I'm never going to get credit for all the good I do for the world. People will only ever hear about my mistakes," I say.

"The werewolf you saved last night will remember," Vivian says.

"Yeah, as the girl who got him into that mess."

"No, as the girl who risked everything to free him. You could've left him to be taken."

"No, I couldn't. I could never live with knowing I left an innocent man for a demon."

"That's why you'll make a great hunter. You care enough about life to fight for it. Human or not. That's where the alliance has gotten it wrong. They believe humans should always come first. In reality, other species need to be saved more often than humans." Vivian leans closer to me. Her powdery, floral perfume reminds me of my mom. I wish she were here to help me.

"But Alana agrees with the alliance. So does Cadence." I stare at the dirt under my nails. The alliance has to have its reasons. It makes sense for humans to come first.

"But it doesn't mean you have to. Just think about it, Cami." The more she speaks, the more it feels like she's expecting me to understand her reasoning, like she senses that I can be more than an ordinary hunter. "While Cadence might've gotten the credit, you're just as brave. You're special. More so than you think."

"I'm not special."

She shrugs. "You'll see it eventually. The more you immerse yourself in the world, the clearer things will get. With your idea of wanting everyone to be safe, you'll be a force to be reckoned with."

"And when will that be, Vivian? I know you have a sense of the future—your stories are real. Will you please just give me a truthful answer?"

She presses her lips together. "Soon, dear. You'll figure things out soon."

My stomach bunches in knots. Vivian's conversation spins around in my mind. Would Cadence and Alana have tried to save Darrius if I hadn't been there? I'd like to think they would. But now, I'm not so sure.

A steaming pot of stew simmers on the stovetop. My stomach growls, upset and hungry. It's hard for me to focus on the present. I can't stop thinking about Dylan and his work for the alliance. Does he know its members don't think he has the right to be protected? What about the werewolves? Is that why they live in this deserted town? Because the alliance won't protect them? I'd like to have a long chat with its members. This isn't right.

I inhale the smell of simmering beef, vegetables, and spices. Vivian sets down a thick ceramic bowl in front of me. I slurp the meaty broth off the spoon, savoring each bite as if it's my last.

Alana strolls into the room, looking like a zombie and

wearing the same clothes from last night. She's a mess with tangles in her short hair and bags under her eyes. She perks up when Vivian hands her a large soup cup full of black coffee. She slumps into the chair across from me, leaning on her elbows.

I reach out and poke her arm. "You haven't even slept yet."

She peeks at me from under her blond lashes. Running a hand through her messy hair, she stifles a yawn into her sleeve. "I've slept. Just not very well," she murmurs after a moment.

"Then you should try again. You look like you haven't slept in a year."

"Thanks a lot. I thought I looked like I was ready to walk a red carpet."

I giggle at her sarcasm. She's in a better mood than she looks. She gulps down the mug of coffee and pours herself another. Color returns to her pale cheeks.

I head back to Cadence's room, leaving Alana and Vivian to talk. I grab her cell phone, which she had left for me on her dresser, and plop on the bed to call Evan.

It goes straight to voicemail, and I leave a quick message to call me when he can. I don't want to seem too needy. I've never even met the boy. But I can't help that he's interesting. Evan knows about so many things I don't. He can teach me things that Alana or Cadence won't.

Thoughts of Dylan flash through my mind. This time I

can't remember what he looks like, just the oily darkness from my latest dream about him. Images of Evan have already replaced him. Dylan has become a blurred spot in my memory that only appears in my sleep. And now, I can't help but get angry because he hasn't called me back. I need to know what's going on. If he's not interested, he needs to just tell me. His lack of contact is the likely the culprit of his recent appearances in my mind—I should get over him.

I circle the room, annoyed that Cadence will be gone until sunset. There's nothing to do in this house, and it's not like I can go anywhere without a car. The closest bus stop is near the grocery store and even that is a car ride away.

I sit back down at the computer and type in "Hunter's Academy" into the search field. Five pages of listings pop up. I scroll through each page and finally spot a phone listing for one in California. I don't think Dylan moved out of state.

I punch the numbers into Cadence's phone and sigh when it goes straight to a recorded menu. I hit the pound key and wait for an operator to pick up.

"Name please," a nasally sounding woman says.

I pause, considering whether or not I should give my name. I would bet anything that the woman is at a computer ready to type my name into the alliance's database. It would look weird if I don't show up, especially since you have to have a password to access the website.

"Cadence Dubois," I say. What if there is a secret question I have to answer?

I can hear the woman clicking the name on her keyboard.

After a second, the woman asks, "What is this regarding?"

"I'm trying to contact a friend of mine who is no longer at the number listed online," I answer.

"Name and species, please," the woman says.

"Dylan...Davidoff, nephilim." I had almost forgotten his last name.

"Good news," the woman says, sounding less like an operator. "He checked in a couple of days ago. I can patch you through to his apartment if you'd like."

"Yes, please." My heart picks up speed at the thought of hearing Dylan's voice again. I don't know why I didn't think of calling the academy before. Maybe it was in my destiny to talk to Evan and not Dylan.

The phone rings three times before I hear the operator click off. A swarm of locusts buzz in my stomach. I'm worried that Dylan doesn't want to talk to me. If he did, wouldn't he have called already?

I'm about to hang up when someone picks up the phone.

"Hell-o-o-o, Katie speaking," a girl drawls.

"Hi," I say. "Is Dylan there?"

"He's unavailable." Her voice sounds overly sweet.

Unavailable? She doesn't say he's out or sleeping. He's just mysteriously unavailable.

"Can I leave a message?" I ask.

"I guess," Katie says.

"Please, tell him Cami called." I rattle off Cadence's number, but it doesn't sound like she's writing it down.

"I'll tell him you've called, Carmen," she says.

The line goes silent as the girl hangs up before I have a chance to correct her. What if she's Dylan's girlfriend?

I put the phone on the pillow next to my head and start to doze off. I hear the front door slam and fast footsteps in the hallway. Cadence flies into the room. She rushes to the closet and tosses her clothes at me.

"Pick out something comfortable," she says. "We have a couple hours of sunlight left, and Alana said I could help you work on your moves."

"Don't you want to, you know, relax a bit?" I ask, slipping into a pair of track pants. "You didn't even tell me how your date went."

"I'm home early," she huffs. "What does that say?"

"That bad?" I ask.

"Worse. I'll tell you more in a minute. I need to work off my anger first."

She rushes from the room like a hummingbird, and I jog to keep up with her. I would think she'd rather get into pajamas and eat ice cream instead of training me, but maybe that only happens in movies. I've never been on a date so I couldn't say.

Cadence flies out the backdoor before I even make it into the kitchen. I pass by Alana and Vivian, who chuckle at my confused expression.

"Good luck," Alana calls.

I scrunch my brows. Why would I need luck practicing with Cadence? Before I have a chance to respond, I step outside and something slams into my back. I topple over the short banister, landing face first in the dirt.

"I'm so mad I can barely think straight." Cadence's voice comes out more like a growl in my ear. She straddles my back, hitting the ground with her fist.

She jumps off me and helps me to my feet. I dust off my stomach, afraid to move. Her knuckles glow white from clenching her fists.

"What happened?" I ask, bringing my hands up to protect my face. "Did Drake do something wrong?"

"It's not what he did," she says, jabbing my open palm with her fist. "It's what he said."

I flinch, pain stinging my palm as she practices her punches. "And that would be?"

"He told me if I wanted to see him again, I couldn't hang out with you. Something changed since last night. He went total alpha on me."

I lower my hands in shock, taking a step back. Yesterday, Drake was nice to me. He even said he wanted to be my friend. What could've changed?

"What did you say?" It feels like Cadence is angrier at me than him. Shouldn't he be the one she's using as a punching bag?

"I told him to screw off," she says.

She smiles with raised eyebrows and holds her hands up for me to attempt to punch. I swing my arm and stumble, missing my target. *I'm so not cut out for this!*

"Good. You're way out of his league anyways." I attempt the move again, grazing her hand.

"Can you believe he accused you of bringing demons here, like you control what they do?" She demonstrates how to throw a punch on target into my palm again.

"Why would he say that?" After all that had happened last night, all that we did for those people. *What a jerk!*

"Because to him, you *smell* like a demon, like one of their minions," she says. "He's so ridiculous it's not even funny."

"You should've told him he smells like a dog," I say with a laugh.

Cadence waggles her eyebrows. "I did. Hence, the reason our date abruptly ended."

I sniff my shirt to double check for the demon odor Drake swears he smells, but I only catch the scent of clean laundry soap.

"Maybe you should stick to humans," I suggest.

"No thanks. Nephilim are cuter," Cadence says.

"Definitely," I agree.

Cadence shows me a couple of easy moves to practice while she burns off leftover anger from her disastrous date. She says if I continue to practice, I'll be at a middle school level in no time.

After an hour of working out, we head back to her room to spend the rest of the night eating ice cream in our pajamas. Even after everything that has happened, I couldn't be happier. I'm not going to waste my time worrying about the past anymore. The only thing I can do now is move forward.

ONE OF US

"DO YOU THINK it's possible?" I ask Cadence.

"About what? The girlfriend or the dream crashing?"

Cadence blows her purple bangs away from her eyes. She gazes over her shoulder at Alana typing away at the computer. She tilts her head to the side in contemplation, absorbing all that I have told her.

"Both."

Alana leans back in the chair, eavesdropping but trying her best to be discreet about it.

"First, he has a girlfriend. All nephilim do. They are simply too irresistible to be single." She picks at her chipped nail polish before glancing up at me. "Second, I don't know. I guess it's possible."

"Well, that sucks." It bothers me more that Dylan might be able to reach me through my dreams. It's like he's trespassing into my private thoughts. My dreams are *my* dreams, and I'd hate to share them with him without my consent.

"My advice is to stop worrying about him. That Evan guy seems to be really into you." Cadence mistakes my look of anguish for heartache, assuming I'm responding to the girlfriend matter. At least she doesn't seem to think the dream invasion is something I should worry about.

"You don't know if that's true. I hardly know him." Evan replaces Dylan in my thoughts once again. I shouldn't be attracted to a boy I don't remember meeting. The boy Alana knows and approves of is more attainable. Not to mention that I'm dying to meet him. Talking to Evan over the phone is like kindling a friendship before dating. You know what you're getting into. Yet, it gives you more to lose if the person isn't who you thought they'd be.

"I'm sure once you lay eyes on Evan you'll think otherwise," Alana says. "When I brought you home, he was the only one able to calm you down. You were in total shock over your parents' death. I was going to keep you two together, but things in the alliance shifted. I had to get you away from all that. It was like your world fell apart all over again." Alana looks over her shoulder at me before swiveling around in the chair. "I do regret the way things have turned out, you know."

I close my eyes to try to remember without success. I can't find a single trace of Evan in my memory, just the burning house and my demon. No Evan. No comfort. Only the raw pain of losing everything. It's given me blurry memories.

"He didn't mention that part," I say.

"Why would he want to? That was like the worst day in your life," Cadence interjects. "I wouldn't want to be re-membered like that either."

"I really wish I could meet him on better terms." I bat my eyelashes at Alana. She has the final decision.

"Maybe next year when we settle down again," Alana says.

"Next year? I have to wait an entire year? He might have a girlfriend by then. I'll have to give Dylan another call. He's more accessible with his wings and all," I say, using Alana's dislike of Dylan in my favor.

Alana crosses her arms. "Dylan is out of the question. I know you think he's cute but so is every other male species associated with the Veiled Realm. Dylan is trouble. Believe me."

"Angel hater," I mutter.

"That's not true and you know it! I've seen a lot of hearts broken because of that boy. Once he sees something better, he goes after it. Evan has never done that," Alana says.

"That you know of," I say under my breath. I don't

know why I keep arguing with Alana over boys. I would love to meet Evan, I really would. But Alana's disdain toward Dylan makes me think about the alliance's motto of humans coming first. And it irritates me.

"Sure feels like you have something against angels." Cadence joins my side of the argument. "Actually, I think you're biased. You want Cami to be with Evan because he's a friend of yours. When in reality, you should be telling her to go after the stranger to save yourself a future of awkwardness if they broke up."

"Hey! To be able to break up, we actually have to be together first. And it's not looking great, not with Ms. Road Block here." Why does this have to be so complicated?

"If Evan can't wait a measly year, he's not worth your time," Alana says.

"A year is fo-o-o-rever," I say.

A chiming noise interrupts our conversation, and Cadence sighs, grabbing her phone. "It's Drake," she mutters as she answers.

I put a finger to my lips to keep Alana from talking. I want to hear the details firsthand. Cadence narrows her eyes even though Drake can't see her and hits a button on the phone. His rumbling voice echoes through the speaker.

"I know our date went terribly wrong, and I'm sorry. I was pretty shaken when I heard about what happened at Hell's Palace," Drake says.

Cadence pushes her hair out of her eyes. "No werewolves were killed or taken. I thought we handled it pretty well. If you would've listened to me, I could've told you firsthand. Instead, you talk trash about my friend and then insult me. There's no excuse for that."

"I said I was sorry." I imagine the room quivering from the deep growl in his voice. "I can't help that Cami's being here makes me uneasy. There hasn't been an upper level demon here in years, and then she shows up and one shows up. I don't live in Desertville for the barren landscape but because it's safe. Did you know five percent of werewolves are forced into submission by demons? Her being here is a risk to the town."

My light mood shatters as anger seizes me. It's not my fault that I'm stuck here. I didn't force the cab driver to abandon us in the middle of the desert. I didn't know I was being followed by my demon, or that he was hell bent on attacking the town to get to me. I didn't even know werewolves existed until yesterday. Alana was right, the more I know about the Veiled Realm, the worse it gets.

"That's why demon hunters exist," Cadence says. "You're lucky to have us. Just be thankful we protect your kind, too."

"I thought you were cool, but I was wrong. All you care about are your precious humans. It's not like they're becoming extinct. The world would be better if they were," Drake mutters.

I gasp, appalled at Drake's words.

"If that's how you really feel, I'm going to go somewhere I'm appreciated. Alana needs a partner anyways. Let's just see how many of you survive the nights I'm gone."

Cadence tosses her phone on the bed before falling face first into her pillow, muffling a long string of werewolf related curse words.

I hover near her, afraid she'll jump up and tackle me. I place my hand on her shoulder to comfort her. She releases a low groan, and I can't help but laugh at her unintentional werewolf impersonation.

I perch on the bed next to her. "I should've warned you. It's hard being my friend. Are you sure you're up to it?"

"Are you kidding me?" Cadence lifts her head from the pillow. "I'd face a million demons if it means I get to have you as a friend. For the first time ever I can trust someone with my life. I meant what I said before about being partners, I want to be your partner." Cadence glances at Alana who listens quietly. "Yours, too."

Alana wrings her hands. She pushes away from the computer and moves to the edge of the bed to sit. She reaches out her slender hands, holding Cadence's and mine in hers.

"We live a hard life," she says. "We don't always have a good meal or a shower. Money is scarce...I work a mundane job when I can. Every night we risk dying. Are you sure you want to give up this?" Alana motions to Cadence's room.

Cadence runs her fingers over her plush comforter. "I

don't care about any of this. I became a demon hunter to keep humanity safe. In this town, I feel like a babysitter. Before a couple of days ago, I'd only destroyed lower level demons, and that's like squishing bugs. I'll serve a better purpose with you. It feels good destroying something intentionally evil. I helped saved so many souls. I want to save more."

I've never felt so selfish in my entire life. All I've ever thought about was saving my own butt, but Cadence is thinking the way I should be—about the bigger picture.

"So, it's settled," I say. "You are one of us."

DEATH SENTENCE

WE'RE NO LONGER welcome in Desertville. It would be selfish to pretend my presence isn't affecting the townspeople. I'm relieved to take my problems elsewhere, yet I'm guilty about leaving Vivian alone with the mess I've caused. Her emotions have been going haywire since Cadence broke the news to her. One minute she hides her face as tears prickle her eyes, then the next she's grinning like a mad woman, throwing praises at Cadence for taking control of her life. If only we were certain of our destination—my bet is one with a low supernatural population.

The landline has been ringing nonstop ever since Cadence hung up on Drake. Vivian swears it's unrelated to the events involving me, but she isn't a very good liar. Her angry expression gives her away every time she slams the phone back into its receiver. The last phone call was the worst. I overheard Vivian yelling at the caller that we'd be gone by morning. I've never felt so rejected in my life. Being hated for reasons outside my control sucks the happiness right out of me. I better toughen up and get used to it.

I help Cadence pack her bag, teaching her the importance of necessities only for easy travel. Jeans are always a must—they last the longest in most unpleasant circumstances and look the cleanest if we're unable to stop to do laundry, which occurs more often than I'd like to admit.

Tomorrow, Cadence's job entails getting us out of town and then returning to finish off the last of the demons in her town. She wants to be certain of Vivian's safety before leaving with us for good. She's packing now for a quick, painless departure.

"I don't think so." I block Cadence from adding a miniskirt to her small pile of clothes.

"Come on! It's my favorite." She tries to toss it over my hand.

I snatch the skirt from her and throw it toward the closet. "It won't be after your legs get gnawed off by razor-sharp teeth."

"Fine," she says, choosing a more appropriate pair of dark denim jeans.

"Better," I say with a smile.

Cadence digs through her oak dresser and pulls out two

pairs of leather gloves. She tosses me a pair for later. They're rough and overused but will help me keep a better grip on the dagger she gave me.

I stuff them into the back pocket of my blue jeans and tug down my green sweater to conceal them.

"This is so surreal. I finally get to do something I want to do," Cadence says. "I just wish I didn't have to drop you off and turn around to come back."

"It'll only be for a week or so. Maybe we'll have an apartment by then."

She swings the small duffle bag over her shoulder, and I follow her outside to the Jaguar. She pops the trunk and thrusts the bag into it. It never hurts to load the car in advance. We need every last minute of sunlight to avoid the possibility of my demon popping in on us.

I shiver, remembering the fear and claustrophobia I felt after being shoved into the trunk by the demon-tainted woman. She had major issues and got herself into that ungodly situation, but I can't shut off my sympathy for her. I hope her soul has found redemption.

I turn to the empty landscape and imagine a cemetery of scattered, unmarked graves. I wouldn't doubt it if there have been demons around here in the past. The human associates of demons aren't as easy to clean up. The bodies don't always make it back to where they belong. It's a sad truth I wish I didn't know, but the Veiled Realm must be kept secret to prevent mass hysteria within the human population.

I brush off the uneasiness I feel about Cadence knowing how to dispose of a body. It could be a subject the academy teaches, but I'll never know for sure, and I'm not going to ask. It's like having bones in the closet—everyone knows they're there, but they choose to hang up their coats instead, hiding the old bones out of sight.

Cadence spins on her feet and dashes back to the house, leaving a small trail of dust behind her. I push the trunk shut and mosey after her. It has to be hard for her. I'm used to charging headfirst into the unknown, but she isn't.

I reach the back porch and climb the creaky steps into the kitchen. Vivian hovers in front of the sink, drying her hands on a colorful kitchen towel. She lifts her worrisome eyes to mine, unable to hide the burden she's carrying.

"Is everything okay?" I ask, closing the distance between us. I wrap my arm around her frail shoulders.

"No," she says.

The muscles in my back tense. I stare into her honey brown eyes trying to decipher what is going on. They shine with tears, and she blinks to keep them from falling.

"We have company," she says.

Before I have a chance to ask who, I hear the front door bang open. Heavy footsteps vibrate the single pane windows, and then a group of oversized, angry men bombard the kitchen.

Vivian steps in front of me as if her small frame could hide me. I gape at the unwelcomed group from over Vivian's head, my heart falling into my stomach when I recognize Drake.

"Get out of my home," Vivian says in the scariest voice I've ever heard. It's raspy and threatening like a horror movie monster, unexpected to have come from the alliance's storyteller.

"Not without the girl," a man says. He looks to be in his mid-thirties. His long brown hair hangs in a braid down his back, showing off the tribal tattoo circling his neck like a collar. He looks like a biker, decked in leather and metal, capable of taking down Vivian if he wanted.

"She hasn't done anything wrong," Vivian says, her voice back to normal. "And she is not a permanent resident of this town. You can't take her. Your laws can't touch her and you know it."

What laws? I press my back into the counter, the sharp edge digging into my skin as the man steps closer. He smells earthy, like fresh chopped wood and crisp greens. It's obvious by his stature that he's a werewolf, and his scent proves it. By the way he speaks to Vivian he must be the pack leader. *So, why does he want me?*

"She'll be the death of my people." His husky voice sends my heart racing in a bad way. "I can't sit back and do nothing as more demons enter our town. If he knows the one he's hunting is dead, he'll leave. Her death will guarantee our safety."

I grip the edge of the countertop to stabilize my shaking

knees. The werewolves aren't here to arrest me and lock me in a dungeon. They're here to deliver a death sentence. *My death sentence.*

I take slow, shallow breaths, peering through the mob of men to see if I can see Alana and Cadence behind them. I pray they're okay. What if the werewolves took them out before coming to me? They don't look like they'd have a problem killing as long as it benefits them. Offing my protectors is a good way to ensure my vulnerability.

I square my shoulders, lifting my head to meet the gaze of the pack. "You'll be the cause of your own destruction," I say, my voice stronger than I feel. I'm thankful it doesn't quiver like the trembling of my hands. "Killing me won't solve anything. It will make my demon angry, and then he'll take it out on you."

"You admit that the demon belongs to you," the man says.

"Yes, in a way. He doesn't want anyone except me, or else you'd all be his little pets by now."

The room fills with suffocating tension. I can almost smell the testosterone emitting from the men. Their pride is hurt because I'm a weak little human who is capable of doing something they can't—like kill a demon. The men growl in unison, and I hold steady to keep from wincing at the inhuman noise. They're truly animals in human form. No wonder Alana and Cadence put humans before everything else; these men would eat me for breakfast if they could.

The man's eyes widen as if a light bulb lights in his mind. He moves closer, inches away from Vivian. She holds her stance, not wavering even as the man towers over us.

Before I have a chance to duck, the man reaches over Vivian and digs his fingers into my arms. My feet dangle as he lifts me up and over her, tossing me on his shoulder. "Then we'll hand you over to the demon ourselves in exchange that he leaves us alone." A deal. Demons rarely refuse a good bargain.

I beat my fists into his taut back, trying to slow him down. The rooms blur past as the werewolf runs through the house and out the front door. Dusky sunlight glares down, stinging my eyes.

The man races to his beat-up pickup truck. I flail my arms to slow down his strides. He yanks the door open and climbs in. My head smacks against the frame as he tosses me across the bench seat.

I peer around as wolves shoot out of Vivian's house and down the gravel driveway. Cadence and Alana are nowhere in sight, and the thought of losing them is more powerful than the thought of losing my life. Salty tears cloud my vision and burn my cheeks, knowing that doom is inevitable.

I never thought my life would end at the hands of werewolves. It seems more ridiculous the more I think about it. I've always thought it would be death by demon, not death by dog.

I scrunch my nose, eyeing the man as he hangs his head out his opened window and releases a loud howl. I guess the wind is irresistible to a canine. I squelch the urge to slap some sense into him, afraid he'd hit me back twice as hard.

The tires crunch the gravel as he accelerates. He won't waste a moment to get out and open the wrought iron gate. I glance over my shoulder as the yellow Victorian house grows smaller and smaller.

"Sheeit," the man mumbles under his breath. "Pesky humans."

The truck swerves as Cadence pops into view from behind a conveniently placed boulder. She crouches low like a cat about to pounce and does exactly that. Her boots slam into the door of the driver's side as she thrusts her arms through the window. Her fingers lock onto the man's neck and small drops of blood bead where her nails dig in.

I flinch as my window shatters. A rock the size of a baseball collides with my arm. I jerk as pain shoots from my shoulder into my fingers. The rock drops next to me, and I lock my fingers around the smooth surface.

The werewolf takes his hands off the wheel to knock Cadence away and the truck bounces out of control. I take the moment of distraction and thrust my foot over the man's leg and under the steering wheel. I'd be embarrassed about straddling a stranger on any other day, but this is life or death, and life always wins.

I use my body weight to step on the brake pedal. The

truck skids to a stop, and my head flies into the windshield. Black stars burst in my vision and dizziness threatens my consciousness. *Oh, God, Cadence!*

The man roars. His face contorts as he transforms into a wolf. His nose elongates, sprouting tufts of fur at random. His jaw cracks as his teeth turn into fangs. When he attempts to bite my face, I gasp and slap his muzzle. I search for Cadence and see her sprawled on the dirt with Alana crouched next to her.

Hairy hands grab for my neck, and I scream. The moment the werewolf has a good hold, I'll be dead. He'll snap my neck in two. I try to roll off him, but there isn't enough room in my awkward position. My foot is lodged under the dash and I'm still pressing the brake pedal.

Angry growls erupt around me. The rest of the pack is back. The man howls in response, and before he can bark a wolf-like command, I pound the rock, still gripped in my hand, against his forehead. He yips and I hit him harder. He slumps forward enough for me to put the truck in park and yank the keys from the ignition.

I gawk through the window at the pack of wolves, wondering how long it'll take them to shred me apart if I get out.

A gunshot rings out, and the wolves scatter, racing from the property. I stumble from the truck. Vivian has a large shotgun propped on her shoulder. She looks like a granny assassin.

"Cami, let's go!" Alana shouts.

I sigh in relief seeing Alana and Cadence standing twenty feet away up the drive. I gather my wits and jet after them in the direction of the Jaguar.

We reach the car, and I jump into the back with Cadence. Alana takes the wheel, floors the throttle, and waves to Vivian as we fly past.

"What about Vivian?" I ask, stunned.

"Grams is a tough lady," Cadence says. "She can take care of herself."

I press my hand to the cool rear window. Vivian heads back into the house and shuts the door behind her. My heart sinks into my stomach as I stare at the fiery sunset. Night will be here soon, and my demon will be free once again. It's going to be a rough night. At least I'm still alive, right?

FLEE

THE STREETLAMPS BLINK on creating an ominous orange glow in the surrounding twilight. The Jag zooms down the freeway. The headlights of passing cars whiz past like a dazzling lightshow of oversized fireflies. I despise nightfall, though I can't help but appreciate the beauty of a glowing cityscape in the distance.

Alana navigates the freeway unaffected by the likelihood of a demon popping up at any moment, which would cause a pileup of cars and trap us on this one-way stretch of winding road.

A cool breeze streams in through Alana's cracked window. It heightens my awareness of demon activity. More often than not, I can now smell a demon before I see it, giving us a small, priceless advantage.

"We have a destination, right?" I ask.

I'd hate to have to stay in another unprotected, unknown town in a dirty motel room. If only all churches could be safe houses for us. Many churches refuse to help us because the humans can't see the darkness that lies in the night. Not to mention that people don't want demons on their doorsteps.

"I always have a destination. The question is whether we can stay there or not. I didn't have time to call in advance." A tight smile plays on Alana's lips. "But I have a good feeling we'll be able to."

I moan and lean into Cadence, who hasn't said much since we left. She did call Vivian to let her know we were safe, but other than that, she's been silent.

"I hope so," I say.

Cadence twirls her dagger between her palms. It's the only weapon we have to fight with that can destroy a demon. Alana has her combat skills to defend herself with. I, on the other hand, have only my sheer will to survive to protect me. It doesn't bother me much since I've never had a weapon before, but now I feel bare and useless if it came down to a demon attack. I hate being useless.

The city lights grow brighter as the night sky darkens. Up ahead, about five miles according to the exit sign, is Fire Mountain Road. Alana merges into the slow lane and eases on the brake pedal to exit. The shady street name is appropriate for our situation. It beats Desertville, though; there's not a single barren desert in sight.

"Good choice. Side streets are safer to drive on at night. More escape routes," Cadence says, breaking the silence.

"Exactly," Alana says.

We roll to a stop at a red light, and I glance out the window. A gas station sits on the corner up ahead, and I remember the millions of spiders from the truck stop. I don't think I'll ever use a public restroom again.

I wrap my arms around my chest, shivering from the freezing air. Cadence shrugs out of her leather jacket and hands it to me since mine was left back at Vivian's. It smells like her verbena-lime fragrance, and I breathe deeply to channel her courage and strength into me.

"Thanks," I murmur, sliding my arms through the soft sleeves.

Alana winks at me in the rearview mirror, her confidence obvious that we'll make it to a safe house before the demon can track us down.

Alana taps the steering wheel. "Not much farther. I think you'll both like it. I used to spend a lot of time here." That must've been before me because nothing looks familiar.

Cadence bobs her head up and down, not quite sure if Alana can tell whether or not she will like it. "We're not far from my house. I thought we'd be going out of state."

She peers in the rearview mirror. "Not tonight. This

place isn't permanent. It'll give us somewhere to stay until we find an apartment. You both can help me decide on where we go from there."

"We should catch a flight and get out of the country. It could be years before the demon finds us again," Cadence says.

Alana lifts her brows. "I'll consider it as long as we can afford it. Plus, I don't think the demon will find us for a couple of we—"

I fly forward as Alana slams the brakes. My seatbelt locks into place. I slap my hands on the front seat to keep it from digging into my ribs. Cinnamon and clove engulf me in a pungent cloud of terror.

The Jag skids to a complete stop. Cadence jumps out of the car with her dagger gripped in her hand before I have a chance to see *him*, my demon. Alana scurries from the driver's seat, and I fumble to unbuckle my seatbelt.

Icy fear runs its fingers up my spine. I pull the gloves from my pocket and shove my fingers into them for protection.

I creep from the car, staying hidden by the wide door. Alana and Cadence circle the demon to keep him from reaching me. He could kill them both in the blink of an eye if he wanted to, and I can't figure out why he hasn't yet.

Cadence rushes at the demon, nicking him on the shoulder with her blade. He dances out of her way, avoiding another slash from her dagger. Cadence is fast, but the demon is faster. Before she has a chance to recuperate from her missed shot, the demon launches a blazing ball of electricity at her. She drops to the pavement. It zooms past her into a small leafless tree, setting it ablaze.

The demon jerks his head and smiles at me. I can see the darkness in his emerald eyes, the malevolent pleasure he gets from wreaking havoc on my life. Alana leaps in to avert his focus from me. The demon thrusts his arm at her, knocking her through the air. She hits the hood of the Jag with a loud bang. Her jacket squeaks as she slides down the hood and back onto her feet.

"Run!" Cadence yells. "I'll keep him busy!"

She soars at the demon, landing on his back. Alana grabs my hand, pulling me away. I plant my feet on the asphalt. I can't leave Cadence to fight my demon alone. It isn't right.

"If we don't go, he'll kill her," Alana says.

I clench my teeth and glance one last time. Cadence's dagger sparkles in the street light before it sinks into the back of the demon's neck.

I'm already on my feet running next to Alana, terrified for my friend's life. Fear and regret seep deep into my soul, tormenting me with bitterness. I wish I could raise my hands in surrender and relieve my friends of their protective duties. The thought passes as quickly as it came. I could never do that. Instead, I flee.

SCENT OF SAFETY

COOL NIGHT AIR clings to my clammy skin. Tendrils of steam radiate from it, swirling into the night sky like wisps from hot asphalt during an icy rainfall. Alana lurks ahead of me, jerking to a stop every time bright, intrusive headlights of a passing car draw near, threatening to expose us.

I dash forward to catch up to her, the loud slaps of my boots ringing out like thunder. I wish I had never bumped into the world of demons—I wish I was either a demon hunter or an ordinary human, not stuck in between like this. That's what I get for stumbling into it instead of dying with my parents like I was supposed to.

"Not so loud," Alana says, raising her open palm to me. "I thought you would be able to keep up with me without so much noise."

"Dirt is easier to move stealthily on," I mumble.

I wipe my forehead against the sleeve of my jacket. If I didn't need it for protection, I would have taken it off already. But I can't afford to expose my bare skin. The last thing I need is to have my arms mutilated by the sharp nails of my demon.

My mind flashes to Cadence. If only she had run with us instead of choosing to be the bait to help us escape. I pray that she is still alive. I can't bear the thought of her death on my hands. She's my only friend apart from Alana.

Alana grabs my hand and pulls me against her. My tense muscles relax under her touch. She wouldn't push me so hard if she didn't think I could handle it. *I can handle this.*

"Don't worry, Cadence is fine. She's a great hunter and can take care of herself." Alana presses her hand against the small of my back to coax me into maintaining her speed. "I'll slow down if you need me too. The demon is still a mile behind us."

"The answer is no. I'd rather not risk it tonight," I say.

"That's what I like to hear. You know, Cami, I think we just may survive this."

"I wasn't planning on anything but surviving," I say, pulling away.

Alana nods her head in agreement. "Same here."

A shiver runs down my spine. The chance of losing my soul is greater and could still happen with my demon more determined to steal me away than ever. Something has shift-ed in his hunts—he's more persistent. After his stunt with the hellhounds, he should've backed off, but he didn't. Ala-na was right in a way. The more I experience the Veiled Realm, the harder it is to be normal. I think my demon is using my newfound knowledge against me.

Alana begins to run. I follow, running on the balls of my feet to eliminate any unwanted noise. The wind gusts around me and cinnamon and clove waft through the air. The hairs on my arms stand on end, and I push my legs to run harder.

"Keep up, Cami," Alana says. "Here comes trouble."

I glance behind me. Two blocks away, the demon kneels with his head lowered to the ground. His sharp, angular nose presses against the concrete. It doesn't look like Ca-dence did much damage. A small black spot stains the back of his collar, but he's moving with just as much finesse and skill as ever.

His sleek, overly gelled hair reflects the blue light of the moon. My heart pounds as his head twitches on his neck like a wind-up doll stuck against a wall.

He lifts his eyes to mine. If I were closer, I'd see his di-amond-shaped pupils, but thankfully I'm not. I'm already close to him as it is.

"He's right behind us!" I yell. It's useless to be quiet now that we've been spotted.

Alana yanks me harder. "We're almost to safety. He'll

never catch us."

The irresistible scent of demon wafts around me. I take a shallow breath, preventing the hypnotic fragrance from invading my lungs. He's tempting me with his pheromones to lure me in.

I shake my head to clear my thoughts. Escaping is easier with a clear mind. I'm less likely to make a deadly mistake if I'm not distracted.

"I see it," I say.

A modern, Gothic-styled church grows in size as my boots pound harder against the pavement. A kaleidoscope of sparkling light shines through the floor to ceiling stained-glass windows. The arched wooden door gleams under the streetlight, its lacquered surface pristinely polished.

The aroma of cinnamon and clove grows stronger, so thick in the air that I can taste it. It leaves a fiery flavor on my tongue. I'm going to need a large glass of water to wash it away. *No wonder I smell like a demon to werewolves.*

"Cami, down!" Alana yells.

I drop to the cracked cement. My gloved fingers scrape against the ground, tearing the thinning leather. My palms begin to sting, and I squeeze my hands into tight fists.

I look up as Alana jumps over my back. She lands in a crouch, prepared to fight my demon and keep it away from me. Her arms spread wide like a hawk's wings about to take flight.

I'm helpless as I stare into the man's demonic, green

eyes. He never takes them off me while he dances around Alana's skillful kicks and jabs. He's just waiting for her to leave an opening.

"Get inside," Alana says as she launches herself at the demon. The collision of the two is louder than rolling thunder on a stormy night. If the weather changed with my moods, it would be pouring rain right about now.

I make my move.

I push up on my hands. The stinging turns into an annoyance. I jerk to my feet, stumbling on the stone steps as I take them two at a time. I might not be as good a fighter as Alana, but I'm good at fleeing. I reach the arched door and bang my bleeding hands against it.

"Please, be open," I whisper. "Please. Please. Please."

I tug on the bronze handle. It doesn't budge. I've always been worried about being trapped in a building, not locked out. *What the heck kind of safe house is this?*

"Let me in!" I yell.

I spin on my heels, wrapping my fingers through the handle from behind. I use the tough heel of my boot and kick. If I keep it up long enough, maybe someone will answer. Sweat trickles down my forehead and streams into my eyes. I blink, my eyes stinging, but I refuse to release my hold on the door.

The demon curls his lips into a smile, slowly showing his teeth. I resist the urge to go to him. It's getting harder and harder to stay away. His charm wears me down. If I just give in, all of this would be over. The chase, the running, the pain. My life. The desire to keep my soul intact outweighs his allure. I turn away from his hypnotic eyes to compose myself.

"Break the window!" Alana yells. By the sound of her voice, he's wearing her down.

I turn sideways, still gripping the door handle. The beautiful stained-glass window sparkles with a warm glow, and I hesitate. I've never had to vandalize a church before. The doors have always been open. I wonder if I'll be arrested for breaking and entering once this is over.

"Just do it," I mumble. "The minister will forgive you."

I swing my leg back to give it enough force to shatter the glass. I lose my balance as something snags my pant leg, yanking me to the ground. My chin smacks each stair as I'm pulled away from the safety of the church. My teeth snap together, and my jaw screams in pain. The metallic taste of blood pours into my mouth, my teeth probably broken beyond repair.

"Alana!" I scream.

The demon slams his foot into my back, forcing the air from my lungs. I cough and spit, cringing at the sight of my blood splattered on the stone steps. I wriggle my body, digging my injured fingers into the ground, searching for anything to grab onto, but the cracks in the concrete are too small. It's useless.

Strong hands wrap around my wrists. The demon's diamond-hard nails threaten to pierce the dirty fabric of my jacket as he yanks me up and over his shoulder.

Tears spill down my face, blending with the tangy blood dripping from my chin. I thrust my legs out, attempting to knock the demon off balance.

"Cami!" Alana screams.

I sweep my eyes over the ground and see her slumped over, her back stiff against the steps. She struggles to her feet and limps as fast as she can behind me. She'll never catch up.

"I've been waiting years for this moment," the demon says into my ear.

My body convulses. My stomach churns at the sweet smell of him. Bile rises in my throat, and I don't bother to try and hold it back. Every time I try to swallow fresh air, my lungs fill with the cinnamon and clove aroma.

"Kill me," I growl. "Finish what you started."

"I have better plans in store for you, Camilla," the demon says.

His melodic voice caresses my ears. I could listen to him speak forever. I shake my head, pushing the unfamiliar thought away. I do *not* want to listen to him at all.

I close my eyes in defeat. I refuse to watch Alana slip from my view. I'm lost now, forever imprisoned by my demon. He has finally won.

My head bobs as the demon quickens his stride. I hold my breath in an attempt to suffocate myself, welcoming death. I listen to my heart thudding, getting slower the longer I hold my breath hostage. The beating in my chest weakens until there is nothing but silence as I welcome my own death. But death doesn't want me. Life refuses to let me go in peaceful bliss.

The demon wails in agony.

My heart drops into my stomach, and I open my eyes in time to see the dark, moonlit grass rushing at me. I hit the damp grass with a thud, jumping to my feet, spinning in search of the demon.

The smell of burning flesh penetrates my nostrils. I cover my nose with the sleeve of my jacket. I look over my arm at a boy dressed in all black, motioning me to run. So I do.

I bite down hard on my swollen lip to keep myself moving even though every part of my body swells with sharp, almost unbearable pain. My boots thud as I pick up speed. I have to find Alana. The demon could be going back to finish her off.

I almost lose my balance when footsteps resonate close behind me. A firm hand grabs my arm and I spin, yanking free. I'm not getting caught again by the demon.

"Don't be afraid," the boy says, huffing in small breaths. He takes a strong hold on my arm and pulls me with him. "I'm here to help."

"Who are you?" I ask instead of saying thank you.

"Evan," he says. "You knocked."

"About time," I growl. I don't care if he just saved my

life. He could've opened the door for me sooner. Now Alana could be dead. *Oh, please, God, let Alana be all right.*

"We're safe," he says, ignoring my sarcasm.

The church, with its pointy spires, looms ahead. I search for Alana but she's nowhere to be seen. My stomach clenches in fear. Alana wouldn't have left unless she was forced to. *Please let her be okay.*

Evan helps me stumble up the steps. I focus on the shiny door instead of the blood stains I know are drying under my feet. I lean against the door frame as Evan pushes it in. The smell of sage and burning incense swirls through the air, and my shot nerves begin to relax. I inhale the perfumed air—the scent of safety.

MALICEVILE

I ENTER THE cavernous room. High vaulted ceilings reach for the heavens and row after row of hardback wooden pews line the marble center aisle. A solemn figure kneels in front of a massive bronze cross supported on a marble pedestal in front of the altar of the empty church. Candlelight reflects off the metal, shooting golden rays of light through the shadows cast by a sobbing woman.

My heart skips a beat when I recognize the short, wispy blond hair and worn leather jacket. *Alana.* I stride up the aisle as fast as I can manage. The slap of my boots on the gleaming marble floor echoes through the enormous room. Alana pushes herself to her feet and turns in my direction.

"You're alive." Her breathless voice wraps me in relief as

she hobbles to me. I break into a painful jog to meet her halfway.

"I wasn't ready to lose my soul." I laugh despite the pain vibrating through my bones, happy because we made it to safety.

"It's just—I saw you being carried off like a field mouse trapped in the talons of a hawk," she says. "Scared the hell out of me."

I kick at the floor with the toe of my boot. Even with the training I've had, that's all I will ever be—a weak little animal, the predator's prey.

Evan's breathing brings my thoughts back to the present. I wrap my arms around Alana, squeezing her. Tears spill from my eyes, and I sob onto her shoulder. If it weren't for this stranger, for Evan, I would've been a slave for all eternity.

Evan clears his throat. I lift my eyes from Alana and meet his startling ocean-blue eyes. His thick lashes, the kind of lashes every girl dreams of, complement the almond shape of his eyes. He holds out a handkerchief, pinching it between his thumb and index finger. The gesture reminds me of something Alana would do. He grasps it the same way she did when I was covered in demon goo. Except this time, it's my own blood I'm cleaning up.

I wipe my eyes, watching as the soft, pale yellow fabric soaks up my sweat, blood, and tears. I'm going to owe Evan a new one after I'm done.

"I didn't get a chance to thank you." I hiccup another sob and try to cover it up with a fake sneeze. "I'm Cami Anders by the way," I add, introducing myself.

"I know," Evan says. "We've talked on the phone."

I smack my hand against my forehead, regretting the gesture. I should've known this boy is *the* Evan. If Alana would've told me we were coming to stay with her friend, I would've been prepared. I feel like an idiot.

"I'm sorry," I say. "I didn't recognize you from the picture."

"I didn't expect you to because of the demon and all. You look like you've had a rough night," he says.

"Try a rough week." Evan's eyes linger on me, and I begin to feel very self-conscious. I can see the blood in my hair and smell the demon all over me. "And thanks again for saving me."

"It's my job," he says with a heart-melting smile.

"No," Alana says. "It was mine, and I failed you, Cami."

My heart clenches. Alana will blame herself for my hesitation in breaking the window. If I would've just done it, none of this would've ever happened.

"Don't you freaking dare blame yourself," I say. "You tried to save me."

"I didn't try hard enough," Alana grumbles.

Evan clears his throat once again to distract Alana and to stop our argument. His liquid blue eyes shine like the glow of soft moonlight. He looks even better in person. I memorize every detail of the boy who has saved my life on numerous occasions.

Day-old stubble shadows his chiseled jaw. Pinkness flushes his cheeks, probably from the run, and his pouty lips puff when he exhales. Prominent muscles bulge from his lean arms, and his broad shoulders look capable of holding me forever. I wish I could remember the first time we met, but the trauma of the death of my parents was all encompassing. He might not be in my memories but my heart knows him. It beats in my chest, begging me to embrace him.

Alana smiles, overcoming her guilt as she watches me study Evan. She cracks her knuckles and holds her arms at her sides, keeping the urge to punch me in the arm under control. It's a sure sign that I should quit gawking and speak up. It's strange, though. I was dying to meet Evan, and now that I have, I'm not sure what to say.

I settle for rolling my eyes at Alana. She chuckles, knowing my thoughts no longer focus on my near loss-of-my-soul experience, but on how sexy Evan looks in his black jeans and T-shirt. If only I can say the same for myself. At the moment, I'm positive I look like a wreck.

"Cuter than the angel," I say.

Evan furrows his brows, taken aback by my comment intended for Alana. He opens and shuts his mouth like a fish looking for water, then presses his lips together.

"Told you," Alana says with a wink.

Heat flushes my cheeks, which I know burn scarlet red, displaying my embarrassment for the world to see.

"Am I missing something?" Evan asks.

I shake my head. Dirty, blood-coated locks of hair smack against my face. I take a clump of my disgusting, once chestnut hair and begin to comb my just-as-dirty fingers through it, pulling the strands loose.

"No," I say before Alana responds. Cadence would love to meet Evan. She wouldn't be as obvious as Alana. *I forgot about Cadence!* "But can I use your phone? My friend is still out there." My voice quivers, and I force the tears to stay put. I can't break down. "And I was hoping I could use your shower."

Evan scratches the back of his neck and nods. He digs into his pocket and pulls out a black cell phone. He hands it to me, and I clutch it in my swollen fingers.

"You can use my bathroom. It's back in the dormitory," he says, using his thumb to point over his shoulder at a door I didn't notice before.

"Thanks," I say, taking a step forward, hoping he'll get the hint that I don't want to stand here all night.

"Follow me," he says, understanding my intentions.

Alana hobbles next to me. Her arm hangs around my shoulder, and I help bear some of her weight. I hope she didn't break anything. That would put us at risk for another attack.

The room leading to his sleeping quarters looks ordinary, nothing like I had expected. The faded brown carpet, about two decades old with threadbare paths leading from door to door, reminds me of an apartment we lived in last year. A dusty, plaid-patterned couch rests against the far wall next to what appears to be the opening to the kitchen. A small battered coffee table is the only other piece of furniture in the room.

I shade my eyes from the bare light bulb hanging from the center of the ceiling as we pad across the carpet. Religious portraits hang on the warm beige walls, giving the room the needed touch to make it feel inhabited.

"It's through the door on the left," Evan says, opening the door to what appears to be his bedroom. "There are clean towels in the cabinet."

Alana and Evan remain in the living room as I make my way through his tiny bedroom. It's about the size of Cadence's walk-in closet. A twin bed rests in the corner across from the bathroom. The stark-white walls contain nothing but an antique cross hanging above the bed.

Stacks of leather bound books take up almost all the available floor space. I squelch the urge to look through them. I enter the tidy bathroom, which consists of a standup shower, pedestal sink, and a toilet with a built-in cabinet above it.

I turn on the shower, allowing the steam to build up. I stare at my reflection in the mirror. Scrapes mar my chin all the way up to bloody, broken lips. My right cheek begins to bruise, the discoloration shadowing my smooth complexion. Rust-colored blood mats my hair, and I smell like a sugary, burnt breakfast pastry.

I flip open Evan's old cell phone and scroll through the contact list. Cadence's number is under my name, and I press the call button. It rings for a painfully long time. My heart pounds in fear. What if she doesn't pick up?

"Hello." Cadence's usually sweet voice sounds scratchy and strained. The weight of the universe lifts off my chest. *She's alive!*

"You're not dead," I say. "It's so good to hear your voice."

"Cami? Oh, my God! I thought I killed you. As soon as you and Alana had started running, the demon knocked me flat on my ass and walked away with my dagger still protruding from his neck. It was gross," she says. "He told me he'd kill me if I followed. I'm such a bad friend. I should've risked it, but I was scared. I've never been so scared in my life. He just wouldn't die." The rush of her words makes me dizzy. It takes me a moment to organize them.

I close my eyes for a moment. "I wouldn't want you to risk your life. You've done so much for me already. I don't know what I would've done if he'd killed you."

"So, you're not mad at me?" she says.

"Of course not," I say. "I couldn't ever be. Just keep yourself safe."

"I'm almost home," she says. "Call me if you need anything."

"Will do," I say.

I snap the phone shut, happy and disappointed at the same time. Happy that Cadence is safe but disappointed that it'll be a while longer until I see her again. *If I ever see her again.*

I shake the thought from my mind and step into the scorching shower. It stings my open wounds, but I don't cool the water down. The heat and the smell of the citrus scented soap is utter bliss.

I listen to the muffled conversation coming through the wall. I only catch bits and pieces of it over the loud spray of water cleansing my demon-tainted skin. It sounds as if Evan and Alana are getting acquainted again, but I also hear a third, anonymous male voice mingling with theirs. It must be Evan's mysterious partner.

Once the water begins to run cold, I dry off and cringe at the sight of my dirty clothes piled on the floor. I refuse to put them back on, not after I just washed away the last bit of foul demon stench.

I wrap a large towel around me, walk to the bedroom door, and crack it open an inch. "Is there anyway one of you can find me something to wear?" I ask.

"Already taken care of," Alana says, shoving a small pile of clothes through the opening.

I click the door shut and put on the flannel pajamas. I guess it's better than nothing. I pull big white socks over my bare feet and tiptoe to the door, pushing it open. I hope to snag the last bit of conversation I've been left out of.

"It's best that she's trained at the academy," Evan says. "I don't think I could do it on my own. What if I accidentally hurt her? She seems so normal."

"She's tough. I'm sure she can handle your methods. It's too risky to send her to the academy. I've spent the last three years keeping her away from them. They'll toss her out before she is ready, and we'll be in the same situation we're in now. I don't want her to go through what I've been through. She's still just a kid," Alana says.

"Come on, Alana," a deep, sultry voice says. The man hides just out of view. His ominous shadow looms on the far wall. "You have known me for a long time. You know I wouldn't be asking you to allow this if I didn't think it would be for the best. Cami needs to learn who she is so she can take advantage of her heritage. Evan can't train her and you know it."

I don't need Evan or the academy to train me. I have Alana and Cadence, and they were doing fine. It's not like I'm going to war. Alana would tell me that, right? As long as I stay out of my demon's way at night, I don't have to fight at all.

Alana rubs her hands over her forearms. I have never seen her seem so fragile or lost before. She has always put on a willful bravado for me. I hate seeing her closing in on herself.

The muscles in Alana's jaw stiffen. She straightens her back, lifting her chin up. "Fine. If this turns out to be a power play, using Cami to benefit the Hunter's Alliance, I'll hand your ass over to Malicevile on a silver platter."

Malicevile?

I take the lull in conversation as an opportunity to make my presence known. I tap the door, letting it fly open. I remain in the doorway, not happy about Alana discussing my life with strangers.

"Shouldn't I have a choice about what happens in my life?" I say.

"Well," the man says.

I raise my hand to him, stopping him from saying more.

"It's not a debate. I'll decide what I want to do as soon as someone tells me what the heck is going on."

I glare at Alana, hurt by discovering she's been keeping more secrets from me. I spin on my socked feet and stomp my way back into the hole of a bedroom. I flounce down onto the bed fit for a child and bury my face in a soft feather pillow that smells of patchouli and amber with a hint of boy.

I listen to whispered arguments outside of the door. Alana will wait for my tantrum to be over before coming to me. It's the same every time I discover something new about the Veiled Realm.

But this is different. This is about me.

I close my eyes, my exhaustion getting the best of me. I

moan into the pillow, my body aching and my chest heavy with heartache. My soul is too tired to care. I whimper one last time and drift to sleep.

I've never been blanketed in white clouds and golden sunshine like this before. It's like I'm surrounded by a little piece of Heaven.

"I thought you could use a peaceful rest after the ordeals you've experienced." Dylan runs his fingers through the puffy clouds, gathering a small bit into the palm of his hand. He blows it, and it dissipates into glittering powder that dusts sparkles onto my pants.

"It's mesmerizing." I twirl around on the balls of my feet, whipping my citrusy-scented hair over my shoulder. "I could stay here forever."

"If it were only that simple, I'd keep you safely tucked away forever from the world."

I sigh, knowing I wouldn't want to even if it were possible. I may dream of Dylan, but Evan is the boy I want to dream about.

"Don't look so sad, love. I can make this last for a while." Dylan wraps his arms around me, shadowing me with his dazzling wings.

"You can't. This isn't real. I have to get back to my life. I can't waste precious time dreaming of you when I could be with him."

The white puffy clouds dim and begin to pulsate with a

roaring storm brewing within them. Dylan kisses my cheek.

"If that's what you want."

A moment later he thrusts me into stormy darkness.

REVELATION

I ROLL OVER and stretch my arms above my head in the warm, homey room. Fragments of a peaceful dream linger in my mind, settling my uneasy nerves. It's like the demon attack last night never happened. My mind wanders to more pleasant recollections like meeting Evan.

The scent of smoky bacon wafts into my nostrils. My stomach rumbles like a freight train speeding through a dark tunnel, and I can't remember the last time I ate.

I twist and turn beneath the wool blanket. My swollen chin aches, and I run the tip of my tongue over my teeth to check the damage. Relief floods through me when I find none of them missing.

I swing my legs over the bed, the pain from last night's

demon battle inflicted injuries intensifying with the movement. My clothes, now clean, sit on a scuffed folding table leaning against the opposite wall next to the bathroom.

I breathe in the smell of lavender-scented laundry detergent before I undress and change. I sigh, staring at a dark bloodstain covering the neckline of my green sweater. I button my jacket all the way to my collarbone. The smooth leather is scraped up but still in decent condition. At least I can return it to Cadence, unlike the shirt.

I turn the doorknob. The cool brass metal soothes the aching skin of my palm. I sneak a peek into the living room to find it empty. Laughter roars from the narrow entryway to the kitchen. *Oh, joy!* I'm left out of the conversation again, and it seems like Alana has picked up where she left off with her family before I came along.

"Come on in, Cami. I can sense you lurking."

I straighten my tender shoulders and stride into the kitchen. It's the size of the living room and bedroom combined. I'm surprised to see updated appliances, the stainless steel gleaming under modern light fixtures. Mahogany cabinets with onyx-colored marble counters line the perimeter of the room. Dark Spanish-styled tiles sparkle in the light. Above the matching center island hangs a pot rack filled with every pot and pan needed to cook a gourmet meal. If I liked to cook, this kitchen would be Heaven. Vivian would love it.

Evan stands in front of the gas stove dishing out delicious-smelling bacon, fried potatoes, and fluffy scrambled eggs onto plates. My mouth waters and I nearly drool on myself. Maybe the werewolf nip did have an effect on me. At a small corner table, Alana sips a gigantic cup of coffee while reading the morning newspaper.

I smirk at the man across from her. The sting of the cuts reopening on my lips prevents me from giving my award-winning smile, so I make do with a closed-lip, pathetic grin.

I bend my bruised knees, almost plopping into the hardback wooden chair. My backside screams for a softer cushion. I close my eyes to try to remember exactly how I ended up injured from head to toe, but I only recall being dragged down the stone steps face first. *I suppose that will do it.*

I take in the appearance of the familiar man for the first time. His black hair curls around his head and his lips hide under a black mustache and beard. It gives him a distinguished look despite his goofy, boyish bone structure. His broad shoulders push against his polo shirt, showing off his sleek, athletic build.

Alana stares wistfully at him, and I can tell there is a long, romantic history between them. This must be Evan's partner.

"Did you sleep well?" Evan plops white ceramic plates on the table.

"Not really. Your bed sucks and my friend isn't coming for a week." My answer would've been different if I wasn't feeling out of place.

I shovel a forkful of fried potatoes in my mouth. The flavor of warm butter, melted cheese, and crispy potato explodes on my tongue, and I take another scrumptious bite before I have even finished swallowing the first. "You're a good cook," I mumble through chewing.

"I told you Cadence would be okay," Alana says to me. She turns to Evan. "Don't bother talking to Cami while she's eating. You're not going to get anything out of her until she finishes. We missed dinner last night." She laughs to herself.

I glare at her from over my glass of orange juice but don't argue. *Why does she love embarrassing me?*

"Then this is the perfect opportunity to introduce myself," the bearded man says. "I'm David Whiteshaw."

I nod my head, continuing to shovel in bite after bite of the delicious breakfast into my sore mouth. "You already know my name," I say. A piece of egg goes down the wrong pipe, and I cough.

I gulp down more orange juice, not even stopping to take a breath. It cools the fire in my throat, erasing all the lingering traces of demonic cinnamon.

I set the empty glass on the table, wincing at the sound of glass smacking wood. I adjust my jacket and cross my arms around my chest. I narrow my eyes, looking like a stubborn child, angry at the adults for not giving into my tantrum.

"Davey the priest, here to preach about the negative effects demons have on my life," I mumble.

"He's far from a priest," Alana says. "He's just a man I've been avoiding for some time now."

"Is that what you've been doing?" David asks.

"I've been doing a damn good job at it. Even after that little stunt you pulled. Sending Dylan to do your dirty work was low," Alana says.

"I'd do it again. If you won't let me be there for you, I can still care for your safety. And I wouldn't complain. You've always performed best on the run." David's tone isn't sarcastic or condescending. It's filled with pride and what almost feels like love.

"Enough with the reminiscing, David. Don't you think we have more pressing matters?" Evan smacks his partner's shoulder.

"Yeah, you're right." He turns to me. "I know you're aware that we've been discussing your life behind your back, and I know it's unfair. Alana's tried so hard to keep you away from the Veiled Realm, but it's now past the time of protecting you. The demon that has been chasing you has been playing games in the past, but things have turned serious."

I stiffen. "He has been relentless."

He rubs his beard. "And there's a reason for that."

I shift my eyes to Alana. "So you know?"

Alana wrings her hands in her lap and nods. "I've always

known, Cami. I didn't just stumble upon you. The alliance has been monitoring you your whole life."

I hold up my hand. "Wait. Why would they monitor me? Doesn't that mean they could've stopped what happened to my parents?" Shadows darken the edges of my vision. "They could've stopped it and they didn't?"

Sadness lines Alana's eyes. "Possibly. I wasn't assigned to you until that night. I'm so, so sorry that I got there too late. You know I'd have done anything I could."

I cover my face with my hands. "This is too much." I lift my gaze to glare at David. "Where were you in all this? You're still working for the alliance right?"

"My hands were tied. I wasn't allowed to intervene. Neither was Alana, but she did."

I grind my teeth, rage swelling into my heart. "You could've helped!"

Alana touches my knee. "Calm down, Cami."

Evan clears his throat, drawing my attention to him. His endless turquoise eyes study me like he's waiting for me to have a nervous breakdown. I wonder where he fits in all this. He can't be much older than me. His relationship with David reminds me of mine with Alana, except David doesn't keep secrets from his partner.

"She has every right to be mad," he says, standing up for me. "I couldn't imagine being in her place."

His words snuff out some of my anger, and I'm annoyed he has that effect on me. I curl my fingers into my palms. "I'll calm down when you tell me the truth. Why me? Why does the demon target me? Why did the alliance monitor me? No more lies or secrets."

The room goes quiet as Evan and David turn to look at Alana. She folds her hands on the table. "I've been trying so hard to keep everything from you, hoping it would protect you, but you were right about it hurting you. If I tell you everything, don't blame me if you don't like what you hear."

I frown. "I can't promise anything."

<hr>

I sit cross-legged on the threadbare, faded brown carpet in the living room. Alana mimics my position sitting next to me, facing the old plaid couch taken by Evan and David. I pick at the loose tufts of carpet, rolling them into tiny balls between my index finger and thumb. The room would be cozier if they would've spent less money in the kitchen and purchased a floor rug for the living room instead.

I nurse my throbbing chin with a small plastic bag filled with ice. I move my lower jaw back and forth, hearing the crack of healed bones in my ear. At least this time nothing feels broken.

"What do you remember about your life before I saved you?" Alana asks.

My eyes widen. She usually doesn't like to discuss my past. She always says that life is about moving forward.

"Not much," I admit. "I remember Mom and Dad. I

can still hear their voices if I think about them long enough. I also remember the house I grew up in before, you know, the demon burned it to the ground."

"That was only three years ago. You were fourteen at the time. There's nothing else you can remember?" David asks, interrupting. *Sure, I remember a lot, but nothing demon-related.*

I shrug my shoulders. What does this have to do with anything? I remember the little things mostly—like Mom's smile and the way Dad's aftershave smelled.

"No. Nothing I can recall that has any importance. Having my life shattered before my eyes kind of ruins things." The snippets of memories from my life before are the only things I have left to hold onto. I'm not sharing them with anyone.

Unanticipated disappointment melts the cheery grin off David's face.

Evan reaches his strong arm out to me and squeezes my shoulder. I lower my eyes to the floor because his simple gesture breaks down the wall I've built in my mind to keep me safe. He's different than Dylan, a good different. He isn't intrusive but comforting. Something about Evan is familiar, but I can't put my finger on it. It's not because I've spoken to him before. It's something more. I shake my head, bringing my focus back to the present.

"I was hoping you would remember something. It would make this easier on you. I'm sick and tired of putting you through this mess, and I'm sorry for not telling you this sooner." Alana swallows to clear her throat. "You are only half human."

Uncontrollable laughter bubbles in my throat. A high-pitched squeal erupts from my mouth, sounding like a hyena sucking on a balloon full of helium. It's impossible for me to be only half human. Both of my parents were human, which means I'm a hundred percent pure human.

And then something in my head clicks. Dylan's words pop into my mind. He said he could help me when I was ready. Only another half human could be able to help me deal with something like this.

"What's my other half? Angel?" It's the only reasonable thing I can think of. I'm not a werewolf. That would be obvious. A person can't transform into a wolf and not know it.

Evan tries to keep a straight face. The corners of his lips smirk into a soft, bemused smile. I'm glad I'm not the only one who thinks this conversation is ludicrous.

"It would make a lot of sense if I were nephilim like Dylan," I add. "No wonder the demons are always trying to bring me down. They are my enemies. But which one of my parents was an angel? Wouldn't one of them still be alive? I thought angels were immortal."

The laughter falls from my lips when three pairs of very serious eyes gaze at me.

"You're not half angel," Alana says.

I breathe a sigh of relief. "That would've been crazy. I

was about to check my back for signs of wings."

"Maybe you should check your forehead for signs of horns," David says with a chuckle.

My heart skips a beat when Alana reaches out and punches him in the leg. My breath quickens, and it feels as if I'm going to pass out. I fold my shaking arms across my chest, trying to smother the fear building in my heart. Vivian's words rush back to me. I guess the day I understand is now. She never mentioned it would be this hard.

"What is that supposed to mean?" I say, louder than I intend to. I try to imagine all the creatures I've learned about from myths, but only one horrible image keeps popping into my mind. This revelation is horrid enough to kill me.

"It means you are half demon," Evan says. "Just like me."

24

TAINTED

THE POPCORN CEILING rolls like a foamy, glittering sea. My stomach churns, nauseated by my blurry vision. My dizziness forces me to remain lying down. Alana hovers above me, tears dripping from her pale gray eyes. She drops to her knees and dabs my forehead with a damp washcloth.

I push up, digging my elbows into the meager carpet. The revelation of who I am rushes back to me. I'm drowning in a tidal wave of emotions—anger, fear, disbelief...confusion. How could I be half demon and not know it? Wouldn't I feel the darkness hovering on the outer edges of my mind? My soul?

"Being a halfie isn't so bad," Evan says.

I squeeze my eyes shut and slowly open them to clear

the fuzzy shadows from my vision.

"You say that like it's something to be proud of. I'm the spawn of a freaking evil demon," I say. "Which one was it? Don't lie to me."

"If you are referring to your parents, you will be highly disappointed to learn that it was neither of them," David says.

"What? But I thought..."

Alana slumps against me, wrapping her arm around my back for support. She's afraid I will faint again. I sit up straighter and rest my head against her shoulder. It's like discovering I've been switched at birth. The people I have loved my entire life, the people who died because of who I am, are not the people I thought them to be.

"It's not what you think, Cami," Alana says, squeezing me tighter. "Your mom is your biological mother, and she is human. But your dad, he couldn't have children, and that's where Malicevile comes in."

"The guy you're going to hand David's ass to?" I roll the name over my tongue, trying to pronounce it correctly, *Ma-li-see-ville.*

Evan smirks. "Yeah, he's the demon who almost got away with snatching you last night. The bastard."

"Wait," I swallow the bitter taste of reality, "That would mean h-he's my fa-father."

A strong series of convulsions begin in my stomach, shaking through my stomach to my limbs. The sound of a child's whimper echoes through the room. I slam my lips closed, stopping the awful noise from escaping. *I'm the spawn of the demon who killed my parents.*

I cover my face with my hands, taking deep breaths of the perfumed air. Finally, the convulsions begin to dissipate, and I find my voice again.

"How is it even possible? My mom would have never deceived my dad like that. Especially with a *demon*," I say.

"I'm so sorry," Alana says. "Demons are the world's greatest predators. And they can be quite persuasive."

My brows furrow, imagining my mother associating with Malicevile, even bearing one of his children—me. My heart aches. The people who loved me the most didn't have a chance. They wanted a normal, happy daughter and were tricked into having me, the spawn of their worst nightmares, and the cause of their deaths. *This can't be happening.* The demon I've been calling my demon truly is *my* demon. Not because he killed my parents, or because he has been hunting me, but because he's my biological father.

"It wasn't by chance that I happened to be driving down your street that night. I was sent to bring you and your parents into protective custody, orders of the alliance. They had never seen anything like it. A fourteen year old demi-demon still living with her human parents had never happened before. Somehow, you were kept off the radar. As it turns out, your parents were tricked into using a demon as a donor when they couldn't conceive," Alana says. "When they found out the truth, they made a deal with the demon to remain as your caretakers, thinking they could outsmart him. They moved clear across the country and after years of not hearing from Mal, thought it was safe. Then he returned for you, and your parents refused to give you up. You know the rest."

"Mal is Malicevile's nickname." I don't ask because I know it's the truth.

I remember my parents talking about a man named Mal. I always assumed he was my uncle because they said I looked like him when I was angry. It never occurred to me that he was my father. That he was a demon.

If Alana would've told me the demon had a name, I would've discovered the truth. She told me demons didn't have names. She knew it all along and kept it from me. Everything she knows about me is straight from a file. Like Dylan, probably like Evan.

I rub my fingers over my jeans to control the fury bubbling inside me. I know Alana was protecting me. She was following the alliance's orders when she found me. I understand why it has taken her so long to tell me. I couldn't imagine having to tell someone that their father is a demon. But still, something about my life being in a file in some dusty room irks me.

"Mal used your parents. Demons have trouble keeping their children alive and need someone else to do it. It was the perfect deal," David says. "That's why he is hunting you. He wants you back."

A shock of excitement sizzles through my veins. I can almost see Malicevile opening his arms, greeting me. I suppress my imagination, bewildered by the happiness I feel knowing that Malicevile wants me. It's the demonic part of me causing this reaction. It's the only valid explanation for these unintentional emotions. Who wouldn't want to know that their real father wanted them? The answer is simple: me. My real father is a murderer, a liar, a fake. He's a demon, the embodiment of evil—an abomination to this world. But what does that make me? My humanity was contaminated the moment I was conceived. I wasn't intended for this world either.

"Resist it," Evan says. "I saw your eyes light up, and you need to resist the twinge of excitement. Trust me."

"I wasn't excited," I say. It's not like I want to feel this way. I'm repulsed by Malicevile. The hate I carry for him seeps deep into my bones. Yet, part of my very being craves the attention I'd receive from him, the knowledge he'd give me that no else one will.

"You are talking to another halfie. You can't lie to me about those things," he says.

"Crap." I groan into my hands. "How'd you know? It's because we're related aren't we? We are the same species and all. I can't believe I was crushing on a relative." I slap my hand over my mouth a little too late. I stare at Evan to find some sort of resemblance to my demon, to me.

Alana laughs, shaking her head at David. They're going to have a lot more comedic memories to reminisce about before the day ends.

"Just because you two are the same species doesn't make you related," David says. "We destroyed Evan's mother years ago. She was a nasty little creature."

I glance through my frizzing hair at Evan. He rolls his eyes at the comment, showing his nonchalance over the demon spawn situation. I wish I could be as composed as he is. I feel like a glass of water filled to the brim. Any sudden word or movement will cause me to lose it.

"Let's not get into the details," David adds. "I'm sure Evan will tell you about it another time." He winks at Alana, and I really hope they're setting me up for a little bonding time with Evan. I'd love it if they did.

"If we can't talk about Evan, then I want to talk about you," I say, nodding at David. "I'm going to assume you aren't a *halfie,* too."

The term Evan referred to us as feels right when I say it. It's kind of like saying, "I'm a jock, or I'm a cheerleader." It puts me into a category I've always been left out of growing up. Now I have my own clique.

"You assume correctly. I'm not a demi-demon, just an ordinary human who has a taste for demon hunting. I grew up knowing about the Veiled Realm. I come from a long line of hunters."

"If you three are hunters, then where do I fit in? I'm not

cut out for this," I say.

I can't picture being a true hunter. It could be because I've known about the Veiled Realm for years, but have never truly been part of it. I knew about demons only because I was being hunted. The rest is still new to me. I'm stuck in Purgatory, between normal and supernatural. I'm super-normal. I think I'll always be this way.

"You are cut out for it. I saw what you could do the other night only using what you know as a human. It's time to discover what your *father* has passed down to you." Alana air quotes the word "father" and I smile. It's like her to make light of the darkest situations.

I cross my arms. "I'm nothing like him. He's powerful and determined. He's a freaking demon."

"So are you. You'd be dead if you weren't. I think it's time we fight. No more running." Alana twists the hem of her shirt.

"I like running, even if I'm not good at it. What about being normal? Or at least semi-normal? I can't do this," I say.

Evan moves closer. "Yes. You. Can. You are destined to fight. The academy can give you the training you need and help you find your power." He smiles, warming my heart with the faith he has in me. If only my confidence mirrored his, I'd be in a better place.

I jab him with my finger. "What about you? You can teach me."

He side glances at Alana. "I can't promise much, but I'll try."

I pout with my bottom lip. "Is that because I don't really have any power? Am I broken?"

"Don't be stupid. You have power." *Alana, always the optimist.* "You have a keen sense of smell and not just with demons. You can tell when someone isn't human. You just have to learn how to recognize it. I bet there's more. Evan can help you find it."

Out of all the cool powers I could have inherited, I get the ability to pick up scents like a dog. How will that ever help me fight a demon? It won't. I can just imagine a demon showing up at the door and me saying, 'Ha! You need a better fragrance because I can smell you, demon! Now get outta here.' *Yeah, totally not going to happen.* This is worse than being an average human. Now, I'm a below-average demi-demon. To top it all off, werewolves share my power. They could tell I was a demi-demon before I even knew. I imagine I would smell similar to my father and not like the rancid-smelling lower level demons...I hope. *This is so unfair.*

My attention draws back to Evan. He smiles, displaying his straight white teeth. No wonder I feel so attracted to him, he's half demon. Completely irresistible. Maybe I have the same effect on him. *Wouldn't that be nice?*

I roll my eyes. "Good luck with helping me, Evan."

"No luck needed when I have this." He opens his hand

and a small flame bursts in his palm.

My mouth drops open as I stare at the bright flame. Its dazzling sunset colors dance in an imaginary breeze. My hand takes on a mind of its own and reaches out, absorbing the heat of the flame. It doesn't burn my skin—it's not even an uncomfortable sensation. I move my fingers closer and caress the flame with my index finger.

I yank my hand back in surprise when nothing happens. There aren't any blisters, not even the rancid smell of burning flesh. I examine my hand, amazed I haven't noticed this before. There's dried blood under my fingernails and dirt embedded in the crevices of my fingerprints but nothing else. I cross my arms over my chest, tucking my hands in the nooks of my underarms.

"Didn't Alana ever tell you to never play with fire?" Evan laughs, pulling my hand back out from its hiding place. He sucks in a breath, noticing exactly what I had noticed. His flame didn't leave a single mark. It didn't even singe the peach fuzz on my knuckles.

"Cool." Evan rubs his long fingers across the back of my hand. "You're immune to fire."

"That's why I survived," I whisper. The only reason I'm not lying in a grave next to my parents is because fire doesn't burn me.

I close my eyes, envisioning the horrible day I discovered the Veiled Realm—the black smoke billowing under my doorway, clouding my vision, and me crawling across the floor, feeling the heat of the doorknob, but not being burned. It was warm, but not hot. I shouldn't have been able to stay in my room as long as I did with the fire surrounding me.

"Yes," Alana says, bringing me back from my past. "I had a feeling after the hellhounds but wasn't sure until now."

"What else can I do?" I need to learn who I really am, what I'm truly capable of. It's the only way to keep Malicevile away from me.

Evan clasps my hand. "Let's find out."

I follow him out of the room, my hand trembling within his, feeling the heat of his power flowing between us. It sends tingles through me, and I can't wait to explore what else he has in store for me. I never thought I'd be this excited about discovering my demon-tainted destiny.

NOT SO NORMAL

THE HUGE TRAINING room with its ceiling rising several stories high is the size of a school gymnasium. The intricately detailed stained-glass windows depict images of angels slaying hideous, sharp-horned demons, and I shiver. *I'm not related to those beasts!* I chant the comforting words like a mantra, begging them to be true.

The bright reds and yellows of the glass flames reflect onto the white tiled floor, dancing across the vast hollow space with the setting sun. A circular, stained-glass rose window accents the wall above a set of wooden double doors, and from the way the window glistens, the doors lead outside. I place the exit in the back of my mind as another escape route out of habit. The part of me who still wants to run remains dominant over everything else.

I've never seen a room this empty yet full of life before. Evan said the Hunter's Alliance walled it off and gutted it years ago, giving warriors a safe place to learn and practice. I can't even imagine what the academy's training facility looks like compared to this. I bet it's gigantic.

Evan stands twenty feet away. He squares his broad shoulders, spreading his boots apart in a fighting stance. His face is calm and collected, almost taunting, with a lopsided smirk and slightly raised eyebrows. My heart's in overdrive because of the excited glint in his bright eyes. His presence screams offense, and I hold my legs steady, resisting the fear slipping through me, begging me to run. I'd do anything to practice with Cadence again.

My eyes travel to the small flame in his hand. It increases in size as he tosses it up and down like a tennis ball. It's both distracting and annoying, toying with the dark emotions I keep buried deep inside a locked box in my soul. My emotions swell like an expanding balloon, threatening to explode at any moment.

I position my feet like Cadence taught me, feeling awkward, the few hours hand-to-hand combat now useless to me because Evan can attack from a distance. It's like having a pocket knife in a gunfight. I'm vulnerable to anything he throws at me.

I drop my arms at my sides. "I'm not going to stand here all day and watch you play with your little ball of fire.

If you plan on being a show off, I'm leaving."

I turn on my heels, stomping my way back to the arched doorway that leads to the altar. Footsteps echo behind me. I barely have time to turn before Evan collides into me. We fall to the floor in a tangle of arms and legs. I land on my back with Evan pressed on top of me. Heat blossoms in my cheeks. I'm angry and embarrassed I was defeated so easily.

I freeze as he watches me, his nose almost touching mine. I can't help breathing deeply. He smells like his pillow—hints of golden amber and raw patchouli mixed with his citrus shampoo.

"Never turn your back on a demon." His deep voice vibrates through me, sending tingles down my spine.

I lie placidly beneath him. "You're not a de—" I begin to say, and then laugh. "Not a whole demon."

"That's beside the point." Evan's words wipe the smile from my lips. "You can never let your guard down for anyone—not even me."

His bright eyes darken like his demon half is raging deep inside him. He rolls off me, breathing heavily, attempting to regain his composure. I push off the floor, knocking him on his back, determined not to make the same mistake twice. I'm tempted to help him up, but I picture him yanking me back onto the floor and yelling at me again. I'm not wild about the idea of him releasing his inner demon. I don't even want to release mine at the risk of losing who I was—who I am, to accept my birthright. I refuse to be like my father.

I walk backwards, putting distance between us. The corner of his mouth quirks into a half smile. I narrow my eyes, taking longer strides backwards, my right hand behind me, guiding my way so I don't bump into the wall I know is coming up behind me.

Evan reaches above his head, pressing his palms flat against the floor, and easily handsprings. His body arches in an elegant swooping motion, and he lands smoothly on his feet. He lurches closer, stalking his prey like a hunter. The predator he is dominates his every movement, every gesture, from his graceful strides to the ferocious glint in his eyes reflecting back at me. *Crap, he's going to try and corner me.*

I steady my pace, taking each step one at a time, reaching out to the cool emptiness of the room behind me. It's a relief to my clammy skin and my tightly wound nerves. I'm not trapped...yet.

The flame flickers in his palm. He tosses it up and down again, teasing me, torturing me, seducing me with its addictive allure. My breath catches when my fingers graze the surface of the wall.

I straighten my back. Lifting my chin smugly, I curl my lips into my most dazzling smile. I focus on the monster living and breathing inside of me that I didn't know was hiding under my pain and heartache. The part dying for attention, craving it, needing it, determined to get it. The demonic side of me no longer content with staying locked up. It's like overlooking a sunburn, numb and painless until you see the pink skin. The moment it's noticed, it comes to life, seething with heat.

Evan hesitates at the sudden change in my demeanor, and my hand balls into a fist at my side. He's expecting fire to bellow out of my palm. He doesn't know that I don't understand the mechanics behind his power. Heck, I don't have any real power. As far as I'm concerned, I'm human. The otherworldly presence only exists in my mind. I don't have magical powers like he does. I'm not even great at throwing a punch, but he doesn't know that. I use his nervousness and dwindling confidence to my advantage.

Swinging my arm over my shoulder like I'm going to pitch a baseball, I throw nothing but empty air. He dives to the floor without realizing I have faked him out. I hurdle forward, jumping over his back. Relief washes over me when he doesn't pull me to the floor. I bolt across the open space, stomping my boots in a way that says, "Ha! Fooled you!"

I swivel my torso to glance behind me. Evan is back on his feet with an alluring smile on his face, the kind of smile that can melt an ice cube. I pause, entranced by his irresistible presence.

Without saying a word, he charges at me. I side step out of his way seconds before his arms can wrap around me. I run to the opposite side of the room. Alana would be proud of my ability to stay on the edge of danger without jumping into it. I'm a fast opponent when I'm not scared out of my wits. I can defeat the feline in Evan's game of cat and mouse.

"You can't run forever. I *will* catch you."

"Want to bet on it?"

"Yes."

Evan jumps into the air higher than I thought possible and throws his fireball at me. I stand helplessly, watching it zoom closer.

Seconds before it strikes me, I remember fire can't technically burn me, and I relax. The warm presence of the flame heats my fingers as I catch his fireball before I drop to the floor, feigning being hit.

I moan before going still. *Plan, please don't fail me now!* If Evan does what I think he will, I'll have him wrapped around my little finger.

Footsteps echo, coming closer, but Evan stops short. My heartbeat falters. He knows I'm up to something.

"Cami? Are you okay?" he says.

I remain frozen in place, still holding my breath. My lungs burn in protest, but I can't let him win. The fire in my palm warms my skin, boosting my confidence.

Evan strides the remaining distance to me. The hurried sound of his footsteps strike a nerve, and guilt nudges my mind for tricking him into thinking he injured me. But the guilt isn't strong enough to give myself away. My eyelids darken, and I can sense him standing over me. His sultry scent drifts over me like a wave of pure heated goodness. His warm hand caresses my cheek, and I make my move.

I kick out my legs, thrusting them into his side. He tumbles over, giving me the opportunity to vault to my feet. His startled eyes blink in astonishment. A devious smile creeps onto my lips, and I throw my new favorite weapon.

The fireball slams into his chest, knocking the wind out of him. Smoke rises from his royal blue cotton shirt, tainting the air with the rancid smell of sizzling fabric. He jumps to his feet and pats the remaining flames off his chest.

"Never trust a demon. They'll use your weapon against you," I say.

Evan laughs, shaking his light brown hair out of his eyes. "You're something else."

"I know. I'm a halfie, remember." I offer my hand to him against my better judgment.

He grabs my hand and pulls me to the floor. Instead of tackling me and singeing my clothes with another fireball, he wraps his arms around me, pulling me against him.

I find my lips inches from his. My breath comes faster, the desire to kiss him overwhelming. I bite my cracked lip, wishing I hadn't just fought for my life less than twenty-four hours ago. Yesterday, I would've never thought I'd be lying on the floor of a church about to kiss the boy I only knew by phone. I suppress the thoughts that think it's wrong to be doing this in a church. *This isn't a church any-*

more. It's a safe house.

Evan tilts my chin down and brushes his lips against my forehead. The heat of his soft lips against my skin makes my hands tremble, and I run my fingers up the sides of his tight stomach. I lift my chin to meet his lips with mine. The draw of my newly found inner demon seeks his, and I find it hard to explain the lust I feel burning within me. I like him. Really, really like him.

"We're floating," Evan says before I can really kiss him.

I look at the floor a foot below us and panic. We drop to the tiles with a thump, my hip smacking the marble, and I wince in pain.

I blush as my leg rests between his and I half straddle him. "Warn me the next time you decide to show off one of your powers."

"I could ask you to do the same because that wasn't me." Evan chuckles and rubs his warm fingers under my chin.

"If it wasn't you, it was me," I say, shocked about our new discovery. "I can levitate!" I squeal, excited at the skill I've inherited from the evil demon I refuse to call Daddy.

I squeeze my eyes shut and will my body to release itself from the heavy pull of gravity. I abandon all my thoughts, imagining my hands grasping the invisible threads tying me down. Sweat breaks out on my brows and drips down my face. I open my eyes expecting to see the floor far below but am disappointed that I'm still lying on Evan. Well, disappointed I'm not cuddling with him in the air.

He studies the frustration in my eyes. "Controlling your power isn't that simple. You can't just close your eyes and hope for the best."

"At least I'm trying," I retort. "I didn't even think I had any powers until now. You make it look easy."

"I've spent almost my entire life practicing. David rescued me when he was the age I am now. I was only five at the time. It's all I've ever known," Evan says.

I stare at him, hoping he goes on.

He takes a breath, continuing. "I can't even remember my family. All I've been told is that my demonic mother wanted to take me away before I would've been able to survive. Like your parents, mine couldn't conceive either, except they had no idea I was half demon. David said that Alana discovered a fiery red-haired demon lurking outside a house. It turned out to be my demon mother. So, don't be hard on yourself. Your powers will come to you."

"How awful. I couldn't imagine being our parents."

"That's life for you. Demons could easily seduce the willing, but they enjoy breaking the strong."

I pat his hand, trying to comfort him about the family memories he never got a chance to make.

"Did your demon mother kill your parents?" I ask, even though I know it's true before he can answer. He wouldn't be with David if the demon hadn't.

"Yeah," he says, sighing. "They're better off anyway.

They'll never have to deal with the fear of demons or with me. They would've probably locked me up in some hospital, unable to deal with me. I would've never become a hunter. Or have met you..." Evan's words trail off. I can't help thinking about my parents. How would they have dealt with me if I wasn't almost normal? Not the way Evan thinks his parents would have treated him, but he doesn't know that. He never got the chance.

"Maybe you can help me get rid of Mal," I say, needing to change the subject. If I continue to think about my parents, I'll break down. I need to be strong to survive.

Evan grips my hand and says, "I'll do everything in my power to make sure you can protect yourself. He won't be able to hurt you anymore."

My heart believes him as much as my mind. A calmness rushes over me as I lose myself in the moment. His words encourage me to believe in myself. He doesn't say he'll protect me like Alana always says. He wants me to protect myself. I'll be my own white knight. "Thanks." I roll off him and sit up. "Now, tell me what's the deal with Alana and Davey," I add, liking my nickname for the mustache man. I'm tired of talking about our demon parents. It's putting a damper on the mood.

Evan pulls his knees to his chest and rests his chin on them. The muscles in his arms bulge as he holds his legs in place. "I'm surprised Alana never mentioned it. They're technically married. When Alana was sent by the alliance to save you, she and David fought a lot about what to do with you. He wanted you to train to be a hunter. She disagreed and left because she wanted you to have a normal life. One she couldn't have given you if she'd stayed behind." *Because I remind her of her sister.*

"I had no idea." My heart aches for Alana. She left everything she loved behind—her husband, Evan, her life—and for what? To protect me. I'll never be able to repay her. I just wish she would've told me.

"It's no big deal," Evan says. "David is a grown man. He knew she'd be back eventually."

"I'm glad they're back together again." At least there was one good thing about being hunted by my demon dad.

"Me too. Now I have the chance to get to know you, too." Reaching his hand out, he gently nudges my knee.

After a minute, he pushes to his feet and pulls me off the floor. He doesn't let go of my hand when I'm standing. We stroll from the training room, past the empty altar, and back into the quaint living quarters.

For the first time in three years, I'm not afraid of the coming night because I know I'll soon be able to fight as good as any other hunter. I can rest in the safety of the church for as long as I want, even if Malicevile is waiting for me on the other side of these holy walls.

I don't want to think about him, about how he helped give me life and now wants to take it away. I don't want to care about him anymore. He can't hurt me any more than he has. Tonight, I'm going to enjoy what it feels like to be part of a normal family, even if I'm not so normal.

AWAKENED

A KNOCK ON the door startles me awake. My bones creak as I stretch my arms over my head. My mind is foggy like I'm in a dream without a care in the world—without a single thought about the future or the past, with only the comforting moment of the here and now.

The stubborn place in my mind refuses to do anything at all except lie here in bed and think about nothing in particular...well, maybe nothing besides sleeping a while longer. I yank the covers over my head, ignoring the early morning summons. By the relaxation settling over my nerves, I can sense it's light out, and since it's morning, I'm not going to rush to get up.

Alana opens the door and enters, and then closes it behind her. Getting a wakeup call from her is more annoying than being harassed by a demon. I try to pretend she isn't hovering in the doorway, and she makes it impossible when she begins tapping her hands on the folding table, drumming to her own beat. I sit up and throw my pillow at her. Her reflexes are a lot faster than mine this early in the morning.

"Get up, Cami." She pounces on the end of the bed. My body bounces in sync with her movement until she stops. "Not fair. No using your powers to keep me from waking you up."

I open my eyes and see that I'm eye level with Alana, lying over the bed instead of on it. I grab at the air, for something to hold onto, but my surprise knocks me back onto the lumpy mattress.

I run my hands over my tired eyes. "Why is this happening now? I could've used it a million times over the years."

She shrugs. "My theory is that it's because you've been exposed to a lot of demonic power lately. I've kept you on the fringes for so long that you've never really needed to use it. Self-awareness might have triggered it as well."

I knit my brows together in confusion. "So, you don't really know?"

She nods. "You can ask Evan. All of the demi-demons I know have taught each other. It's the one piece of information they refuse to give to the Hunter's Alliance, and

Evan has been around long enough to know. His training session might've been just to awaken your power."

"He has awakened a lot more than that. Is it weird that I like him so much so fast? It feels like I've known him forever." I imagine the heat of our bodies lying on the floor of the training room, his soft touch and fathomless, liquid blue eyes.

"Part of you has. The part I've kept from you. From what I understand, people in the Veiled Realm have always been able to find their kind and band together. It's a survival tactic along with a million other reasons. Also, attraction is a funny thing. I can't give you the best advice when it comes to dating in the Veiled Realm, but what I can tell you is to follow what you think is right. What feels right. It's the only way to be happy."

I laugh. "You sound like an after school special."

"I know, right? If this helps, Evan really likes you. He told me so himself."

"Do you think that's why I liked Dylan as well? Because he's part of the Veiled Realm?" Dylan flashes into my mind, pushing my thoughts of Evan away. I remember the fear I felt gazing into Dylan's eyes, like he could see the wounds on my soul before trying to heal them. How he left without turning back, without calling me. Maybe Dylan can repair my soul with his angelic powers, but Evan makes me feel stronger and more alive than I've ever felt. It's like he fills the holes in my life instead of just mending them.

"I have no idea. I'm of no use when it comes to nephilim. Demons are my specialty," Alana says.

I scrunch my brows in consideration. Evan is a demi-demon like me. Dylan is the exact opposite in a way. I'd like to think the human half of me would have more of a say in who I like and choose to be around. Of course, none of this matters now. I don't think I'll ever see Dylan again. If I do, he won't be getting a hello hug—more like a fist-in-the-face. It really bothers me that he never called me back.

"Besides, any man who can make a girl walk on air must be special," Alana adds.

I blow hair from my face. "I'd like him a lot more if he didn't throw fireballs at me. He burned a hole the size of a baseball in the back of my only sweater, which isn't even mine."

She lifts an eyebrow. "Don't even go there. I saw the one in the front of his shirt."

"He deserved it. No one throws a fireball at me and gets away with it."

Laughter erupts from her mouth, shaking her shoulders. When she composes herself, she says, "I agree."

Forcing myself to function through my exhaustion, I finally roll out of bed and look at my neatly folded clothes on the table. I shake out my sweater and stick my arm through the newly made hole. I hope this isn't Cadence's favorite. If Evan would've hit me with the fireball any higher, I would've lost my bra, too. Then he would be in serious trouble.

"Think of it as a third arm hole." She covers her mouth with her hand to hide her oncoming smile. I'm glad one of us is amused.

"That would be okay if I were a three-armed halfie," I say. "But no. I'm just a girl with a large hole in the back of her shirt and a massive blood stain on the front."

Reaching out, she pulls at the hem of the sweater. "It's unfortunate. I'd thought you would appreciate that we get to go shopping for a new wardrobe."

My agitation melts away. I don't know why I was getting worked up over a hole in an already ruined shirt. I knew Alana wouldn't force me to wear the same clothes over and over for who knows how long.

"Sorry. All of this is strange to me," I say.

Alana pats my back. "I understand. Now, get ready. We'll go as soon as you're dressed. If you'd like, you can pick out a new sweater for Cadence, too."

I grin. "Sounds good." I can really get used to this normalcy.

***

David finally puts his foot down six blissful shopping hours later. Evan carries my bags as I carry the pile of clothes I've tried on to the register.

The first store I went into I left wearing an impractical, as David referred to it, sundress. Pink lace covers the airy, black cotton material. The sweetheart neckline and the black satin ribbon around my waist emphasizes my curves. My new black satin ballet flats feel smooth against my feet. I can't resist the occasional spin or two. I'm excited to be out of restricting jeans and holey sweaters.

I ignore the gawking eyes of strangers, staring at my beaten and bruised body. I'm not ashamed of surviving a demon attack, and I refuse to cover up. No one would believe me if I told them anyway. They can think whatever gives them peaceful dreams at night for all I care.

I shuffle behind Alana and David, clutching Evan's hand on the way back to the car. My heart skips a beat when I notice the sun sinking below the horizon. Soon, the demons will be coming out to play.

"The sun is going down," I say to Evan, even though he is aware of it. "We're running out of daylight."

"Don't worry so much, Cami," he says. "We'll be home soon."

"Not before it gets dark." I pick up my pace, half running, half dragging Evan to the car. "The demons will come after us."

"I'm not too worried about that," David says, hearing the fear in my voice. He underestimates Malicevile. Or he overestimates his abilities. Malicevile isn't one to give up. Not even if I'm a billion miles away.

My hands become clammy, and I wipe them on my new dress. I throw my bags into the trunk of the car and jump into the backseat. My hands tremble as I try to latch my seatbelt. After several failed attempts at buckling, Evan pulls the seatbelt from my grip and latches it into place.

Alana starts the car and backs out of the space. After being abandoned by the taxi in Desertville, I doubt she'd let anyone else drive us again. David doesn't seem to mind her need to control the wheel, though.

Her knuckles turn white as she clutches the steering wheel. At least she knows what to expect. I lace my fingers together and whisper a prayer for a safe ride home.

"You girls sure are jumpy tonight," David remarks, holding onto the grab handle above his window.

Alana accelerates, the electronic speedometer exceeding the speed limit. The headlights automatically blink on as the last precious rays of sunlight disappear, announcing the arrival of the night.

LUCKY

MY EYES NEVER waver from the windshield. I'm afraid to see what's lurking on the sides of the road. The more intelligent lower level demons wait for pedestrians, for cars to break down, or for the more oblivious targets to take advantage of. But it's not them I'm afraid of. Evan rubs my bare leg, relaxing my stiff tension.

We exit the freeway and turn onto the dark road that leads to the safety of our church. Alana releases her lead foot from the throttle and slows down to the neighborhood speed limit.

A relieved smile crosses my scabbed lips, cracking them open for the hundredth time since yesterday when I see the spires of our sanctuary. I bow my head, thankful for making it safely.

"Crap," Alana breathes.

I jerk my head up. A man stands in the center of the road ahead of us, blocking the street leading home. It isn't Malicevile or a human either. His eyes reflect the orange glow of the streetlamp, making my skin crawl.

The tires squeal as Alana slams the brakes and shoves the car into reverse. I almost miss the movement in the man's legs as he scuttles towards us. He shuffles his feet at an inhuman speed, like a roadrunner speeding away from a coyote, except the demon is speeding straight toward us.

He stretches his arms out like a zombie on steroids, attempting to grab the car. His thin silver hair flies from his head in tufts. By the time he is close enough for me to get a good look at, he's almost bald. He's shifting into his true body, using the fear factor against us. That's how he gets his prey. When ordinary humans see something inexplicable, they hesitate, trying to put things together. It slows them down and makes them vulnerable.

"On the count of three, I want you to turn the wheel sharply to the left, put the gear in drive, and floor it," David says.

Alana nods her head, acknowledging his instructions. I squeeze Evan's hand, heat building in the palms of our hands as he releases a small flame. I cup my fingers around the fire, sealing it in my hand until I have to use it.

"One. Two. Three!"

The seatbelt tightens, locking me to the seat like a mouse caught in a trap. My legs slide freely into Evan as the force of the turn sends us sprawling to the side of the car. I lose control of my movements. I can't prepare to flee from the car if I have to.

The demon runs past us, unable to control the directions of his diminishing legs. His head twitches erratically, turning sharply like the swivel of an owl's head.

Alana jabs the gear into drive and accelerates. She maneuvers the wheel, aiming to take the demon out with sheer force.

The demon's shark-like teeth savagely rake at the flimsy skin of what used to be his lips. He's more monster than man, playing with the raw fear of seeing something so unnatural and evil. Alana narrowly misses him. He runs his greasy fingers over my window, leaving behind a sludgy trail of slime.

I turn my head to stare out the back window. The demon is nowhere to be seen. Mid-level demons are infamous for giving up after failing their first attempt to get their prey. Instead, they search for an easier target.

"I think we lost him," Evan says.

I lean my head against his shoulder, taking a deep breath to keep from getting sick. His citrus scented shampoo wafts into my nostrils, overpowering the rancid smell of demon. I hope I smell just as good as he does and less like my father. I'm not keen on the idea of smelling like an exploding bakery.

I sniff my shoulder, smelling nothing but the scent of skin. "I hope so. I hate mid-level demons. They are nasty."

Turning away from Evan, I look out the window. An ear-piercing scream shatters the silence, and I slap my hand over my mouth. The demon's beady, lidless eyes peek into my window from on top of the roof.

Foamy saliva drips from its distorted lips as it flicks its two-pronged tongue against the glass. Bile rises in my throat. I can smell the demon. Decaying cedar and burning rosemary pours in from the vents, polluting the sterile air. No one seems affected except me. I truly hate my supernatural sense of smell with a passion. It may alert me of a demon, but it hinders my ability to do anything else.

Alana slams the brakes and the demon rolls off the roof with a thud. The car shakes like its running over a massive speed bump as Alana hits the demon. She thrusts the car in reverse and runs over it again to make sure it stays down.

The demon wails in frustration. I cover my ears. I can't let my fear of this demon overwhelm me. I've fought scarier, more powerful ones before. *But I had a weapon!*

David opens the glove compartment and grabs a stainless steel flask that has a delicate cross embossed on it. He jets from the car, and Alana and Evan follow him.

I pull on the handle, reluctant to join in on the destruction of the demon. They'd think it was ridiculous if they knew I was afraid of getting my dress dirty. I don't want to get demon gunk all over me again. Pushing the door the rest of the way open, I step out onto the black asphalt. A slimy hand grabs my ankle, and I scream like a girl from a B-rated horror flick—the kind of girl that always screams the loudest and ends up dead first.

The demon clutches my ankle as I stumble back. I kick furiously to loosen its hold, but it's determined to take a bite out of my unprotected bare leg.

"You look delicious." I stare in horror as the demon talks to me. This entire situation screams wrong.

"Malicevile will destroy you if you eat me." I never thought I'd have to persuade a demon with my father's name. But I'll do anything to keep myself alive.

"He said I had to bring you in alive, not whole," the demon says.

My mouth drops open in shock. *This can't be happening!* I scream again.

Standing on one foot, I scrape my shoe against my leg to pry the demon's determined fingers open. He nips at my skin with his sharp, pointy teeth but doesn't puncture my flesh. I kick the demon in its distorted head, the same move I used on the Bird Man when I was without a weapon. Only this time, I'm not wearing boots. I need a new signature move, one I can do even if I were naked.

The demon transforms into a disturbing version of a reptile. It opens its mouth to try to eat my foot. The cracking sound it makes as it dislocates its jaw sends a shiver through my spine. Rows of razor-sharp teeth glisten with frothy saliva, dripping down its flat chin.

"Alana!"

I haven't paid attention to the others since I stepped out of the car. I snap my head away from the demon for a split second to see if they're okay. I'm not the only one having issues. Two other reptilian demons scuttle around trying to separate us. *Please, please, please let us get away.*

There has never been a better moment for my ability to kick in. It feels like I'm standing on my tiptoes on an invisible barrier. I flap my arms, envisioning the world getting farther and farther below, but I'm stuck. I can levitate, not fly. The demon's grubby fingers lock tightly around my ankle, preventing me from moving.

The flame, still locked in my fingers, glows like a tiny star about to explode. It's hardly big enough to torch the demon, let alone kill it, but it's my last option. I need to do something before I lose an important body part.

The demon dislocates its jaw again. Its gaping mouth opens wide. My throat burns as I hold back another scream. Its tongue caresses the satin of my new shoes, coiling around my toes, slowing pulling my foot closer to the sharp teeth that will snap jaggedly through my bones.

I bend over, grabbing the loose skin on the demon's forehead and position my other hand in front of its salivating mouth. Releasing the flame in one swift motion, I pray that it doesn't sputter out on contact with the moisture of the saliva. Like a tiny spark hitting a canister of gasoline, the demon ignites in rancid-smelling flames. It screams before it drops to the ground, twitching as it dies.

"I killed it!" My feet touch the solid ground, adrenaline flowing through my veins. I can taste the power inside of me like a caffeine tablet stuck to the back of my palate.

I run over to Evan, who is facing off with another demon. Its body is blackened with burn marks from his flames. The demon shakes his head to keep the fireballs away from its flammable saliva. *Smart little demon.*

"Throw me a fireball," I say.

Evan tosses me a glowing fireball. I dangle my foot out in front of me like a worm on a fisherman's hook to lure the demon closer.

"Come here, stupid demon," I say, egging the demon on.

The demon's attention focuses on me and it scampers closer. Rotting flesh falls off its body, and it takes all my will power not to vomit.

Dislocating its jaw with an odd clicking sound, the demon prepares to swallow my leg. The demon might be fast, but I'm faster. Before it gets the opportunity to taste my flesh, I jam the fireball into its mouth, millimeters from grazing my fingers against its poisonous teeth. Its head explodes, forming a mushroom cloud of guts and demon blood. The flames flash, momentarily blinding me before the demon dissipates into a pile of rotting mush.

Evan scoops me into his arms and twirls me around, my dress flowing around me. I can take on an army of demons at this very moment. I feel invincible, incredible. I've never felt so alive. But a foreboding dark cloud lingers in the back of my mind. These were only mid-level demons. I don't think the outcome would be the same if I faced Malicevile. He is my weak spot, but maybe with the others by my side—*no!* I could never ask them to be part of this nightmare.

Caught up in the moment, Evan brings his lips to mine and kisses me, washing the darkness away. My heart flutters, and I pull away, afraid. The night isn't over yet. The demons could be planning another attack. Next time, I might not be so lucky.

The smell of rotting flesh circulates through the air as David and Alana finish their kill. David pours the flask of holy water over the demon's melting head with the same effect as the demon fire. I should carry around gallons of it in case Evan isn't with me. Not all demons have abilities I can use against them. Some use brute force to subdue prey.

"Nice work, Cami. You've killed three demons in less than a week," Alana says.

I curtsy, bowing my head. "I'd like to thank my fear and sheer will to survive for helping me succeed."

Evan laughs. Throwing me over his shoulder, he rushes to the car. The air is heavy with adrenaline and excitement. I never imagined it would feel this good keeping humanity safe by killing one demon at a time. Maybe Alana is right, and I'm not cut out for a desk job. If only I was strong enough to face my own personal demon—my father.

Alana parks the car near the curb instead of in the parking lot. I skip ahead of her, rushing to the door. The excitement of fighting demons diminishes the closer I get to safety. The door shuts behind us, and I can't help falling to my knees to kiss the floor. I'd be okay if I never stepped out of the church after dark again.

DEMON BLOOD

THE ROUND TABLETOP lamp glows, shadowing the small room. I sit erect with my back flat against the wall. Evan perches on the edge of the bed, his torso turned, facing me. We're close enough that if I moved my legs, they'd be in his lap, but instead I sprawl them at his side.

He focuses on the new blackish bruises entwining my ankle like an old tribal band tattoo. His bare chest, tense with bunched muscles, rises and falls with every breath. Lightly running his index finger down my leg, he caresses the tender skin of my ankle, tracing the marks left behind by the demon that was determined to take me.

I lean forward and clutch his hand, pulling him next to me on the bed made for a single body. Our legs dangle over the edge, his bare feet covered by the hem of his baggy sweatpants.

His firm arm drapes across my stomach, and I can feel his warmth through the cotton material of my tight fitting night shirt. He rests his head on my breast bone, while I run my fingers through his ear-length, golden blond hair.

"You were great tonight," Evan says. "So confident and held together. You weren't even scared."

I tilt his chin up to look into his shadowed blue eyes. "I was terrified," I admit. "I felt vulnerable without Alana by my side. I'm used to her protecting me, I just...I don't know. It was horrible."

"I'm sorry for that. I should've stayed with you. I didn't think you would leave the car," Evan says.

"I wasn't going to get trapped if something went wrong. I'm a runner remember? I was taught to flee."

"You didn't run after killing the first demon." Evan brushes my cheek with his hand. "You charged in and killed another."

"Because I didn't want you to get hurt. I was only able to do it because you gave me your ultimate weapon. Unlike you, I'm weaponless."

Evan presses his lips together. "I don't believe that."

"You're right. I once kicked in a demon's face because I lost my dagger." I sigh. "It really sucks having to rely on something I can easily lose."

"It's a good thing you can't lose me." Evan's fingers run

a line over the curve of my cheekbone and find the tender skin of my swollen lips, caressing them.

I can only smile because it's the cheesiest, yet sweetest thing someone has ever said to me. I consider cracking a joke out of nervousness, but instead I just rest my head against the wall.

Evan adjusts his body, finding a comfortable position, and wraps his arms around me. I snuggle into his chest, breathing in his freshly showered scent underlined with his demon smell, patchouli and amber—a comforting, familiar scent.

The primal side of me recognizes him and wants him. Everything about Evan feels right to me, like we are meant to be together. It was fate that Dylan never returned my calls and that I reached Evan instead. It's not his looks or his determination to be a great hunter. The feeling is something darker, rawer. It's an irrevocable desire igniting my power, my strength, my inner demon.

I push away my desire. As much as I want it to be real, I must decipher whether or not these emotions are true. I've never been a believer of love at first sight, but the easiness of my budding relationship with Evan leads me to question everything.

"You know, there was something really odd about the demon attack tonight," Evan says, breaking the confusing thoughts consuming me. *I've only known him for a short time.* "It was like we were set up. The demons knew we were gone and they waited. I've never seen so many demons at-tack at once."

"It's because you've never hung around me after dark." I take a deep breath. "Malicevile is sending his demonic army after us until he recuperates from the injuries you inflicted on him. Just because he can't get to me doesn't mean he won't stop trying. He never stops."

Evan nods his head, letting my words sink in. "That's why you need more training. Together, we can put an end to him."

I want to argue with Evan, to tell him this isn't his fight, but the words refuse to come. I bring my lips to his and kiss him softly. He shifts his body, pressing it into mine. His hot fingers trail down my sides to rest on my lower back. He kisses me back desperately. His tongue slips into my mouth, and he twirls it around mine. His kisses aren't sloppy or forceful, and I can't imagine a kiss being more perfect than this.

My hands explore the curves of his bare chest, the tight muscles of his abdomen, the indented curve of his hips. His fingers run over the soft fabric of my pajamas, trailing to the smooth bare skin of my leg. I gasp at the tingling sensation of the tiny flame in his palm, heating my skin.

My breath quickens, intoxicated by his lips against mine. Heat travels up my bare leg to my thighs.

I gasp. "Wait, too fast."

I shift my body away from Evan, creating space between

us. I run my fingers through the tangles in my hair, pulling it out of my face. Training my eyes downward, I'm afraid of seeing the disappointment in Evan's eyes. I can't jump into something I'm not ready for.

"I'm sorry," I add as I wriggle to the edge of the bed, never taking my back from the wall. I stand up, planting my bare, polished toes on the carpet.

"You're apologizing?" Confusion arches Evan's eyebrows. "You did nothing wrong. I should be the one apologizing. I was the one moving too fast."

I huff in relief. "It's fine. We're both at fault. It's the adrenaline and maybe our demon blood getting the best of us."

Evan chuckles and sits up. He reaches out his arms, beckoning me to fall back into them. I can't resist. I uncross my arms and shuffle to him. Standing over him, I gaze down into his hypnotic eyes and allow him to wrap his arms around my waist.

"I'm sure you're just making excuses," he says. "It has nothing to do with the attack or our blood. I know for a fact it's because I like you. A lot."

My cheeks flush. Not from embarrassment, but from the excitement squeezing my chest. "I like you, too," I say, planting my lips on his forehead.

<hr>

I sit at the table, enjoying another hot breakfast. I could get used to this. I sip my glass of orange juice, savoring the tangy citrus as it dances across my tongue.

Alana drinks her giant cup of coffee, while David flips through the yellowing pages of one of his many research books. Evan follows along with David, reading over his shoulder.

"Men," Alana mumbles under her breath. "Can't even take the time to enjoy breakfast with us lonely girls. Always busy, busy, busy."

I swallow before my orange juice sprays over the table and laugh when Alana narrows her eyes at David.

"Doesn't even hear a word I'm saying," Alana continues. "All I ever get is a 'huh' or a grumble."

David grumbles, bringing his eyes away from the page and says, "What?"

Alana and I burst into laughter. She really does know her husband. I hope one day to have the same special relationship that David and Alana share.

"Find anything good, Davey?" I ask, taking advantage of his attention being on us.

"Actually, yes," he says. "It says here a demi-demon's power will increase around another demon. It's a defense mechanism."

"Is that why I can occasionally levitate? Because Malicevile is lurking around?"

"It's possible, but I think it could be because of Evan. He is in full control of his demonic powers, which would be the reason for triggering yours," David says.

"It's true. I've been around halfies almost my entire life, hence the reason for my control," Evan adds.

"It's possible that your powers will increase the longer you are around each other. I've also considered the idea of trying to increase your powers by bringing in reinforcements," David says.

I scrunch my brows, intrigued by where his thoughts are going. "Which would be?"

"My good friend Jacie. She's a demi-demon, too," David says.

I nod my head, bringing my eyes back to my breakfast. My stunted abilities are embarrassing. I would hate to make a fool of myself in front of another demi-demon besides Evan. What if she laughs at me or says that I'm worthless? I couldn't live with the knowledge that I can't take advantage of my heritage—or protect myself from Dear Old Dad.

"There's nothing to be nervous about. Jacie is a very nice person who's happy to help you grow into who you were born to be," Alana says, reading my expression.

"I don't want to fail. It's bad enough I'm half human, half evil," I say.

"I don't know about you, but I'm not half evil. I may have been conceived by a demon, but I'm standing in this church, and that proves something," Evan says.

I twirl my fork through my scrambled eggs. Evan's right. Just because I'm Malicevile's daughter doesn't mean anything. Being able to step into a church proves I'm not malevolent.

"You're right," I say, still unsure if I believe it.

I push away from the table without another word and shuffle into my bedroom. A moment of peace might be the thing I need to clear my mind. I strip down and toss my pajamas onto the bed before pulling out a pair of white track pants and a black tank top from the dresser. When I'm ready, I jog through the church, running on the balls of my feet to mute the sound of my footsteps.

The training room glistens in dazzling rainbow light cast through the stained-glass windows. My boots pound on the marble floor as I run laps around the open space, warming up. I steady my pace, keeping my breathing under control to maintain my stamina.

After my warm up, I sit cross-legged on the floor, calming my nerves in deep meditation. I take cleansing breaths, imagining the weight of my body is as light as a cool breeze blowing through fluffy clouds. My legs begin to tingle, the sensation crawling from my toes into my hands, and lastly to my head.

I peek through my eyelashes. It worked. I'm floating a foot off the ground. Squeezing my eyes shut again, I focus on lifting myself higher like a balloon filled with helium, floating into the sky.

The boom of the lacquered door closing breaks my concentration. I crash to the floor and the wind is knocked from my lungs. Pushing through the pain, I catapult to my feet to meet the person who interrupted me head on.

A feminine, muscular silhouette graces the doorway. She saunters into the training room and as she comes closer she looks several inches shorter than my five and a half feet. Mahogany brown hair accentuates high cheekbones and full lips, and curls around her shoulders. Her coffee brown eyes are lined with heavy black eyeliner, reminding me of Cadence. She smiles at me and I force myself to smile back.

"Can I help you?" I ask as politely as possible, hiding my irritation from her intrusion.

"Not really," the girl says, shaking her head, "but I can help you."

She opens her fisted hand, showing off a neon green ball of crackling electricity. It flashes in her palm like a tiny lightning storm, and my blood cools. Her power is reminiscent of Malicevile's. It looks like she has enough of it in a single finger to light an entire city.

Hypnotized by the ball of energy, my eyes widen like a deer transfixed by headlights. The girl twirls her arm and releases the sizzling ball at me. I don't scream. I don't even try to run. All I can do is watch as the ball of glowing electricity flies toward my stomach.

STRANGE ABILITIES

"NICE WORK," THE girl says.

The ball of crackling electricity rests in the palm of my hand. I squeeze my hand shut, snuffing it out with a puff.

"I'm Jacie Hallowitz." She moves forward, her feet barely making a sound on the tiles. "You must be Cami. I've heard a lot of good things about you."

"I've heard nothing about you," I say, offering her my hand.

Jacie grips my hand between hers and pulls me into an awkward hug. My arms remain at my sides when she releases me. She takes a step back, giving me a curious once-over and smiles.

"You're even more beautiful than Evan described. That

boy is really fond of you, you know."

She must not look in the mirror often. Jacie looks like she stepped straight out of a movie. If Cadence were here, she and Jacie would have every man in town drooling at their feet.

"Thanks," I say, uncomfortable with the idea of people talking about me behind my back, even if it is all positive. "People used to say I looked like my mother."

"Don't kid yourself, hon, you have Daddy Demon all over you," Jacie says.

I open and close my mouth, not sure of how to respond to Jacie's insensitive comment. I turn on my heels and stomp away with tears lining my eyes. The last thing I need is to be compared to *him*. His attractiveness is a disguise. It's not real. Under his green eyes and perfect smile is a dark, evil creature.

"Cami, wait!"

"Why?" I ask, turning around. "So you can put me down? Rub in the fact that I'm the spawn of a demon? There is just as much human in me as there is demon. I don't know why everyone insists on bringing out the darker side of me."

Jacie's smile fades. "Because that darker side is the only way you'll survive in this world." She lowers her gaze to the floor. "Being part demon is a gift you shouldn't take for granted or despise. It's why I'm still alive."

My shoulders sag. Jacie and Evan grew up knowing that

they were half demon. It's something they accept and even enjoy. It's always been their life but not mine. If staying alive is the only good thing about being a demon then I'd rather give it up. I wouldn't have to worry in the first place. It's frustrating they can't see what I see. I bet Dylan would understand.

I fold my arms over my chest. "Can you blame me for having a hard time adjusting to this? I've spent the last three years running for my life from a demon who turns out to be my father *and* the man who killed my mom and dad. I've been abducted and harassed by wolves—all of which would have never happened if I wasn't a demi-demon. I just don't think being one is so great right now."

"I didn't know." Jacie reaches her hand out and squeezes my shoulder. "David never explained your history to me. He only said he needed me to bring out your powers."

I can't help but laugh. "My powers? They're such a joke. I've inherited useless crap from Daddy Dear. So, I can smell a demon coming. Big. Freaking. Deal. I'd say my abilities are defective. I got ripped off." I roll my eyes. "No wonder Alana was able to keep my identity a secret for so long."

A heavy weight lifts from my chest. I've been dying to rant to someone who isn't partial to my situation. I've been through so much and haven't gained anything from it. I'm not even stronger—just really, really irritated.

"You do realize you're levitating." Jacie chuckles instead of pitying me. "Don't tell David, but his theory is right."

I glance down at Jacie, who now seems shorter than before. I shrug my shoulders, no longer surprised by my power. I stretch my arms above my head and propel a foot higher.

"I thought it was cool too, until I saw what you could do," I say. "It's not like it's useful. All I can do is hang above a demon and taunt him. I'd make really good bait though."

"You're forgetting that you can deflect and absorb abilities, too. I thought you may have been a fire demon after my conversation with Evan, but after seeing my own electric orb in your fingers, I'm positive you can deflect anything." Jacie tosses an energy orb to me, and I catch it.

"Which means I'm screwed if a demon comes charging at me with a knife," I say, snuffing the electricity out. I wish I knew how to control these strange abilities and what to do with them.

"Don't be silly. Demons are conceited. They wouldn't dare use a human-made weapon. It would scream weakness." She's probably right. I have yet to witness a weapon wielding demon. I know Malicevile wouldn't dare. He's too good for that.

"I guess that's a good thing." I allow my body to glide to the floor. My boots thump on the tile, echoing through the open space.

"It is. Just because demons won't carry a weapon doesn't mean you can't. You'll be unstoppable with your advantage," Jacie says.

"I doubt it."

"Oh, come on." Jacie nudges my arm. "You'll change your mind when I'm through with you. You'll be dying to get out of here to kick some demon butt."

I raise my eyebrows. I'm not convinced I'll be storming out of the safety of the church in search of a fight any time soon. I'm content where I am, even if I'll never see the outside world again.

⁂

My hair buzzes with electricity. Standing on end, it floats into my eyes. The static from Jacie's energy orbs clings to me like the static created from rubbing a balloon against your hair.

Jacie races towards me, the crackling light in her palm notched up to high voltage. The power is strong enough to kill a human. I'd have been dead an hour ago if I wasn't only half.

I spin on my heels, ducking as the sizzling ball soars over my head and crashes into the wall. The lighting overhead dims and flashes back on. The neighbors probably think something is wrong with the electricity. It's the first thing I'd think, being raised a human and all.

Another energy ball soars at me. I catch it, unable to move from the corner. Before I have a chance to snuff it out, Jacie throws another sparkling ball, and I add it to the first, doubling it in size.

I throw the ball low, aiming for her feet. She does what

I expect her to do. She reaches down to grab it, giving me the moment I need to evade her.

As I lunge past her, I trip over the arm she thrusts out to stop me. Somersaulting back to my feet, I hurdle over another energy ball. Static crackles through my chocolate colored hair, and I flinch, expecting it to shock me, but it doesn't. I'd be worse off if Cadence hadn't taught me a couple of combat moves. *God, I miss her.* But this is how it has always been. I'm never in one place long enough to hold onto a friendship.

I turn to face Jacie, Evan's words echo in my ear: *Never turn your back on a demon.*

She springs for me. I slam my feet into the floor and push off, vaulting over her using my ability to my advantage. The more I attempt to levitate, the easier it becomes, but for some reason unknown to me, it doesn't always do what I want it to. It's hard work keeping my ability under control.

I flip my body around midair and use the force of my spin to kick Jacie off her feet. She falls forward, losing her balance. I watch in amazement as she folds in her arms and tucks in her head. She rolls on the ground and lands back on her feet ready to launch another energy ball.

Swinging my arms like I'm swimming in the air, I try to force myself to levitate higher, but it's no use. The energy ball speeds at me at a rate too fast to avoid. I squeeze my eyes shut and brace myself for the impact.

It slams into my legs, propelling me backwards. Losing control, I spin through the air like a helicopter after losing engine function. Glass shatters around me in a kaleidoscope of colors, and I crash to a stone walkway outside in a small courtyard.

Stars burst in my vision and my lungs complain as the air whooshes from my chest. Warm liquid drips from the back of my head, and I rub my fingers over a knot on my scalp, cringing when my fingers come back bloody. I'd think that whoever designed the training room wouldn't have used so much glass. It isn't safe to practice around even if I wasn't floating. My arms sting from shards of glass lodged in my skin. Ignoring the black haze rimming my vision, I blink slowly, holding on tight to my view of the world as it closes in on me.

The sound of a slamming door and thunderous footsteps dull the pounding in my head. I close my eyes, feeling my muscles going limp.

I try to open my eyes at the roar of voices surrounding me, but my eyelids are like sandbags, too heavy to lift after a storm. It must be Alana and Jacie, maybe even Evan, but they sound too far away. A weird buzzing noise blocks out all sound, and I press my fingers to my ears to make sure I'm not getting attacked by killer bees.

A dark purple silhouette hovers over me. *Cadence! She came!* Her soft fingers caress my arms, and I grab them. Her nail polish matches the dark purple of her hair. I'm so happy she made it here. I didn't even know she was coming yet.

"Cadence? Did you know I'm a demon? The werewolf was right. You *are* a demon lover," I say. "Also, tell Dylan I understand what he meant." My tongue lolls from my mouth. "God, we have so much to talk about, you know. I finally met Evan, and I think love at first sight might be real." The words spill from my mouth incoherently as I try to catch Cadence up as quickly as possible before the world disappears.

Everything is a big blur as I struggle to sit up. I can't see Cadence anymore. The world spins around me, and I thump back to the ground.

I try to open my eyes again, but the stupid black fog thickens around me. I can't hear the voices either. My body no longer reacts to what my head tells it to do, and I start to panic, thinking I'm paralyzed. I'm vulnerable to demon attacks that could happen at any second. I focus on moving my fingers, but I can't find my hands.

And then, I don't feel or see anything at all.

RESPONSIBLE

DYLAN'S SILHOUETTE TOWERS over me. I strain to see his gorgeous features through the miserable fog. I can tell it's him because of the golden halo surrounding him. His wings flap, twirling the fog around us in a tight funnel. It's like we're the only two left in the world.

"Where am I?" My voice sounds small, lost in the whoosh of his wings.

"With me." He stretches his ethereal wings, wrapping me in their sunny warmth. "I promised I'd protect you."

"How? I thought you were afraid of demons?" I step closer to Dylan until our fingers brush against each other. His skin is as soft as powder, almost as if he's not solid in front of me.

"I have my ways, love." Dylan leans closer. I can smell sweet sunshine radiating from him. "You only have to trust me."

"Cami!" Evan's voice echoes in the distance, barely audible through the fog. "Come back to me."

I close my eyes, warming to the sound of Evan's voice. Dylan kisses my cheek before letting me go. The world blurs, and I lose my balance, falling into a black void. The fog swallows me, ripping me away from Dylan—away from my angel.

⁓ ✿ ⁓

"She's waking up," a velvety voice says near my ear.

The back of my head throbs with an annoying ache. I blink, agitated by the bare light bulb hanging from the ceiling. Dylan's image lingers, dancing in the harsh glow.

A blurry silhouette hovers over me, and I thrust my arm out, pushing it away. "Feisty little thing," a sweeter voice purrs.

I shift onto my side, throwing my legs onto the floor. Sitting up, I rub my fists in my eyes to wipe away the fuzziness from my vision. Circular blobs begin to morph into figures. Alana and Jacie kneel on the carpet in front of me. The bed shifts under me, and a heavy arm falls over my shoulders.

"I bet you feel like crap," Evan says. "You flew through a window."

I nod, having trouble finding my voice. The last thing I

remember is the glorious waterfall of rainbow-colored glass and seeing my friend's purple nail polish. And Dylan.

"Where's Cadence? I need to talk to her." She'll be able to sort things out.

"Here," Alana says, setting a cup into my hands, "drink this. You hit your head hard. Cadence was never here."

I scrunch my brows. It felt like she was with me, holding my hand. I need to call her to tell her about everything she has missed. What will she say when I tell her about my demon father? She wouldn't end our friendship because of it, would she?

"I need your phone," I say, focusing on Evan.

He points to the glass in my hands. "After you drink."

Helping guide the glass, he holds it to my lips until I take a sip. I swallow a sip of lukewarm water and then run my tongue over my teeth and across my bottom lip to keep from dribbling.

"Take these, too." Alana hands me two bright orange pills. "It'll help your headache."

I pop the tablets onto my tongue and wash away the powdery texture with another gulp of water. I hand the glass to Evan. After finding my bearings, I wipe my sweaty hands on my pants and adjust my sleep-twisted tank top. My back creaks as I find my footing to stand.

"Good girl." Alana pats my hand like I'm a child. "You did well tonight. I'm proud of you."

"What are you talking about? I failed," I say. "If Jacie

was a whole demon, I'd be dead...or worse."

I can't stand the concerned looks anymore, so I hobble the five feet it takes to get to the door. I use the wall for support and drag my feet across the living room and into the kitchen. The lack of natural light means that I've been out for hours.

The moment I step into the kitchen, David plops a plate of spaghetti in front of me. "You must be hungry. Eat up." He sits across from me with his own plate. "It'll help you regain your strength."

"Thanks," I murmur, appreciating David's unobtrusive attitude. He's great at pretending nothing is wrong. He's never once told me how I should feel. He only encourages me to do what I have to do, rather than forcing me to like it.

Voices echo through the arched doorway, and I stop chewing to eavesdrop. Alana begs Jacie to spend the night for safety reasons, but it sounds like her pleas are useless.

"I'll be back in a couple days," Jacie says from the doorway. "Eric is on his way."

"I'd advise you to call him and tell him to come in the morning," David says, calling out instead of getting up. "It isn't safe for a human to be seen associating with us after dark."

"Aren't you human?" I ask David.

"I'm a highly trained demon hunter. Eric is an accountant. There's a difference," he says to me.

"An accountant," I mutter. "How does a halfie end up with an accountant?"

Jacie pops her head into the doorway. "It's a long, boring story. But I love him anyways."

A buzzing noise sounds from Jacie's pocket, and she yanks out a cell phone. She answers it and shouts, "Coming!" She shrugs her shoulders, noticing my curious expression. "Call me if you need anything." Without another word, she rushes out of the kitchen. The front door creaks open and booms shut. Goosebumps prickle on my arms, and I jump at the sound of squealing tires peeling away.

"Don't look so worried. Jacie will be fine," David mumbles.

I nod, only half believing it. I've seen Jacie's skills, and I know she is capable of taking care of herself, yet I have a bad feeling about her leaving after dark. I struggle to push the distressed feeling from my mind. Something's wrong.

The aroma of cinnamon tickles my nostrils, and I breathe in deeply. "Are you baking something?" I ask, perplexed that I just noticed the tantalizing scent.

"No," David says. "Why?"

"I smell cinna—" My lips snap shut.

I inhale again, sucking in a hint of clove as well. The dull ache in my head begins to pound like a sledgehammer against concrete. My heart races, while fingers of icy fear glide up my spine. *Malicevile.*

I jump out of my chair, toppling it onto the tiled floor.

My demonic father is outside. I'd know his scent anywhere. Gripping the counter below the only window, I stand on my tiptoes to peek through the curtain. I brace myself in case he decides to pop into view to scare me.

Nothing is visible in the darkness except for hedges bathed in soft, silvery moonlight. I lean over the sink and press my nose to the cool glass, using my hands to shield the surrounding light from the kitchen.

A firm hand grabs my shoulder, and I yelp, jabbing my elbow behind me. Fingers lock onto my forearm, and David spins me around.

"Let go," I growl, spinning to gaze back through the window. The nauseating, spicy smell overpowers my senses. Malicevile is nearby, I can sense it.

"Not until you tell me what you're searching for." He yanks me away from the window.

"I smell Mal. He's outside the window."

"That's impossible," David argues. "The ground up to the hedges is blessed."

"Then he's behind the hedges."

David pulls me farther away from the window. "It's nothing to worry about. You are safe within these walls. He's not going to hurt you."

I swallow hard, forcing my rising gorge back down. My stomach churns, tumbling like an unbalanced spinner on a washing machine. My hands begin to tremble, and I close my fingers into fists, embedding my nails into the palms of my hands.

David wraps his arm around my shoulders and pulls me into a hug. He pats my back, fissuring the strength keeping me together, and I fall apart in his arms. Salty tears sting my eyes and I hiccup, gasping for breath through my runny nose. My chest clenches, making it impossible to calm down. My shoulders jerk with uncontrollable sobs.

"I hate this," I cry. "Just when I was starting to feel safe again, *he* comes back to taunt me. I wish he would leave me alone. I'm not interested in a reunion."

"He won't stop. Not until he is sent back into the fiery depths of Hell," David says. "That's what demons do."

A moan gurgles in my throat as I try to pull myself together. My knees buckle under me. I slide from David's grip, crumbling to the floor. I pull my legs to my chest and cradle myself.

Light footsteps tap against the tile, and I can sense Alana's presence in the doorway.

"I've never been good at comforting," David mumbles.

"I'll say." Alana kneels next to me, rubbing her hand along my back. "Please, don't cry, Cami. Whatever David said, he didn't mean it. I promise."

David huffs.

"Tell her you're sorry," Evan says. I squint through my wet eyelashes and see him lurking behind Alana. "I heard that always works."

Laughter bubbles in my throat, replacing my sobs. I

wipe my eyes with my palms. "I-I'm s-s-sorry. It's j-just I'm sc-scared," I stutter.

"What did you say to her?" Alana glares in David's direction.

"Hey!" David raises his hands in surrender. "I was trying to help. She has to understand the truth even if she doesn't want to."

Alana scrunches her brows and takes a good look at me. I smile to show her I'm okay for now. As good as I'll ever be, knowing what waits for me beyond these walls.

"Davey really did try to help," I say. "It's not his fault that Malicevile is lurking somewhere around here."

"Mali—"

The sound of metal scraping concrete jolts me to my feet, cutting Alana off. I bolt to the kitchen doorway and into Evan's chest, knocking us both to the floor. I lunge to my feet and topple over again when Evan grabs onto my ankle.

"Where do you think you're going?" he asks.

A scream rips through the air, sending panic to my heart, and I struggle to kick Evan away. Alana and David rush from the kitchen when another scream sounds out, but this time it sounds as if it's coming from the back of the church where the parking lot is.

"Stay here, you two," Alana demands. Before I have a chance to argue, she races after David.

"Let me go!" I snap. "We have to help. Jacie's out

there." I yank my foot from his grip.

"You heard Alana."

"Don't you think we're more skilled for the job? You can create fireballs." I motion my hand to him. "Now, give me one."

Fire ignites in his palm, and he tosses one my way before getting to his feet. Instead of heading in the direction where Alana and David went, I head toward the front door.

My footsteps ring out as I run down the center aisle, past the rows of pews to the grand entrance of the church. I could never live with myself if my demon hurt someone who was trying to help me. I know it's stupid and crazy, and I hesitate for a second, hearing Evan stomping behind me. It doesn't stop me, though. I fling open the door, knowing he'll be right here to help me.

I stagger down the stone steps, nearly tripping. Slowing my pace, I cautiously stroll down the path to the street and glance in both directions. My heart stops when I see a metal dumpster tipped over in the middle of the street, garbage spewing out of the open lid and littering the ground. It would've taken someone with extreme strength to throw it.

"Cami!" Evan yells.

I freeze in my tracks, though I see no obvious signs of danger. Jacie isn't anywhere either. I take a slow step back, surveying my surroundings, regretting that I let my fear of Jacie's safety draw me from the church. I'd have done the same for Cadence, Evan, and even Dylan, too. I can't help it. I feel responsible for my demon dad.

The overflowing garbage moves inside of the dumpster, catching my eye. A scream burns in my throat but dies quickly as an adorable, silver-coated cat claws its way through a heap of trash and climbs out of the dumpster.

TRICKY DEMON

THE CAT'S BEAUTIFUL slender body shimmers, reflecting the moon's silvery glow. Its emerald green eyes sparkle in the luminous light of the streetlamp, flashing like two precious stones. As it pads closer, the muscles on its haunches twitch. Its tail sways with every step it takes. The poor thing probably got caught in whatever happened when Jacie left.

The fireball warming my fingers sputters out when I drop it to the moist ground. "Here, kitty-kitty," I say, clicking my tongue on the dry roof of my mouth. "It's okay, baby."

Twitching its ears, the cat tilts its head to the side, listening to my soft voice. It's curious and cautious, staying a good distance away. Alana has never allowed me to have a pet, but maybe this time she'll make an exception.

"Come here, baby," I say. "It's not safe for you out here."

I crouch low, my knees inches away from the pavement, and snap my fingers. The clicks echo through the still night. I shiver, forcing the imaginary bugs crawling on my skin to stop. I need to get this poor stray inside.

"Stop drawing attention to us. We need to get back inside. Now."

I vault to my feet. "It's just a ca—"

A deep purr vibrates the ground, and my knees lock into place. I jerk my head up, losing my words. The cat is twenty feet closer, and I never saw it move. It sits back on its haunches and nudges its nose against its paw. A breeze carries the rancid smell of demon, sending me reeling back. *Stupid, tricky demon.* I've never known a demon to appear as a normal animal—they're either hideous creatures or human.

The cat morphs, shifting and cracking as it grows into the size of a miniature schnauzer. Its sleek, muscular legs have stretched another six inches. I hold my breath, every muscle in my body seizing up.

"Move as slowly as you can," Evan says.

"That isn't a cat is it?" I don't know why I ask. I just need to say something to get my mind off the demon stalking me.

I rub my hand over my forehead, brushing hair from my eyes. Inching to the sidewalk, I shuffle with my back against Evan. His fingers lock onto my clavicle, easing me along.

The creature lurches forward, stalking us. The sound of its snapping bones is louder than the blood pounding in my head. The demon's claws snap out three deadly inches, looking awkward on its delicate paws. Each step it takes falls in sync with my pounding heart.

"Throw a fireball at it," I beg.

"It's not a good idea." Annoyance coats his words. I thought he could take on anything.

"Why not?" I ask. My stupid absorption ability doesn't allow me to do anything unless the demon attacks first, and even then if it uses blunt force, I'm not match.

"I hope you never find out," Evan says. If I wasn't so tense, I'd turn around and slap him. I thought the mystery was over, and I could know the truth.

My heel hits the curb. Evan guides me back to the church. The creature remains an uncomfortable ten feet away.

The only feline resemblance left lies in its flat triangular face and sharp pointed ears. Its once silver coat has morphed into dull gray elephant skin.

My stomach churns, staring into the glowing green eyes of the small demon. It's a cross between a cat and a monkey with dagger-like claws. It's more disturbing than the lizard men.

The demon bares its fangs. Black foam glistens from every sharp tooth. *Oh, crap! It's smiling at me.*

A screeching, guttural sound erupts from the demon's savage mouth. The hairs on the back of my neck bristle. I wish the werewolves would've taken me into their pack. I'm sure they could take out this demon. I clamp my hands over my ears as if I'm hearing the ear piercing noise for the first time. The demon is trying to knock me off my feet.

I can't find my bearings and stop in place. My legs refuse to move. My head is about to explode like a balloon being filled with icy air, pushing on the inside of my skull. Warm liquid streams over my fingers, and I lean my head against my shoulder. A pool of blood seeps into the fabric of my shirt. If the demon doesn't stop screaming, I'll lose my hearing.

"Run!" Evan sounds like he's yelling underwater, his voice barely audible over the noise. He yanks on my arm, but my body refuses to cooperate. I crash to the cement walkway, folding in on myself.

My lungs rage with fire as the air is knocked out of me. I fling my arms out and claw at the ground, scratching the cement for anything to stabilize the convulsions running through me. I can sense Evan above me, but I can't see him. My eyes lock on the demon in front of me, unable to look away.

The demon ignites. Lava-like red liquid oozes from its

pores, consuming its gray skin. Evan pulls me by my wrists to help me stand, but the demon slashes at my legs, and I squirm from Evan's arms, trying to fight the demon off.

"Evan, help!"

It lunges and lands on my chest, singeing the fabric of my hoodie. The smell of putrid sulfur chokes me. Growling in my face, the demon drips foamy, black saliva onto my cheek. Gorge rises in my throat, making me sick.

Evan kicks his leg out, trying to push the demon away, but it slashes its dagger claws at him to keep him away.

I cringe as the demon's head lowers, its fangs inches from my lips. I squeeze my eyes shut. I can't bear to stare into its glowing, sadistic eyes. It sniffs my sweat-soaked skin. It's becoming harder and harder to breathe.

My body jerks as Evan tries to kick the demon off me. His jeans smoke with every ineffective move. It's no use. The demon is too heavy, and I have no will to fight. Black fog rims my vision. At any minute now, the fog will consume me.

"Holy water," I say through clenched teeth, using the last ounce of my determination to live before my resolve melts into the black shadows soaking into my soul.

"Where the hell are David and Alana? I won't leave you," Evan growls.

"Just go." I won't let Evan die because of me. If he stays and the demon kills me, he'll be its next victim, and I won't accept that. I have to get him out of here, even if it means I die alone. It's funny how romantic it is in movies when lovers die together, but in reality, it's ridiculous. I'd never want that to happen. As long as Evan is safe and won't die with me, I can go peacefully.

The demon steals my next words, devouring each gasp of breath I let escape. I want to tell Evan something insightful, something that'll stay with him forever—beautiful last words to remember me by, but death isn't romantic. Dying is brutal and painful. I just want it to be over.

Evan pauses, shifting his weight between his feet as he stares at the door. He's reluctant to leave me at the mercy of the demon, but he doesn't have a choice. My limbs hang placidly at my sides while my soul struggles to hold on. As the demon devours my breath, I'm fading fast.

A scream rips from my burning throat, though the sound can't make it past the demon as it swallows the sound. My skin feels like it is being ripped off even though the demon hasn't budged an inch. I blink; there's a strange, translucent light flowing from my lips, mingling with the inky fog. *What is that?*

I jerk as the front door booms closed. My eyelids hang like lead weights, struggling to remain open. It's lonely being this close to death with only my nightmares to comfort me. But it's better this way. I couldn't bear the thought of anyone watching me go, including Alana. I wouldn't be able to console anyone. I can't even comfort myself.

I gasp as the demon shifts off me, the pressure of its

weight subsiding. It paces the length of my body, stopping at my feet.

The fog clears, and I can see the world again. I no longer see death's door right in front of me. I don't have the urge to bang it down.

I flip onto my stomach and claw at the pavement, inching away. A sharp pain explodes in my ankles as the demon's dagger-like talons slash through my pants, nicking my flesh.

I flail my arms as the demon begins to drag me. My fingernails scratch the pavement, filing down to the quick. My hands catch on a large crack in the curb, but the demon tugs me free. It's stronger than I could ever imagine for its small frame. Loose gravel embeds in my bare stomach. My burned and shredded shirt is unable to protect me from road rash.

My blood begins to boil, heating the chill in my veins. Angry tears leak from my stinging eyes. This is the second time within a week that a demon has dragged me away from my safety. *Not again!*

I relax my tense muscles, harnessing my powers. Cold wind whips at my scraped stomach instead of the ground rubbing my bare skin raw. Four inches of air hangs between my nose and the ground. The street begins to move faster, and my heart sinks into my stomach. I've made it easier for the demon to kidnap me. I'm like a balloon trailing behind an excited child, tugged along, waiting to be popped.

Footsteps sound behind me. I pull my head up and see Evan a block away. The demon breaks into a sprint, blurring the world around me. Perspiration freezes my forehead as the demon hurries inhumanly fast. Evan grows smaller and smaller as the distance between us grows.

"Let go of me," I growl, struggling to kick my legs free.

I concentrate on levitating higher, my muscles screaming in anticipation.

My ankles ache from the weight of the demon clinging onto my feet. If I go any higher I might grow an inch taller, but it would be worth it if I can get away. I continue to ascend until the demon can no longer touch the ground without releasing me from its grip.

But it doesn't let go.

"Hold still." Evan's deep voice echoes out. Relief floods through me.

"I'm trying." I gasp as the demon attempts to crawl its way up my legs.

"Not you," Evan says.

Smoke rises from my burning pant legs. My lungs seize as I cough. A cold breeze lashes at my back. I cling onto my waistband as the demon begins to tug my pants down as it climbs up me like a cat climbing a tree to escape from Evan.

I blush as my underwear starts to show, and I thrash my body. The power of embarrassment is stronger than my anger. The smoldering fabric of my pants begins to rip. The demon roars as it falls to the ground with a thud.

An ear shattering scream rips through the night when Evan thrusts a cup of holy water into the demon's face. The stench of unnatural rotting flesh makes me gag as I drop to the ground, finding my gravity.

The demon flails, gouging its melting face with its claws. I watch it struggling to rip the holy water-burned flesh away.

Evan grabs my arm, yanking me away. My ankles buckle, and I hurtle to the pavement. Without a second thought, he scoops me into his arms. His pace doesn't falter with my added weight.

"Please, let us make it," Evan says.

"I think we're safe," I say. "You killed it."

"No. I just pissed it off."

A screech rings out, and my blood cools in fear. I stare over Evan's shoulder in shock. My eyes bulge from my head as the demon shifts back into a cat. Its rotting flesh transforms into a sleek, silvery coat as it dashes behind us.

"Can you run any faster?" I ask. Fear quickens my heartbeat. "The kitty is coming."

Evan grunts. His muscles tense as he tosses me over his shoulder. He swings his free arms to gain speed, while I cling to his back.

Alana and David stand in the doorway of the church, calling their encouragement. A scream escapes from my sealed lips as the demonic cat hisses only feet behind us. Evan jerks me over his shoulders and tosses me through the doorway. I fall onto the marble floor of the church, rolling until I hit a pew. Evan vaults up the stone steps, skidding through the doorway before crashing into me.

Unable to stop, the demon hits the invisible protective shield. I squeeze my eyes shut as demon guts explode onto the pristine stone steps.

I scramble to my feet and lunge for the door. My heart stops when I catch a glimpse of Malicevile's vibrant green eyes. He lurks in the shadows on the other side of the street.

DEMON WITHIN

ALANA'S FINGERS LOCK around my arm as she tugs me away from the door before slamming it shut. I turn in her arms and sob. I'm a complete wreck, afraid and ashamed. It was so easy for me to give up on life—on everything. The relief I felt knowing I was about to die goes against everything I have ever believed in. I thought death would be hard, but at that moment, life was unbearable. Alana would be disappointed if she knew that less than ten minutes ago, I stopped being who she taught me to be. I became weak and tempted by an easy way out.

My stomach heaves while I fight to restrain the aching in my chest. Alana holds me, my knees turning into Jell-O. *Stop thinking this way! Stop it!*

I hiccup, trying to catch my breath. I can't keep the dark shadows away. It's unsettling to feel my death wish so tangibly, the way a blanket feels good when it's cold. The morbid thoughts of how much easier life would be for everyone if I were gone consume me.

"God, Cami, you were so lucky," Alana says. "And we were all a little stupid for falling for that trap. Mal's watching this church non-stop, and he knows we can't resist trying to save innocent people."

She rubs comforting circles on my back, though my body aches in agony. I knew Mal would be around. I smelled him. But Alana's right. I couldn't stop myself from trying to save the day—not because I think I'm some amazing demon hunter, but because Malicevile is my problem.

I groan through my pain. "At least you didn't try to coax a demon cat from a dumpster."

She laughs, petting my hair.

I probe the scraped skin on my stomach. Tiny embedded pebbles feel rough under my bloody fingertips. I accept the pain as my punishment for being a demon's daughter. I'd rather it be me who suffers than Evan.

My legs throb, and I slip back to the floor and out of Alana's hold. Evan scoops me into his arms like a fragile child.

"That looks painful." Evan breathes his warm breath into my hair.

I dig my chin into my chest to look at the extent of the

damage. My stomach looks even worse in the light of the living room.

"It's not so bad." I grind my teeth, praying my lie to turn true. "It could've been worse."

Evan sets me on the couch, my tender skin throbbing as I settle down awkwardly with my ankles hanging over the arm of the small sofa. David hustles into the room carrying a large bowl of soapy water. A first-aid kit dangles from his fingers. He sets the bowl on the table and opens the kit next to it.

He takes stainless steel tweezers from a small compartment and spreads a paper towel on my lap. I grit my teeth as he begins to pluck bloodstained gravel from my skin.

"Talk to me." Alana brushes her fingers through my frazzled hair.

"About what?" I flinch as David plucks a rock the size of a dime from my stomach.

"Anything." She shifts my head away from Dr. David with her hand.

"Why was I lucky?" I ask. I know Alana better than anyone, and she didn't say I was lucky because I survived. There's something more to her words.

"You faced Malicevile's right hand demon. It's what kept me in the church when it was chasing you," she answers. "I feel awful for not doing more."

"I don't get it." I wince as David dislodges another rock. "You've faced off with Malicevile at least a handful of times over the last three years, and you're afraid of the cat?"

"Malicevile doesn't kill me for a reason. That *cat* was a soul sucker. It doesn't have a reason not to. I'm fortunate he hasn't unleashed it sooner," Alana says.

"It was stealing my soul?" That's why I couldn't breathe. The demon was forcing me to submit to it by taking the thing most precious to me.

"If it wanted your soul, it would've taken it. All it wanted to do was wear you down," Evan says from behind my head.

"You're afraid of a soul sucking demon but not Mal. I still don't get it. He can take your soul. He will eventually try to kill you." *Once you're no longer useful.* He keeps her alive to stay on my good side. He hopes to win me over by letting her live, I just know it—Malicevile is clever, and that's why he is an upper-level demon.

"Death is better than being trapped for eternity inside a demon like that. Who knows how many souls were freed tonight because of you two," Alana says with a smile.

"I didn't do anything," I say. "Curiosity killed the cat."

"You mean stupidity," Evan corrects.

Warm water drips onto my stomach while David cleans my open wounds. I bite my lip as cold peroxide flushes out any lingering dirt. He coats my cuts with an antiseptic cream and covers them with a thick layer of gauze, taping the loose ends to my sides. Before I'm able to sit up, Alana puts her hand on my arm to keep me in place.

"I'm not finished," David says. "There are demon scratches to take care of."

Tears burst from my eyes at the thought. Demon scratches are the worst to take care of...and the most painful.

David grabs a sharp pair of sewing scissors from the first-aid kit and begins to cut the tattered, singed remains of my pants. He cuts the material at my knees, turning my track pants into sweat shorts.

"Oh, ew," I say, gawking at my feet. "Please, don't tell me I'm going to lose my legs, Dr. Davey."

He chuckles. "You're not going to lose your legs."

The once smooth skin around my ankles is covered in fine, black spider web lines. It looks like dark sludge is pumping through my veins. Jagged gashes run up my calves from when the demon was scurrying up my legs. The poison from its talons is causing a serious infection.

"Don't watch."

I look above me, locking eyes with Evan. He frowns and I jerk my attention back to David, who holds a flask of holy water over the wounds. He begins to pour the clear liquid onto my legs.

I scream.

It's as if I'm feeling fire for the first time. The liquid rushes into my veins, burning me from within. I bite my tongue. The salty, coppery taste of blood gushes down my throat. The pain intensifies, as if acid is eating through my insides. The room fades into a world of my worst nightmares—demons, burning buildings, my real father.

"Love, you're hallucinating." Behind the horrifying images, Dylan stands in all his miraculous glory. "You need to fight this."

"I can't," I whisper. "It hurts too much. Please, just let me die."

"You're stronger than that. I've seen it. Now, let me help you."

Dylan extends his wings and wraps them around me, leaving me standing in white light. The ethereal caress of his wings tickles my face. The nightmares, the pain, and the need to give up vanishes, cast away like the night come early dawn. Dylan's angelic light seeps into every pore, giving me the courage to face the hardships life is throwing at me.

"How do you do that? I know you're not really here," I say.

Dylan presses his lips to my forehead. "I've seen your soul. I can always protect you no matter how far away I am." But it's not the same. Evan is physically here, and that's what I truly need—someone who can always be here. I'm not even sure if Dylan is real anymore. Choosing Evan doesn't mean I want to push Dylan out of my life forever; he's my guardian angel, but it means that he could never be anything more to me than this...a dream.

I don't have the heart to tell Dylan this. His touch is soothing, and I think I might fall apart without it. "Please, don't let go of me," I beg. "I want to stay with you. It hurts too much. I think I might die."

"Listen to me, I could never leave you, love, but I have to release you. You must go back. The pain will go away, I promise." Dylan fades away, leaving behind only a memory of his presence.

I regain my vision, but I can't move. I'm paralyzed with fiery pain. Heat scorches my legs, but I can't kick David away. My body convulses. Alana presses her palm over my mouth, muting the screams ripping from my throat.

I stare at Evan, begging him with my eyes to do something, anything, but all he does is grip my fingers. Bile rises in my throat at the smell of sizzling flesh, *my* sizzling flesh, wafting into my nostrils, gagging me.

Black shadows haze the room; the poison is working its way into my brain. I can't fight it off. I can't do anything except pray that Dylan was right, that I'm strong enough to handle this.

"It'll be over soon," Alana whispers.

I can see her rubbing my arm, but I don't feel her touch. Excruciating pain overwhelms me. My back arches as my body begins to lose gravity. Evan holds my arms while David's firm hands clasp my feet, keeping me stabilized. Alana carefully presses on my waist, forcing me back down completely.

Suddenly, my blood runs cold, as if ice water is gushing through my veins to stem the flow of molten lava inside of me. I shiver uncontrollably, frozen by the cleansing water. The black haze closes around me, shielding me from the world. I'm terrified and alone, trapped in a place of utter darkness, unsure and unaware of where I am, or even if I'm still alive.

And then...all I see are wings.

⁓⟡⁓

"Cami," Alana says. "Cami, wake up."

I open my eyes. Dazzling rainbow colors dance off the ceiling, reflections from the stained-glass rose window. I'm lying on a blanket on the hard floor of the altar overlooking the rows of wooden pews. My back creaks as I sit up.

"David said this would be the best place for you to sleep while your body fought off the poison," she says.

I rub the sleep from my eyes and press my aching hands against the floor to push to my feet. Last night comes rushing back—the demon, the burning of the holy water...Dylan.

"Let me help you."

I grab her hand to stand. My legs wobble, threatening to send me crashing back to the floor. She puts my arm around her shoulders to steady me. I stare over the cavernous room and blink. A figure is bundled up, sleeping on the first pew. I didn't think this church was open to the public anymore.

"He stayed with you all night."

I blink again. The person sleeping on the pew isn't a random stranger—it's Evan. He breathes heavily, probably exhausted from last night.

"Help me walk to him."

Alana guides me down the steps of the stage to Evan. I bend over and press my chapped lips against his cheek. His eyes flash open, and he beams a radiant smile.

"Good morning." His deep, husky voice sends excited shivers down my spine.

"Morning," I mumble. My throat is sore and my voice is hoarse due to my uncontrollable screaming last night.

"Why don't you take Cami for a walk around the block," Alana says to Evan. "David said it'll help you gain the strength back in your legs," she adds, glancing at me.

"Sounds good." Evan smiles at me again.

"I guess." I'm not even sure I can walk.

"Don't worry. I'm used to carrying you." Evan's laugh falls flat as his joke doesn't even make me crack a smile.

I frown. "Let's not make a habit of that."

<hr>

The sun warms my face as Evan helps me shuffle down the sidewalk. All the evidence from last night's battle has been removed. The dumpster is gone, back to wherever it came from, and there are no signs of struggle anywhere—not a drop of blood or scrap of clothing, not even a single trace of the pulverized demon remains on the church steps. The sun took care of the demon bits; David must've taken care of the rest.

The neighborhood hums with life, completely opposite

of its nightlife. Most lucky humans can sense when evil is lurking and they avoid those areas. A little fear never hurt anyone. Humans who have a taste for danger or are desperate for something attract demons to them—my mother did. She wanted a child, and Malicevile knew it. She was lost long before I was born and took my father with her. My birth only sealed their fates.

"I never got a chance to thank you for saving my life again," I say, lacing my fingers with Evan's.

He gently squeezes my hand. "I'd say you did a pretty good job keeping the demon from taking you. If you wouldn't have fought so hard, I'd have never caught up with the holy water."

"Thanks for that, too. I know you didn't want to go."

"I didn't want us to be outside in the first place. You risked a lot, you know."

I purse my lips. "I thought Jacie had been attacked."

His narrowed eyes soften. "You're smart, caring, and quick thinking—I admire that about you—but you're also reckless. You can't let the Veiled Realm get the best of you. If Jacie was hurt by a demon, it would've been her own fault for leaving after sunset."

I huff a small breath through my lips. "It would've been my demon who'd have hurt her because she was here to help me."

He halts in place, forcing me to stop with him. "Your demon?" He raises his eyebrows like what I've said was the craziest thing. "Taking ownership of a demon is dangerous. I know you think you're responsible because he's your biological father, but he's nothing to you."

Heat crawls up my neck. "I don't know if I can stop. I'm aware of him more than ever. His blood created the demon within me, and I can't ignore it. The allure scares me. It's kind of like how I feel about you."

He tilts his head slightly. "I scare you?"

I swallow. "I'm scared of the feelings you awaken within me. I barely know you, but your presence does something to me. I—I like you. A lot."

He peers into my eyes before tucking a dark curl behind my ear. "I feel the same, Cami. I have since the day I first met you. I always thought it was weird, but you confirmed my feelings yesterday after flying through the window. You said after meeting me, you believed in love at first sight."

He's referring to when I was hallucinating and thought I was talking to Cadence. It's hard to control the embarrassment flowing through me. "Is this crazy? Are we crazy?"

He scratches his jaw. "No crazier than the world we live in."

My heart races as I stare into his oceanic eyes. It takes everything in me not to sling my arms around him and kiss him. Instead, I start walking.

Guiding me along again, he strolls with me around the block. We stop at an empty park the next street over. Sprawling green grass surrounds a small play area, and flower beds and trees decorate the rest of the place. It's a pretty spot to hang out. I kneel under a large tree, the shade cooling my skin. Playing with the loose threads of my cutoffs, I wonder how terrible I look.

I lean back on my hands. "Wouldn't it be nice if life were always like this?"

Evan stretches his legs out next to me. "It can be."

I twist my lips to the side. "No, that's not what I meant. It'd be nice if things could always be normal. I wish I didn't have to track the sun in the sky or worry about my friends' souls getting sucked out by demons. I wish it were safe for people to be around me. I miss Cadence. I haven't known her long, but she's my only friend besides Alana...and now you."

His eyes brighten. "Oh, I forgot to tell you. Cadence called while you were sleeping."

I don't blame him for forgetting. Things haven't exactly been easy, and I know Alana pushed me to walk things off because she's afraid I'll be too injured to protect myself if something goes wrong.

Evan digs into his pocket and pulls out his cell phone. He sets it in my hand before I can even ask to use it. I have so much to tell Cadence, but with Evan sitting next to me, I'm going to have to limit my conversation.

"Thanks," I say, blushing. *Are you reading my mind?*

His eyes say they don't. "You're welcome."

I browse through Evan's long list of contacts, not really

looking at the names. My brows furrow when I don't see her number in his phone, and then I remember it's under my name.

"How is she?" Cadence answers before the line even rings. She must've been waiting for him to call her back.

"She's alive," I say.

"Oh, my God, Cami!" Cadence cries. I yank the phone from my ear a split second before her shrill voice can hurt my ear. "Evan told me what happened. I wanted to come right away but he told me not to. For some reason your little boyfriend doesn't think I can take care of myself after dark."

I raise my brows and smile at Evan.

"I'm surprised you listened," I say. "But it's good that you did. Malicevile was waiting outside. Probably all night."

"Who's that?" she asks. I forgot that Cadence doesn't know.

"My demonic father." I close my eyes and wait a moment for the yelling to start, but Cadence remains quiet.

"So, you finally know," Cadence says after a long pause. "Alana did the right thing and told you."

"You knew," I say. Why wouldn't she not know? It's like everyone knew except for me. "And you still protected me, even though the number one rule for a hunter is humans first?"

"Rules can be broken, especially if it involves my best friend. Anyways, before we get all mushy on each other,

Dylan called. He knew you'd been hurt. He was worried."
So, now he calls? I only had to be on my deathbed for a response.

My heart skips a beat. I thought I'd imagined him being with me. I suppress the urge to smile because I shouldn't feel this excited about Dylan. He's too late anyway—even if he can keep my nightmares away. Evan is the one who's been here for me, and I'm not going to just forget about him the moment Dylan is brought up.

"I'm sure he was worried," I say. "I'll let Evan know he said hello," I add to let Cadence know I'm not alone.

"Oh," she says, getting the hint. "I'll tell you more tomorrow when I see you."

"See me?" I ask.

"Yes, see you. I took care of the last remaining demon last night. That's the main reason I called. I'm leaving here first thing in the morning. It's time to get out of this town."

"I can't wait," I say.

I snap the phone shut and hand it back to Evan. He shoves it into his pocket and pushes to his feet. He helps me up, and we make our way back to the church in time to watch the somber sun setting from the doorway.

Even though the day is over, night has just begun. I hope I can survive another one.

SURVIVOR

WHEN EVAN AND I enter the church, David and Alana are rushing around the kitchen cooking dinner. The delicious aroma of lasagna swirls through the air, making my mouth water. My stomach growls; I'm starving because the only thing I've eaten today was an energy bar. Meals haven't been that important, at least not lately, what with the high occurrence of demon attacks.

Evan helps move my chair out, and we take our places at the table. I grab a hot piece of garlic bread from a basket in the middle of the table. I take a bite, savoring the fluffiness of the bread.

Alana and David join us, setting the glass dish of lasagna on the table. Alana piles a large heap onto my plate, and I dig in.

"Cadence is coming tomorrow," I mumble through chewing.

"Great!" Alana says, smiling wide. "We could definitely use her skills."

David grunts a response I can't understand.

"Not like *we* don't have any skills," Alana says, turning to David, "but I've taken her up on a partnership with Cami. She's even faced off with Malicevile by herself."

"So did I," Evan says.

"After I wore him down first," Alana says.

The phone rings from the living room, interrupting the competition of egos. I don't remember seeing one there, but David grumbles and leaves the table. I hear him answer, keeping his responses short and to the point.

"Cami," David calls. "It's Jacie."

"She knows to call my cell," David mumbles, walking past me as I go to pick up the receiver.

"Hello," I say, pressing the phone to my ear.

"Hey, Cami," Jacie says. "I wanted to see how you were doing after last night."

I lean against the wall. "I'm alive. There's not really much to say. I'm lucky, I guess."

Her breath creates static on the line. "That's one of the reasons I hate cats. Especially demonic ones."

I pause, taking in her words. I assumed she was asking me about practice. David must've told her what had happened. I press the mute button on the keypad. *Something doesn't feel right.*

"Davey," I call. "Did you tell Jacie about the demon attack last night?"

"No, why?" he asks.

"She knows."

David grumbles, and I hear the dial tone of his cell phone as he puts it on speaker phone. My stomach drops when I hear the same voice, Jacie's voice, on David's phone.

"Cami, you there?" Jacie asks.

I click the phone off mute and say "Yeah, sorry."

"Anyway, I was saying I'm on your street. I'll be at the church in two minutes. Come outside."

The hairs on the back of my neck prickle. This Jacie-wannabe is insane to think I'll be stepping even an inch out of the church after dark.

I swallow to stop my voice from cracking. "I don't think that's a good idea."

"There aren't any signs of demons. Come on, I'll keep you safe," she responds.

I clench my hand at my side. "No. You won't." My voice comes out more like a husky growl, and the tone surprises me.

"Stop acting like a child."

I force myself to continue talking instead of hanging up on the imposter. "I'm not being a child. How's your husband by the way? What's his name again?"

"He's fine, the same as usual," she says.

"What's his name again?" I repeat.

"Uh. John," she says.

Oh, crap! I take a breath, releasing it, creating noise in the receiver. David waves from the doorway, making goofy hand signals I can't understand.

"Who is this?" My voice quivers with fear.

"Jacie," the imposter says.

"You're lying. Who is this, really?"

A sharp breath comes through the line. My hands tremble, and I clutch the phone to my shoulder to keep from dropping it. Whoever is on the other line knows who I am. Knows what I am. This whole phone call screams demon.

A throaty laugh erupts on the line, sending ice through my veins. "I should've known you'd be smart, and I couldn't fool you so easily," a man says.

My stomach lurches, the voice imprinting on my brain.

"Like father, like daughter," he says.

I collapse to the floor, terrified to hang up the phone. David dashes into the room and tries to snatch it from my fingers, but I can't let it go. I won't let it go.

"My dad's dead," I whisper. "He was murdered."

"What a shame," Malicevile says. His sultry voice rings sweet in my ear. I can almost smell a hint of cinnamon in the air. "He would've made a fine minion."

My voice sticks in my throat as my lip quivers, remembering the horrible night of my parents' deaths. I pull myself together. I'm not that frightened little girl anymore. I won't let him get to me.

"You wouldn't have succeeded. My father was a good man."

"That's why he lost. Good doesn't stand a chance against me. Everything good in your life was a mistake. You are meant for better things. Darker things," Malicevile says. "And I'm running out of patience waiting for you."

"Well, you better find some then. You'll be waiting for the rest of eternity." Anger strengthens my voice.

"I'm through being nice, Camilla. I've given you ample opportunity to give me the chance to show you a beautiful future by my side. I've even been nice enough to leave your friends alone, but your stubbornness is messing up my reputation. I won't stand for this teenage angst anymore."

My eyebrows peak on my forehead. The more he speaks, the less fear and anger I have. He sounds so normal. *Clever, clever demon, remember?*

"Why me? There are dozens of people willing to trade their souls to be by your side. Pick one of them."

He whistles into the phone. "Camilla, my daughter. My blood runs through your veins. Your power—it's mine."

"I don't have any power. Leave me alone." I pull the phone from my ear and start to hang it up.

"Camilla!" His deep voice booms through the phone. "This isn't a discussion!" The scent of cinnamon wafts through the air. "Now, I want you to listen, and listen carefully. You have until fifteen minutes before dawn to pack your things and leave the church. If you choose not to, your little humans will pay the price. They'll share the same fate as your parents. As for the half-breed, he'll spend eternity with his mother."

"His mother is dead," I say. "Just like you're going to be."

"Where do you think a demon goes after it is banished from this world?" Malicevile asks, ignoring my comment.

My heart clenches in my chest. Evan would never end up where his demonic mother is...would he?

"You can't hurt us." Tears roll down my cheeks.

"Oh, I can. Take my advice and make things easy," Malicevile says. "See you soon, daughter of mine."

The phone goes silent.

I scream in frustration, pitching the phone at the wall. It smashes to pieces like my breaking heart.

<hr>

I glare at the digital clock on the microwave, trying to freeze time. Its neon green numbers read just after one. I have a little over four hours to figure out how I'm going to get my friends, my protectors, out of this mess. I can't ask them to sacrifice their lives for mine. The human world needs their skills. I have nothing to offer. Levitation and deflecting powers to save my own butt isn't useful. The only gift I will ever bring is destruction and doom.

Another minute flashes by. I've wasted three hundred

and sixty-five precious minutes trying to find the words to tell David and Alana the truth, explain to them that the chase is over and the predator has won. I have to tell Evan it's over. Our budding relationship will never go anywhere. I'll never have a chance to find the courage to tell him how much he means to me, not with Daddy Demon in the picture.

I baby my tall glass of water, imagining hot flames licking the walls, disintegrating this beautiful church. I envision the furniture igniting, the thick smoke contaminating the air, the screams. The memory of the death of my parents prevents me from thinking about anything else.

"You should get some sleep," Alana says, leaning against the arched entrance that leads to the living room.

"I can't," I say. "I have a problem, and I think I've made it worse."

"What is it?" Alana pulls the chair away from the table and takes a seat. "It can't be as bad as you think it is."

"Bad doesn't even describe it," I say. Horrible, terrifying, catastrophic—those are better word choices.

She reaches out and pats my knee. "Does this have something to do with the mysterious caller?"

"Yes. It has everything to do with him."

"So, it was a man," Alana confirms.

"No. It was a demon. My father to be more specific." The word father feels wrong on my lips.

"I was afraid of this. How long do we have?"

"A little over four hours." I glance at the clock like a ticking time bomb. "Then the war begins. Or I can stop it all together if I just pack my belongings and leave with him."

I hold my breath, praying Alana tells me to do the latter. I wouldn't argue if she asks me to leave. I'd understand completely. I was ready to die last night. I'm sure I could be ready again. But I doubt dying is an option, well, at least physically dying. I can't say the same about my soul.

Alana wrings her hands together before setting them flat on the table. She looks me straight in the eyes, her brows furrowed.

I suck in a deep breath. "I understand if you want me to go. I've been nothing but a burden on you."

Alana pounds her fists against the table. She rises to her feet, yanking on her short, sunny blond hair. I cringe in alarm, terrified she'll lash out at me and confirm my deepest fear.

"That's out of the question. We're in this together." The hurt in her voice matches the ache in my heart. I know Alana loves me like a sister, and I've hurt her feelings. But I'd rather see her alive with hurt feelings instead of dead with none at all.

"I don't want you to get killed because of me," I say.

"Don't you get it, Cami? You'll never be the death of me. None of this is your fault. You didn't choose to be born a demi-demon. You didn't choose to have Malicevile hunting you, and you're not going to choose to give up. You're a survivor. *We* are survivors, and we will make it through this."

"But I can choose to sacrifice my life for yours, like you've done for me over the last three years. You gave up everything—your job, your husband, your life. For what? To keep me, the spawn of a demon, safe? Now, it's my turn to do the same."

"I gave up nothing. If anything, I've gained more than I could have ever asked for." Tears rim her light eyelashes. "And I'm not going to lose you."

I cross my arms over my chest. Alana has always been stubborn, putting others before herself. I need to figure out a way to convince her to think of herself for once. I'd never forgive myself if Malicevile hurts her to get to me. I don't care if it was never truly my fault. I'm guilty by association.

"Then we need to figure something out. Officially, we have four and a half hours before death comes knocking on our door."

FIGHT ALONE

DAVID'S ANGRY PHONE conversation leaks through the open door of his bedroom. His tone becomes louder and more upset the longer he stays on the line with the Hunter's Alliance. A thud sounds, and a small crack emerges on the wall, causing flakes of plaster to fall to the floor.

David comes from his room, rubbing his bleeding fist. He shakes his fingers, dabbing the wounds on the hem of his dark T-shirt.

He paces in front of me. "They're a bunch of idiots. I don't even know why I bothered."

"They might be idiots, but they have good intentions," Alana says.

"They've ordered us to stay out of it. Said Cami must

deal with her 'personal matters' on her own."

I lower my head, covering my face with my hands. I agree with the alliance, yet a tiny part of me wishes they would help. Not for me, but for the others. They didn't do anything to deserve this. *I don't deserve this.*

"The alliance can't order me to do anything," Alana says. "I quit a long time ago."

Evan sits next to me. His hand rests on my knee, showing his support. I know he's here for me no matter what the outcome is.

"I thought they would protect us," Evan says. "Cami is one of us."

"Cami isn't human," Alana says. "In their mind, she'll never be worth risking human lives for. The same goes for you, Evan."

Anger creases his forehead as he scowls. "They'd be nothing without us! Humans can't destroy all demons."

"I know," David says. "They know it, too. But the alliance was made for humans. Pure humans. It's been that way for as long as anyone can remember."

"It's ridiculous." His voice nearly sounds like a growl.

I squeeze Evan's hand, and he falls silent. This isn't the time to argue about what is right or wrong. The alliance has the right to have its opinion, even if it means we're left alone to fight this on our own. And if it goes the way I plan, I'll fight this alone.

"It's okay. I don't want anyone to fight my battles," I

say.

I watch David pace around the table again. Dark stubble shadows his face, disheveling his usual distinguished appearance. He presses his lips together, which are partly hidden beneath his mustache. He pauses, and his eyes meet mine.

"What exactly did Malicevile say?" he asks.

"He said if I'm not packed and ready to go with him before sunrise, you and Alana will suffer the same fate as my parents." I bite my lip, forcing the rest of my words free. "And Evan will be spending some quality time with his mother—his real mother."

"Your parents died in a fire," Evan says. "That's great!"

My mouth falls agape.

"No, no, no," he says, waving his arms in surrender. "That came out wrong. I meant to say your parents died in a demon-related fire. Mal can't touch this church. His powers can't hurt us."

"Evan might be right," Alana says. "But are we willing to risk it?"

"What better choice do we have?" David says. "It's not like we can sneak out the backdoor. Malicevile will expect that."

My heart jumps. He might expect us all to try to sneak out the back, but he won't expect the others to leave without me. If I can distract him long enough, no one will get hurt. I can run back inside when Malicevile realizes I'm not going with him. Fire can't hurt me. *Thanks for the deflective power, Daddy Demon.* It might save my life.

"I have an idea," I say. "You're not going to like it, but I think it will work."

I excitedly explain my fireproof plan to the others. Alana's eyes darken when she realizes I'm not going to escape with them. David scrunches his eyebrows, worried, but doesn't argue. Evan sits silently, shaking his head.

"I can stay with you," Evan says. "I can protect you if the plan fails."

"You need to protect Davey and Alana. I'll be okay on my own." It's time to learn how to take care of myself. "I'll meet you when the sun comes up."

"If the church doesn't burn down first," Evan remarks.

I squeeze my hands into fists. Tiny crescent moons form where my nails dig in. This will never work unless Evan gets over his hero-complex. I'm plenty capable of taking care of myself. *I hope.*

"Don't jinx me. I'll deal with the worst case scenarios as they come crashing my way," I say. "Stop worrying about me."

Evan pushes away from the table, knocking his chair to the floor as he storms from the kitchen. My planning overrides my ability to comfort him. He just needs a moment to sulk.

I trace invisible circles on the tabletop. This is the scariest decision I've ever made. Somehow, I'm okay with it. I'm willing to do anything to keep the others out of harm's way...even if it means I'm jumping directly in its path.

Alana scribbles on a pad of paper. Her pen scratches over the surface, creating an illegible mess. David hands me a cup of steaming coffee, and I gladly accept. I'm going to need all the extra energy I can take. Evan stalks back into the room, and I rub a smile from my lips.

"Here, take this." He hands me a small ivory colored flask with a detailed cross embossed on the front of it. "If all else fails, toss it in Malicevile's face, then run like hell. Better yet, fly like hell."

I pop the cap open, taking a sniff of its contents. Water, or holy water, to be more exact. My stomach churns, remembering the fire coursing through my veins as the holy water cleansed the demon poison from my body. This is enough to stop a demon in its tracks.

"Thanks." I tuck the flask into the waist of my jeans. I'm never going to risk wearing sweatpants again in public, my fear of nudity outweighing practicality.

Evan kisses my forehead, and I lift my chin so he can reach my lips. His soft kiss is like the feathery lightness of a butterfly's wings. I grab his shirt and pull him closer, desperate for the heat of his skin against mine. I kiss him like it's the last one we'll ever share. It just might be. His fingers tangle in my hair as he pulls me closer, kissing me deeper.

David clears his throat, and I reluctantly pull away.

"Sorry," we say in unison.

Alana rips the top page from her notepad and hands it to me. "These are directions to the closest safe house and the next three after that. The phone numbers on the bottom are a list of contacts, people who'll help you if we lose touch with each other. We can't stay more than a night or two in each house. We need to be as far from here as possible before Malicevile enters the human world again."

I shove the list in my pocket.

"We need to pack," David interrupts.

My eyes jerk to the clock on the microwave. My heart races. We have less than an hour left.

<hr>

I put the last of my meek belongings into the small duffle bag I borrowed from Evan. Living life on the run makes packing easy. Sometimes I don't even pack at all. The zipper is loud in the calm quiet of the church. I lift the light bag onto my arm and take one last look around at the room that was starting to feel like mine.

Alana knocks on the doorframe. I turn to face her worried eyes. She glides in and pulls me into a hug. Tears threaten to escape, but I blink them back. Alana is the most important person in the world to me. My heart aches because I'm putting her through this with less than an ounce of hope I'll succeed.

"I love you so much," Alana whispers into my hair. "I wouldn't have changed anything."

"I love you, too," I say with a heavy heart. "Thanks for

being there for me when I needed you and still being here for me. It means a lot."

She squeezes me tighter, hurting my shoulders, but I don't complain. "Remember this isn't the end, Cami, just another bump in the road."

The smell of clove and cinnamon trickles through the room, tainting the air around me. My fingers shake and my palms begin to sweat. Malicevile is early.

"No," I whisper. "We still have ten minutes."

The smoky aroma of a burning fireplace overpowers the scent of nauseating spices. I pull Alana with me, my boots thumping hard on the carpet.

Evan paces the living room. His fisted hands punch the air in frustration every few steps. He looks up at me with wild eyes, part anger and part fear. David rushes into the room and drops his bag on the floor.

"The training room is on fire. We forgot about the broken window. The back door is blocked. We can't escape."

REVENGE

I RUSH PAST the altar. Thick, black smoke curls through the air. Bright flames crackle, licking the wooden doorframe. Glass shatters in the intense heat. The only other exit from the church is through the flames. Alana and David could never make it without being seriously injured.

I stare at the stained-glass windows. The only way to escape through them is with a ladder, which we don't have, or with levitation. And I have to be the distraction.

I turn on my heels and rush back to the living room. David gasps heavily, already affected by the smoke. He wouldn't survive the burning of the church even if we were able to keep the flames away.

Alana sits at the table, her head bowed and her hands

clasped in prayer as she keeps herself under control. If I don't do something soon, my friends will all die.

"I have a plan B," I say. "I'm going to step out of the church as we had planned before. Only I'm going to go to him."

I have to deal with the fact that I'm demon bound. I'm not going to let Alana protect me anymore. It's my turn to return the favor. I can't think of any other way around this inevitable situation. I always knew in my heart that I would have to face my demons. I'm not doing this because it's an easy way out of life or because I've decided to be evil. My decision is simple. I have to do everything I can to save my friends. They can survive without me. At least they'll have a chance to live, a chance to save others. I'm the only one who can save me. If I have to die, I can at least save my soul.

"You can't," Alana cries. "I won't let you."

"Yes, you will," David says. "You'll have to trust her judgment. Cami isn't the little girl you rescued anymore. She is a fully capable demi-demon."

Alana begins to sob in her hands, and David pats her back. Grasping my hands in his, Evan peers down at me. I stare into his aquamarine eyes, seeing his inner flame shining through.

"No matter what happens, get them out of here. I trust you to keep Alana safe for me," I say. "And do *not* try to save me. You'll just end up getting yourself killed."

"Okay," he says.

"Will you promise me one more thing?" I ask.

"Anything." His voice is as rich as creamy chocolate, making it difficult to share my final request.

"If I can't save myself—if I have to go with Malicevile and lose my soul, I want you to kill me. Hunt me down and destroy me. I can't live without my humanity."

Evan reluctantly nods his head. He knows I would do the same for him. I couldn't live in this world fully consumed with evil. I wouldn't want Evan to risk human lives like that, not after I've seen what Malicevile is capable of.

<hr>

I squeeze Alana's hand. Her lip quivers as I turn to go. David coughs, breathing into a damp cloth. The fire looms closer, devouring the pews. We can no longer stay in the burning church. The vaulted ceiling is close to caving in.

I timidly open the door. David gasps for the fresh air trickling in. I straighten my back, lifting my head high. I will not allow Malicevile the pleasure of seeing me distraught.

The demon shimmers into view across the street. He saunters from the thick greenery, his appearance screaming predator. I descend the steps. Every hair on my body rises with fear. Goosebumps prickle over my skin. *This is it.*

Malicevile's lips curl into a smile. His blocky, white teeth shine in the streetlamp light. He stretches his arm out to me. I cross my arms over my chest, keeping myself together.

"I'm here." I circle around him. His eyes never leave mine as I turn his back to the entrance to the church.

"For revenge, I hope." His voice is like a silky caress. I could listen to him all day.

I shake my head, both answering him and trying to keep from being hypnotized by his alluring presence.

"I thought you'd be angry at me for killing your humans. Just be thankful I don't want your little boyfriend."

I close my eyes, concentrating on not looking around Malicevile to see Evan guiding Alana and David to safety. Malicevile believes he has killed them, and I'm not going to let him know otherwise.

"I'm not angry. I'm not even surprised." I keep my voice low to hide the quiver of my rising panic. "You did exactly what I expected you to do."

"What can I say," he says, shrugging his shoulders. "I got tired of waiting."

The flash of headlights surrounds Malicevile in glowing white light and fades away as David's car screeches down the street.

"I'm a survivor," I mouth, hoping Alana can see me through the back window.

"What was that?" Malicevile asks.

"I'm a survivor," I say out loud, my voice surprisingly strong.

His diamond-shaped pupils expand and retract; a hint of irritation crosses his face. He narrows his eyes. I pray one of his powers isn't mind reading, or he will expect what I'm about to do next.

I bend my knees and launch into the air. The wind whips at my face, tossing my hair over my eyes. If I can stay out of Malicevile's reach for twenty more minutes, I'll be safe.

A firm hand tugs on my leg. I stare dumbfounded at Malicevile levitating under me. I should have expected this. I did get my power from him.

My arms propel in circles as Malicevile jerks me to the ground. I tuck my head in my arms as I crash into the concrete. I somersault out of his reach, nearly knocking my head on the curb of the sidewalk.

An orb of dazzling purple energy erupts in his palm. He launches the crackling ball at my head. I try to catch it but it sails past my outstretched fingertips, colliding with the roaring fire of the church behind me.

Strong hands clutch my hair and yank me to my feet. Pain shocks my scalp as a patch of my hair is ripped out. I grit my teeth while Malicevile forces my head back, exposing my neck.

Every vampire movie I have ever seen flashes through my head like a film reel. Except, having my neck exposed to a demon is ten times worse. Liquid terror drenches me in a cold sweat. Malicevile's teeth won't prick my neck. He'd have to savagely tear a chunk of my flesh away with his blunt teeth.

I flail in an attempt to kick Malicevile's legs out from under him, but I'm inches shy of my mark. I clutch his hands tangled in my hair, trying to pry his fingers apart.

He yanks me higher. My scalp aches as I try to rip my hair free. My feet dangle an inch from the ground. I concentrate on releasing gravity. The pain in my scalp subsides as I levitate unnoticed, like I'm standing on an invisible barrier. I bash my head against Malicevile's, but he doesn't even budge. My head throbs even more. It's becoming difficult to resist the black fog closing in on me.

Malicevile leans closer and I squeeze my eyes shut. A sharp pain explodes in my cheek as his open palm makes contact with my face. The coppery taste of blood floods my mouth, and I spit, aiming for Malicevile's cat-like eyes.

The sound of crunching bones, followed by more excruciating pain, creates black stars in my vision. The roaring wind cools the hot blood rushing from my nose as my limp body flies through the air.

My back hits the sidewalk, and the sudden loss of breath leaves me suffocating, gulping air, but not breathing. I open my eyes in time to see another vibrant energy ball whizzing my way. I gasp and cover my face with my palms outward to catch the crackling globe. It slams into my open hands with a slight sting. Another energy ball sails in my direction, and I catch it, adding its electrifying energy to the first one. I'm determined to create a weapon to defeat him.

I blindly launch the sizzling ball. A growl of aggravation

echoes through the air like I'm trapped in a hollow room. Malicevile smiles, tossing the basketball-sized energy ball up and down in his hands. He heaves the ball again. It flies at me, too fast for me to catch. It plows into my chest, launching me into the air. I crash into the stone steps of the fiery church.

I claw the cracks with my fingers and drag my heavy legs up the steps ramming my aching knees. If I can't beat him, I need to run. I crawl into the safety of the burning church.

Malicevile throws another energy ball at my back and I lose my balance. I topple down the steps, smacking my cheek against the bottom step before hitting the pavement. I shake my pounding head. If I survive this, I'm never going to live in a place with stairs again.

"Had enough da-a-a-a-ughter?" Malicevile drawls. "Are you going to let me take you home now?"

"Never," I say. My nose aches, the bone probably shattered from the abuse. "I'd rather die."

"Father's don't always give their little girls what they want. If they give in, it's harder to train them. Now's the perfect time for your first lesson."

"And what's that?" I whisper.

"Daddy will always win."

Malicevile slams his fist into my face, snapping my head to the side. A pain like the pinpricks of a thousand needles rushes over my skin. Malicevile pumps his power into me and it flows through my blood, boiling me from within. He is trying to force me to submit to him.

My deflective power absorbs every last drop of energy he has to throw at me. The flow of power arches my back as I begin to run out of room to store it. I wriggle, uncomfortable from the mass of power zinging through my veins. It's like dying of thirst while drowning underwater. I crave the power, need it, but it's too much. I'm overloaded, floating in a pool of sizzling electricity.

It's killing me.

My entire body tingles with his power. My skin glows with electrifying light running through my veins. Black fog clouds my vision and I grasp at tiny threads of consciousness. I can't do anything but wait for it to be over. This time I have no one to save me.

I stare at the beautiful lightening sky. White, puffy clouds swirl carelessly in the breeze. I imagine what it would feel like to levitate into the clouds to experience the moist air on my skin.

My eyes grow heavy. My chest tightens, the air forced out of my lungs with every new stream of energy Malicevile shoots into me. I close my eyes and see Alana with tears in her eyes. They glisten with sunlight, dripping onto my face.

Imagining Alana helps me find the will to push my weakening hand under my back. A hard object digs into my spine. If I'm going to die, I'm going to make myself as comfortable as possible.

My fingers caress the smooth flask. *If I'm going to die,*

Malicevile is not going to get off pain free.

I flick open the cap of the flask and use the last bit of my remaining strength to splash holy water in his face.

I wince at the ear shattering screams exploding from my demon. The sickly sweet smell of burning cinnamon tickles my nostrils, and I inhale, coating my lungs with the scent of my own personal revenge.

I squint through my lashes to stare at my demon father jerking around with smoke pouring from his burning face.

A bright white light flashes in the distance, bathing me in its heavenly glow. The world goes quiet around me. Death is here to take me away. I can't escape my fate any longer. I'm tainted with demon blood. There is only one place to go.

I wait for the agonizing screams of banished demons, for the gates of Hell to open and swallow me into its fiery depth, but only white light and silence greets me. I can die peacefully knowing that my friends are safe. And that I'm not my father's daughter.

My eyes clear as the black haze dissipates. The radiant, heavenly sun peeks over the horizon, embracing me in its luminous light. I force myself to sit up and look around. My father isn't dead. He's been banished by the sun for another day. His pride and overconfidence has given me a second chance at life.

A car slows down, stopping in front of me. A woman rushes out, looking at me and then the smoldering church.

"Are you all right?" she asks.

I nod my head.

"I'm going to call 911," she says, digging through her purse.

I reach out my hand, grabbing her arm. "No, I'm fine. Can I just use your phone?"

The woman hesitates before she hands it over. I pull out the contact paper from my pocket. Alana's number is the first one on the list. I fumble, pressing the tiny buttons with my swollen fingers. The phone rings, and a smile stretches across my lips when she answers.

"I need a ride," I mumble.

"Cami! Thank God you're alive. I was so scared," she cries.

"For now," I say. "Malicevile is still out there."

"We'll get him. I promise."

"I know. I'm no longer just a survivor. I'm a fighter."

MORE TO LOSE

I'M SITTING ON a fluffy cloud, haloed in a ring of golden sunlight. It's peaceful with the wind caressing my hair, the smell of ripe apples and rain showers swirling around me.

"I want to stay here forever," I say, petting the airy cloud. It's the softest thing I've ever felt.

"I thought you preferred the real world?" Dylan says, gripping my fingers between his.

"It's overrated. I like this much better." I laugh, tugging my hands away. I brush the clouds with my fingers, and they begin to dissipate.

Dylan frowns. "You can't stay here, love. It's not right. You have your life to live."

"I'm scared, Dylan."

"Don't be. I'm here for you."

"In my dreams," I say.

"No, not this time. I'm really here. I promise." Dylan kisses my cheek. "You just have to wake up."

A rhythmic beeping stirs me awake. I peek through my lashes at the stark white room. I rub my fingers over the annoying pain on the top of my hand. An IV is stuck into my vein, dripping a clear liquid. I wince, expecting my hand to feel an intense, liquid fire, but it isn't holy water. It's something medicinal.

The beeping comes from a heart monitor placed next to my hospital bed. The sound is in perfect sync with my heartbeat.

I push the button on the railing of the bed. It whines as it raises me into a sitting position. I blink, realizing I'm not alone. Alana sleeps in a chair in the far corner of the room.

A soft hand rests on my leg, and I jump in surprise. Cadence smiles down at me. Her purple hair gleams in the fluorescent lighting. She places a single finger against her lips and motions to the figures sitting on both sides of my bed.

The beeping picks up pace as I see Evan fast asleep. I glance at the other figure, and my mouth falls open. A pain shocks my jaw, and I snap my lips closed. I can't believe Dylan's here. I thought I was dreaming, but no, here he is, sleeping next to my bed with his head resting against the wall.

"How do you like an angel and a demon sitting on both sides of you?" Cadence whispers.

"Weird," I say. "What is Dylan doing here?"

"He lives here. You're in the infirmary of the academy."

"Oh." I'm at the academy? I thought they wanted me to deal with my problems on my own. I wonder what's changed.

"You've been out for three weeks. The doctors induced a coma to help you heal. You almost died," she says.

"I don't remember much." *Just all the power Malicevile forced into me. I can feel it zinging under my skin.* It's awful.

"That's a good thing. You were in really bad shape."

I still feel in really bad shape. My head aches, my skin is tender, and I still feel an uncomfortable amount of energy flowing through my veins.

I stare at Dylan. His black hair has fallen over his eyes, covering his face. I suppress the attraction I had felt for him before I met Evan. After everything, how is it that I still feel anything for him? But it's hard to resist his angelic charm, even when he's sleeping.

"I know he lives here and all, but what is he doing in my room?" I ask. I can't remove my eyes from Dylan. *What am I doing? I want to be with Evan.*

"Moral support, I suppose," Cadence says. "Or maybe because the poor guy likes you."

"He has a funny way of showing it," I grumble.

"Besides, I've chosen Evan."

"I like the bad boys, too." Cadence giggles into her hand.

"He's not bad," I argue.

I slam my hands on the side rails, accidentally hitting the power button for the television. It blinks on and the sound blares through the side speakers. I glance around and see three startled faces look towards me.

"You're awake," Alana says, yawning into her hand.

I half smile and nod. The door to my room flies open, and David comes bustling in with his hands full of flowers. I wiggle my finger in a wave, feeling claustrophobic with Dylan and Evan flanking my sides.

"The doctor told me you'd be waking up today," David says. "So, I brought you these."

"Thanks. I mean for everything. All of you."

David drops a card into my lap, and I run my finger through the seal to open it. I pull out a thick paper and gaze at the emblem at the top. It's a lightning bolt through a small triangle, a symbol I've never seen before, yet it's somehow familiar.

"It was delivered to the church's mailbox," David says. "Addressed to you."

I can't hear anything over the rapid beeping of the heart monitor. "Congratulations on your escape, Camilla. Enjoy your new home while you still can," I read out loud. "The hunters won't protect you forever. Not after they see what you are capable of. But don't worry—I have big plans for you." I drop the note as if it'll explode in my hand at any second. "It's signed from Malicevile."

Alana snatches it and tosses it in the trash. "He's trying to scare you. He knows he's lost."

I close my eyes for a second. "You're right. I won't let him hurt me again."

My words reverberate through me as I try to decide if I believe them. When I open my eyes and see the faces of those who love me, I find the strength to know I'm right. Malicevile might be my demonic father, but he's nothing more than that.

He won't ever catch me off guard again. He'll regret it if he even tries.

Because I'm stronger than him. I'm more determined. I have more to lose.

A demon might swirl inside of me, but my humanity is stronger than ever before, and I'll never let him take my soul. I'll never even let him try.

TO BE CONTINUED...

ACKNOWLEDGMENTS

I OWE SO many thanks to the people who helped make this book possible. Without so many special people in my life, this writing journey would be lonely and not as amazing as it has been.

A big thanks to Jan Moran for her unwavering support and superb editing and critique skills. She always drops everything she's doing to come to my rescue when I need her. You're the best mother-in-law in the world!

I also owe a big thanks to Katie Harder-Schauer from Proofreading by Katie for her editorial guidance, feedback, and help in polishing Tainted. You're fabulous!

More thanks to Jamie Hall and Jazmin Garcia for being my first readers. Your encouraging words, honesty, and feedback mean the world to me.

Thanks to my mom, Elaine, who let me read this entire book to her out loud even though demons scare her. Without your love and support, my world wouldn't be as bright.

A special thanks to Melissa Hardy, who made a name suggestion that sparked the idea for Cami Anders. Also thanks to all those who participated by voting for Cami's name. Without your help, Cami would've probably ended up being named Demon Girl, DG for short.

I also want to give big hugs to my family and friends who have given me the love and support I needed to get through the bad days—to Eric, who lets me sit at the computer for far too long. To Tami, Lily, and Eric H. You three rock! To Amy H. and Lyndsay W. for your enthusiasm and kind words. I'm so happy we've reconnected and that you love my books. Also, thanks to my friends that I haven't personally met yet but have been such a support throughout my indie journey—Nikki Godwin, Karen Laird, and Courtney Whittamore, much love to you all!

Lastly, I'd like to thank my readers. Thanks so much for taking a chance on my books. Thank you for reaching out to me through social media and letting me know you enjoy reading my books. While I initially write for myself, I publish for you. So thanks! Your excitement and love for the worlds I create make this journey worthwhile. For you, I'm truly grateful.

GINNA MORAN IS a writer from sunny Southern California. She started writing poetry as a teenager in a spiral notebook that she still has tucked away on her desk today. Her love of writing grew after she graduated high school, and she completed her first unpublished manuscript at age eighteen.

When she realized her love of writing was her life's passion, she studied literature at Mira Costa College in Northern San Diego. Besides writing novels, she was senior editor, content manager, and image coordinator for Crescent House Publishing Inc. for four years.

Aside from Ginna's professional life, she enjoys binge watching television shows, playing pretend with her daughter, and cuddling with her dogs. Some of her favorite things include chocolate, anything that glitters, cheesy jokes, and organizing her bookshelf.

Ginna Moran loves to hear from her readers so visit her online at www.GinnaMoran.com. You can also find her on Facebook, Twitter, Instagram, and Snapchat (@Ginna Moran). To stay up-to-date on new releases, sign up to her newsletter. You'll not only get a FREE book, but you'll be able to participate in monthly giveaways!

Ginna Moran is currently hard at work on her next novel.

MORE BY GINNA MORAN

PARANORMAL

Destined for Dreams Series
Demon Within Series
Finding Nate Series
Going Ghostly Series
Spark of Life Series
When Souls Collide Series
Demon Watcher Series
Call of the Ocean Series

CONTEMPORARY

Falling into Fame Series

STANDALONES

Life After Lila